The Consciousness of Cats

Nigel J Borthwick

Matador
9 Priory Business Park,
Wistow Road, Kibworth Beauchamp,
Leicestershire. LE8 0RX
Tel: 0116 279 2299
Email: books@troubador.co.uk
Web: www.troubador.co.uk/matador
Twitter: @matadorbooks

ISBN 978 1784625 184

British Library Cataloguing in Publication Data.
A catalogue record for this book is available from the British Library.

Printed and bound by CPI Group (UK) Ltd, Croydon, CR0 4YY
Typeset in 11.5pt Bembo by Troubador Publishing Ltd, Leicester, UK

Matador is an imprint of Troubador Publishing Ltd

Dedicated to deep thinkers everywhere. Your quest is insatiable, long may you provide essence to the complexities of human nature.

INTRODUCTION

To contemplate the idea of human beings without a higher level of consciousness would be the same as imagining the earth without the sun, implausible. And, whilst consciousness is almost impossible to define, we cannot ignore its consequence to our existence. Neither should we overlook its relevance to our story.

Freud proposed the idea of the 'iceberg mind', so-called because most of our thoughts and urges lie beneath the surface, thus implying that our behaviour is determined by thoughts repressed into the unconscious mind. So why is it that most of us tend to go about our everyday lives in some kind of taken for granted stupor, without ever questioning the magnitude of such phenomena?

Whereas, philosophers have theorised about the mystical entity of the soul for centuries, and there are those who believe that if we could pinpoint the soul, then consciousness itself might finally be explained. Plato believed the soul was a higher reality than the physical self and is an entirely separate entity to the body; therefore the real identity of the person lies within the soul itself. John Locke took the notion further, offering us the idea that consciousness could be transferred from one soul to another. If this were to be true, then our beliefs and understanding of the world continue on after our physical body has died. For those of us who look deeper into ourselves, questioning our very being becomes not only a way to find meaning in our lives, but an attempt to write ourselves into eternity, through choice.

As interesting as this debate is, we do not wish to make the basis for our story a plethora of unintelligible questions, albeit the consequence is a platform on which the story about the main individuals concerned has been constructed.

The fascination of these ideas has long been the subject of many of my conversations with Nathan. Whatever mediums of communication have evolved since Nathan and I have been acquainted, we have always managed to discuss our mutual interest on the wonder of consciousness – and its implication on the soul of the thoughtful.

PART ONE

AND SO THE ICEBERGS MELT

I should say that in my opinion, Nathan is one of the few people who could be said to possess a 'consciousness of soul'. In that only a minority of people have the belief and capability to recognise the call from our inner-core, where within it lies our true identity, purpose and possible immortality.

Perhaps it is also relevant to say who I am, or where I fit into this story. Albeit at this point in our narrative the detail of my relationship with Nathan is not important; though what probably is, is the fact that I know him better than anyone. On an intellectual level, we are two like-minded, would-be philosophers who share similar thoughts about life's great mysteries.

Nathan Blakemore reminisced over his junior school essay on life in England: the land of unfinished Test matches and steamy fish and chip shops that gave off a warm, inviting glow at the end of cobbled streets. He'd always thought it to be an articulate observation for a ten-year-old; one that unleashed his prowess for metaphorical descriptivism. More importantly, it awoke his conscious awareness to the hidden enigmas of ordinary life.

At thirty-three, he'd arrived at the unpopular conception that there had to be more to life than Friday night binge-drinking with tenuously connected friends. Nathan sarcastically referred to them as 'head turners', due to the amount of attention they gave to following the movements of well-enhanced females in the local pub, whilst pretending to find each other's jokes funny.

Reality can be cruel. If we never assess our purpose then

we are captured forever in predictability. Nathan was all too aware of this, but fleeing the oncoming starkness was not as easy as he imagined.

Nathan hated the uneasiness within himself that tugged on his conscience like an egocentric child pulls on his mother's sleeve. This was made worse after he had recently seen a disabled couple riding tandem in motorised wheelchairs along the canal bank. They had looked so full of *joie de vivre* and appeared totally unperturbed by their predicament as they mingled with skateboarders, stopping briefly to feed the weather-beaten pigeons. The sight of them had even broken his most sacred habit: nipping the skin above his top lip using one finger, a characteristic he adopted when deep in thought – an anxiety-laden fallout from his conflicted teen years.

It wasn't a Ferrari or a yacht in the South of France that would provide total fulfilment for Nathan. It was something more simplistic and tangible, which he needed to make his life reflect, some ultimate goal. Three hours of rewinding his life against the backdrop of the city centre canal atmosphere was enough. Nathan decided to head home to his cognitive safe haven.

Something about writing that essay all those years ago had triggered him into questioning what life was all about. It was like a self-induced electrode probing deep into his psyche, leaving him with a permanent scar of unconscious deliberation. His teacher had complimented him on the essay, which had been entered into a schools literary competition. He had received second prize, though Miss Reynolds told him that he should be encouraged and that she was sure he would write a book one day.

Even as a normal, healthy, growing boy, there was no contentment in the fact that he merely existed. He often wondered if the clue to his whole existence lay in the fact that he was born who he was, and not one of those unfortunate children from Biafra who he'd seen on the news. How could one essay affect the trajectory of his life plan? It had left him with the vital urge to suck the bone marrow out of life rather than to just eat, drink and daze through it with a lack of cerebral inertia. Sunday was a grim event; the eighties were on their way out but even with the pretentious promise of nineties leisure speak, it was still a black cloud day. *Just what was God thinking when he proposed a day of rest? He never thought of the consequences it would have on the common man; even drinking beer on Sundays is tarnished by some underlying thought of guilt. He obviously never considered the onset of Monday morning for the working classes.*

Nathan never expected another playback of his underachievements. It was a harsh reflection of his past, somehow attempting to time warp the solution into the future. How did he not manage to become a professional footballer when everyone else around him believed that was his destiny?

A brief stint at Huddersfield Town as a junior never materialised into full-time status. It was easy to blame the lack of parental encouragement, or the comfort too easily found in swilling away the night in music-laden bars with desirable females on tap. It was not in these places where his dissuasion from sporting greatness lay, but somewhere in the recess of his unconscious. What happened to those bold aspirations of a boy who became all too aware of a hope, a dream? These were the haunting questions posed by a lack of self-actualisation.

The motivating sound of the doorbell made Nathan cut his shower short. Charmaine had a particular expertise in calling round unexpectedly.

"Not caught you at a bad time I hope?" she said, trying hard not to stare at his towelled body.

"Make some tea if you like, I'll join you in a minute," Nathan suggested. The concoction of Charmaine's problematic life and her determined aspirations created a welcome deflection from his own anxieties. She was twelve years younger than him and had been left without a father for as long as she could remember; a misfortune they both shared. Only Charmaine's neurotic mother had been there to guide her through the growing pains of teenage angst. Her plain beauty proposed an aura of innocence, yet her social perceptions were finely tuned. Although their relationship was one of platonic respect, there was an obligatory sexual tension; it dangled temptingly in front of them like a chord waiting for one of them to pull on it. To Charmaine, it was far from a geographical coincidence that Nathan had moved into the house at the end of her street. She often deluded herself with the notion that he had arrived to lead her to the looking glass of salvation, where the pitiful drudgery of her existence would be transposed into a world less fearful. The fact that Nathan had a degree in philosophy fuelled her interest in him further. She was in her second year of a psychology degree, at the same time as running the cocktail bar in the nearby Bistro.

By the time Nathan got out of the shower for the second time, Charmaine had his agenda arranged in the usual fashion: his favourite England football team mug was placed perfectly at arm's length on the side table; she knew he preferred to watch football with coffee rather than tea. The football was already underway as she half-lay on the sofa, flicking incessantly through some promotional mail from Greenpeace.

"So how was your Sunday?" she asked, as he watched the game uninterestedly.

"Well, it was a Sunday, bleak prospect of Monday hanging over."

"Hmm, who was it that said 'Mondays are the sand-traps on the golf course of life'?" Charmaine posed.

"No idea." He twisted his head away from the match, before supplementing his thoughts.

"Sounds like a line from a Seventies sitcom." She liked to

prise conversation out of him. She was also fascinated by the way he could never sit still when he spoke; his hand gestures matched his head movements – twitchy and changeable.

There was another small thing about Nathan that amused her – his unique modesty when it came to showing flesh. If his T-shirt pulled up whilst lounging around he would quickly tug it back down over his tummy and shift his eyes to see if she had noticed. Charmaine would feel herself blush if she caught sight of his hamster-coloured skin. But it was his cleanliness that impressed her most about him; he was always appropriately attired and carried a freshness that most grown men just don't keep. She found it pleasing to cater for his mundane habitual pleasures, expecting in return only the reward of meaningful conversation; anything to take her away from the inner seclusion of her own psychical detention.

"Oh I remember, it was Snoopy," Charmaine quipped as Nathan flicked through his diary to check his whereabouts for the coming week.

"What?" he asked, turning his head sharply in all directions.

"I had it on a Snoopy poster on my bedroom wall when I was twelve."

"Snoopy," Nathan retorted satirically, "oh well, if Snoopy said it – it must be true!" He sat back down in his chair and slipped into his broody mode, ready to accept Sunday's victory over him.

Although her arrival could at times seem like an intrusion, he was aware of the mutual gratification they both gained from being together. It seemed to provide them both with some much needed affection and intimacy; it grew into a form of psychological escapism. They could tug on each other's belief strings; sharing their dreams meant they could hold onto them tightly, letting the unpleasantness of life fray all by itself. He liked her being there, in her soulful realness, with her extremities of jovial pursuit and shared solitude. Then she would leave without guilt or expectancy; leave him to be himself.

Charmaine had first met Nathan when he had visited the Bistro with a girlfriend. She remembered thinking how mismatched they seemed. The woman portrayed the look of a power dresser who spent most of her time stood up beside her desk spouting orders to someone on the other end of the phone. Nathan however, held an aura of the typical boy next door; he looked comfortable in his own skin, in a stylish, checked shirt and jeans with the boyish mannerisms of a bashful eighteen-year-old. Charmaine estimated his height as five foot eight, making him an inch taller than her, though a good two inches smaller than his date. His athletic frame was more noticeable through his skittish affectations. Moreover, she noticed an incredible relaxation of spirit that protruded his immediate anxiousness. It was the woman, *that black hearted sacred cow in Versace clothing*, who insisted they both order a cocktail, and then proceeded to present an over self-indulgent communiqué on how a White Russian should be prepared. She had complained to Charmaine that the cream was sour and demanded the cocktails be replaced. The woman strutted away to the restroom with the pretentious precision of a catwalk model.

Charmaine was delighted and touched when Nathan leaned sympathetically over the bar and apologised to her. She immediately detected a sensitivity in him. She convinced herself that he was far too sensitive, intelligent and handsome – if somewhat unconventionally – for such a plastic person, who spat venomous remarks all too easily.

Nathan's first date in the Bistro had ended in a cascade of embarrassment. The woman finally declared that Charmaine 'wouldn't know a fucking Orgasm from a Slow Screw', to which Charmaine had fittingly replied that the woman 'had probably never experienced either without faking it'.

Nathan held his hands to his face in the way that a

professional footballer does after missing an open goal; his potential one-night-stand poured the remaining contents of her cocktail into Charmaine's face.

"Bitch!" she had screamed before storming off with stilettos screeching across the polished floor, leaving tainted droplets of dignity spilling onto her empty stage. Nathan immediately diffused the situation by reassuring the manager that Charmaine was in no way to blame for his companion's overplayed performance.

"You okay? Sorry about that!" Nathan said, handing her a napkin from the end of the bar.

"A combination of PMT and too much memo writing I guess."

"I'll survive; anyway it's not as bad as the pints of bitter you can get thrown in your face down at the Duck and Drake." Nathan couldn't help noticing how erotic it had made her look. She stood unblemished by the offending liquid, calmly padding her glazed skin with the napkin as a trickle of cream seeped sensually down her neck, gradually seeping through her white blouse to expose her firm, milky breasts. After a few moments of small talk he offered to walk her home whereupon the conversation became less hampered by enforced predicament. That was the moment they became part of each other's world. From then on it was as if neither of them had any choice.

★

He had acquired a certain amount of contentment in his work as a sales representative for a musical equipment manufacturer, though he loathed the driving. To Nathan, cars were the scourge of mankind, private dormitories of frustration, anger and cynicism. *They were roaming the earth in their millions; a nauseating intruder of social culture. The world was evolving dangerously fast.*

Whatever happened to the simple life? Nathan would have been perfectly suited to life in Fifties Britain, when the pace of life was never at odds with its simplicity. He could have melted safely into the background of tree-lined avenues and country clubs – driving around cautiously in a metallic blue Ford Anglia.

Selling guitars, keyboards, amplifiers and microphones created at least some aesthetic value to his profession. It was the one remaining link to part of his previous life. However, the common toil of working for a living still managed to tie him to the ransom chair of normality. His part-time lecturing post at the local college did give him a sense of satisfaction and altruism, surpassed only by the pure essence of worthiness.

Lecturing in philosophy had given him back his much needed stage; here he was admired, revered, even inspiring. Nathan had spent much of the early Eighties touring Europe as the sound engineer for a contemporary rock band called Shelter in a Suitcase. They enjoyed a modicum of success with a top forty album and three top thirty singles, although only one reached the elusive Top Twenty.

Then, like many bands, they just split, claiming 'managerial mishaps' had created 'artistic differences'. The only member of the band he had remained friends with was the unusually nicknamed Schmarko, who now lived and worked in New York. He made his living writing monotonous jingles for radio stations and TV companies who were prepared to pay extortionate amounts of money for what they believed to be radical compositions.

Nathan was never seduced by the archetypal rock band pastimes. He preferred instead to limit his substances to cold beer and the very occasional puff on someone else's joint. The AIDS scare during the era had also ensured he kept his sexual exploits to a minimum. Schmarko often used to accuse him of being timid, with a bequest intention to avoid life in the fast lane. Nathan's counter argument was to advocate his independent right to free will and self-control. He was more than happy to dip his toe into hedonism but not to wallow in it. He had come across too many bedraggled folks who had allowed self-gratification to paint them into a caricature of themselves.

The five-year ordeal of sound recording work had led to various personal projects, including session and studio work. However, as with Shelter in a Suitcase, he always seemed to be working with bands bordering on the verge of major success, but never quite turning out to be the next U2 or Simple Minds. The last thing he needed was the obligatory reminder of how persistence pays off. Five years of sleeping on stacks of amplifiers in the back of fart-contaminated transit vans and squalid, semen-stained hotel rooms had quelled his desire to become a record producer. The fortuitous hand on the shoulder that invited you through the door of reputability had somehow eluded him.

When the inevitable split happened, it was to Nathan the welcome corrosion of effervescent relationships, cast from what he believed to be the most volatile occupation in the world. There had been some colourful memories; those created from the half-hearted antics of precocious young men, which arise from collective testosterone levels. Nathan believed that the continuous high jinks flowed from a contrived existence. The petty pilfering of stale French sticks and cheap beer from the back of café bars was borne of stereotypical behaviour, rather than as a quest for survival. They were hardly on the brink of malnutrition. Such actions did nothing to enamour him to the lifestyle others seemed to crave.

There had been other moments, those which are placed deliberately in the unconscious lock up of long term memory until our failings and disappointments seek for us to evoke the memory as a form of psychological compensation for our current disappointments. On one particular hot Paris day inbetween gigs,

Nathan lost himself in the episodic subsistence of the city. Sitting under the Arc de Triomphe, inhaling all its grandeur, he visualised the prolific footsteps that had once been trodden there: Napoleon, and Hitler after he conquered France in that act of defiance. Countless world leaders and other notorious people had stood there and pondered the curvature of their lives, probably long before they became known to the world. They had all passed through this very same dimension which only time separated him from. Then for some unknown reason, he thought of that council estate house he once shared with two other people when he was unemployed. He tried to rationalise the direction of his thinking. What was the significance of him being able to stand where eminence had once prevailed? Next, he thought about the threadbare carpet in that same house and the old sofa that was on the brink of collapse when someone had the nerve to actually sit on it; it was later found to be the loving home for a family of mice. It seemed an absurdity, that in his physical realm of existence he could contemplate the contrast between that sofa and the Arc de Triomphe. Rubbing shoulders with historical greatness spurred him into questioning his place in the world. It was no longer good enough to just simply live. He needed to find a reason, or faith. There was an obligation to leave his mark in some way.

After strolling along the North Bank of the Seine, by Notre-Dame Cathedral, he eventually headed for the surreal diversion of the Place du Tertre. Painters beckoned him to sit for a portrait, as mime artists cordially invited him into their performance. He never knew what had lured him to sit at that café bar. It might have been the refreshing mimicry of the Stella Artois sign, or simply the sheer thirst for liquid refreshment. Perhaps it was something else – something that dwells deep in the libido of us all.

He swigged the crisp, ice-cold lager with the prudence of a man trapped at the oasis of life.

Placing the half-empty glass on the table he noticed a woman sitting a few seats away who appeared to be casting a warm smile in his direction. Her dress was soft peach; it hung onto her physique lightly – almost as light as the cause of the early warnings of an unwanted erection, which Nathan did his best to conceal. Nathan judged her to be in her early forties. He scanned her outline as if pre-sketching oil paint on the canvas of his arousal. She licked her forefinger with a well-practised sexual etiquette, before peering over her designer sunglasses with the confidence to encapsulate Nathan's awareness of her.

"Hello," she gestured. "You are English, yes?"

"Is it that obvious?" he replied after thinking that she had the typically accented vocalisation of the English language, like the ones often portrayed in British comedy sketches.

"No no," she held up a hand in apology, "I overheard you talking to the waiter." No sooner than the introductory body language had altered its form, she ambled across to sit at his table. "May I join you?" she asked, dragging the chintzy, wrought iron chair out from the opposite side of the table.

"Yes, please do." Although the onset of crow's feet had begun to establish a pattern around her dark, exotic, brown eyes, her strong, sensual lips and slicked back, jet black hair provided the perfect erotic accessories.

Nathan soon learned that she was a fashion photographer. She had sexual liberation oozing out of her every pore. Her intentions were not at first sexual in motivation; only when she had discovered an allure for his veracity and sensitivity, did she feel the overwhelming urge to bestow her carnal expertise on him. Nathan was uplifted by having a conversation with someone who knew things about the world, other than what was on the front pages of tabloid newspapers. They discussed everything from music, art and literature to the state of the Third World. Two hours and three drinks later, they were almost counting down the inescapability of what was to come.

Back at the woman's apartment, Nathan imagined himself to give off a scent of virginity.

He was happy to let her take on the responsibility of seductress. She skilfully undid the brass fly buttons on his fading jeans; she took him eloquently between her lips, clasping her hands together around the base of her spine, which accentuated the eroticism and equalised the sense of sexual power. Nathan exploded into spasms of excitation. It was as if every shadow of any innocence he still clung to had finally merged with all his darkest fantasies. They continued to make love all through that afternoon; hardly any conversation was needed. There was no need for questions about each other's aspirations or likes and dislikes. This was what it was – a rendezvous of lust. Sauntering through the Paris night, a sensual fulfilment flowed through him. *If the rest of the tour was over tomorrow it had at least served a purpose;* although what the purpose was, he wasn't sure.

We could conclude that Nathan had experienced his iceberg melting for the first time, where conscious thoughts melt into unconscious desires, meaning we cannot always distinguish between our actions and our dreams. Our unwanted thoughts sink, until desire causes them to float to the surface once again. It is this melting process that confuses us, because when our thoughts fuse we can never find what we are looking for. Instead, we swim back to the depth where we feel secure. This is because what we want most rests on the ocean floor of our insatiability; it belongs to a different sea that we have not yet navigated. But the tide of life will carry us out to sea and wash us back up on the shore. The cycle will not end unless we can find the right wave; only then will we recognise the purpose of our actions.

★

14

We have already learned that Charmaine possesses an immensely sharp perception of the world, which is incredible given her mother's constant battle with psychiatric disorders. The constant emotive turmoil created by her mother guided Charmaine towards a saner reality, rather than a darkened seclusion. She was determined not to let her mother's troubles quell her appreciation of finding peace. Or at least that was her front; internally, Charmaine carried fragilities of her own, which could creep into her otherwise strong-minded outlook.

Auntie Norma had been her 'Rock of Gibraltar' in recent years. She was the one trustworthy member of the family who had always afforded Charmaine some necessary attention. Her mother did have good points and was always eager to jump on the bandwagon of praise with regard to Charmaine's academic achievements. It was just a shame that her frail psychological condition never really allowed her to be a reliable source of inspiration.

In order to vacate herself from the four wall torment at home, Charmaine found excessive studying to be the best form of escapism. This stupendous self-discipline had resulted in ten grade A GCSEs at school and three straight As in A-levels at college. Her strategic life plan was mapped out with precision: first A levels, then a BSc in Psychology, MSc in Social Psychology followed by a PhD, which she thought would be based on mental illness in socially deprived communities, leading up to a position as a clinical psychologist. She had waded through the usual girly teenage friendships with some of her ex school mates, although it never amounted to more than a temporary outlet. Most of her friends proclaimed the more obvious route to self-fulfilment: meet a boy, fall in love and get married; then assume divorce after ten years whereupon the goal would be to have regular sunbed sessions and to frequent popular suburban pubs, looking for Mr Second Time Around. The dull prospect of mapped-out mediocrity persuaded

Charmaine to drop out of the reckoning fairly early on. She did however have the obligatory boyfriend, who for a short time offered her an appealing alternative to Saturday nights in alone. For most of her relationship with Leonard, she spent too much time pretending to be interested in his ambitions of owning his own graphic design studio and 4x4 complete with tow bar to pull his windsurfing equipment. Although she enjoyed their nights out together, the impeding closeness highlighted their obvious differences. She thought of the gap between their expectations as two trains at the same station that are bound for different destinations.

Sometimes the confusion of life weighed her down heavily, as if it was a disguised burden placed on her by her mother's psychological problems. Even a holiday romance had left her with a moral teething. She could never accept it as a typical healthy necessity or rite of passage; instead she chose to pry deep into her own reasoning until all she found was a shallow emptiness that echoed around her conscience. Those nights of lovemaking with an Adonis of a man had only served to flood her mind with unanswerable questions… *What am I doing; what am I trying to prove to myself; is this really me?* She convinced herself with an explanation; she had succumbed to her sexual needs at a conscious level, yet her soul or unconscious mind had not participated willingly. The dualism between her mind and body had been at war; she needed them to make peace. One evening after lying awake beside her Cypriot lover, she decided to walk down to the beach. As she trampled her way across the night sand she raised her arms aloft as if inviting the salted sea air to evaporate her physical body, leaving only her soul to soak up the sea moisture. Charmaine began to talk aloud.

"Life shouldn't be based around desires. There has to be a better way to love than this." It was like a splash of guilt had woken her from a morally perfect dream. Charmaine had soothed her conscience, though her soul was no longer white. Any further stains would be enough to change everything. *The cleansing would have to begin.*

After her first full year at university, Charmaine had become a virtual stranger to social life. Five nights a week waitressing at The Flying Pasta restaurant during summer holidays had limited her daytime activity to reading, watching daytime TV and the occasional walk into town. When Toto, the restaurant manager, offered her the chance to train as a cocktail waitress she seized the opportunity with a delighted honesty. The new job would mean she had one less night to work for slightly more money.

Toto's amorous intentions were a side dish to his disguised lust. He showered her with flowers and chocolates before peaking at a gold bracelet. At first, she blocked the transparent affection she received from him. For some unknown reason she endorsed his false charm, just enough to reignite the spark in herself that had dimmed since the start of the summer break. She decided that liking his company might just generate other feelings she had stored away. She meandered through the relationship with a casual disregard of his efforts to woo her, until the formality of dead end love dimmed her perceptions just enough to let her lose sight. A rare evening out with a couple of university friends had been interrupted by the arrival of an anxious-looking Auntie Norma.

"Charmaine, it's your mum!" Her aunt bellowed over the girly gossip.

"What's happened?"

"She's been assaulted; come on, we need to go to the hospital." Charmaine's mother had been physically and sexually assaulted by one of the drunks who frequented the local working men's club, where her mother was also a regular.

At the infirmary, Charmaine tried to focus on the bruised and bloody distortions of her mother's face. "Hey," she whispered, as she reached out caringly for her mother's blackened hand. "Everything's okay, Mum, don't worry." She knew her words were a meaningless comfort, if they even registered at all.

She felt she was in the middle of a sorry scenario; it was ludicrous yet unsurprising at the same time. Charmaine and her Auntie Norma had always feared this kind of occurrence, due to the type of crowd her mother associated with. They had always tried to allow her to make her own judgments as it meant she had some claim to her self-sufficiency and independence. The long night in the atmosphere of the intensive care unit ground guilt into the minds of Charmaine and Auntie Norma; they locked it away, as if sealed by a mutual conscience where only they would hold the key.

When her mother returned from hospital, Charmaine and Auntie Norma took turns at being on-call for nursing duties. Despite her mother's neurosis she was a hardy woman, with an eggshell-like lifejacket. She insisted she didn't need a twenty-four hour bedside vigil and had actually passed the whole incident off as a misunderstanding. She also claimed that the drunk, known as Sad Sid, had tried it on for years, only this time he had gone too far. Charmaine couldn't agree with the attitude of denial that her mother had adopted. She believed that despite her mother's irrational behaviour, it should be natural for her to want vindication. To Charmaine, the whole affair was an embarrassing absurdity; it highlighted her mother's pitiful social life and the circle of rapacious individuals who infiltrated it. The police had strongly advised her mother to press charges, believing they could almost guarantee a conviction for sexual assault. Her mother did not have the psychological armour to withstand another stressful life incident – especially one which had the potential to drag on for months.

Toto, whilst proclaiming his total sympathy for Charmaine's

predicament, was unhappy at being seemingly ignored for a whole two weeks. He could cope with her absence from the cocktail bar, but the fact that she had other people higher up her priority list bothered him. Every telephone conversation between them ended in disharmony; his lack of patience and understanding, which he had managed to keep submerged, now began to surface in a tide of selfishness.

It had been the longest time she had ever spent in that house without stepping into the outside world. The closest she had come to any human contact other than her mother and Auntie Norma, during that time, was to wave to Demetri the Greengrocer across the street whilst managing to escape into the front garden. Demetri embraced the mandatory routine of asking how her mother was, then immediately slipped into his usual sexist but harmless remarks.

"Hey Charmaine, you want to come and feel my fresh grapes, yes?" he shouted over to her.

"No thanks, not after seeing what your nuts are like!" Their repartee carved out the first smile across her face since the attack on her mother. She had developed a healthy banter of sexual innuendos with Demetri. His routine was well known amongst the local female community. Though it bordered on being mildly offensive at worst, most people accepted it as part of his natural Greek allure and basic grasp of English. Only Charmaine was able to equal his double entendre without showing any hint of humiliation. She could never decide if this was an innate skill or one she had refined through her daily verbal intercourse with him. She looked to him for laughs, accepting that he had somehow equipped her with some optional extras to her profile of sublime virtuousness. That brief and throwaway rapport with Demetri blew the fuse to her boredom; she felt the need to get out into the world again. It was time to fold back the carpet under which she had swept leaves of guilt, and blow them into oblivion.

19

She decided to take a shower and dress for summer. Charmaine's personal motivation was harmonised by her compassion for others. Now though, she needed some time for herself. She found an old, red, patterned dress in her wardrobe. The shoulder straps were thin, revealing the glossy skin on her shoulders. She chose to wear her canvas pumps that gave her legs an athletic look. Throwing her shoulder bag over her head, she was ready for the outside world.

"Mum, will you be okay on your own if I go out for a while? I need to walk, breathe some fresh air."

"Don't you worry about me, love, I'm fine. It's about time you got yourself out. There's no need for all this nurse-y stuff, you know. Go on – get yourself off!"

"Okay, bye, I'll bring you something nice back!"

The gaiety of her personal suburbia seemed to be coloured with an extravagance she had not recognised before. She was ready to indulge in a freedom of spirit. She bought a selection of magazines and some natural beauty products from the nearby arcade. She fingered through a selection of men's ties in one of the local clothes shops and giggled out loud as one with a Flintstones cartoon design caught her eye. She decided it would be a nice peace offering for Toto.

There was a bounce in her step as she edged her way past the morning delivery of Italian beers. By the time she tiptoed into the kitchen of the Bistro she was actually excited at the prospect of seeing his face light up; that is if he could tear himself away from cleaning the store cupboard, which was where all the noise appeared to be coming from.

"Hello!" Charmaine parroted, lightly. The illicit groans of pleasure drifted over towards her in a wind of deceit. Toto was lost in the stormy skies of lovemaking; he writhed at the new waitress from the rear with the intensity of a dutiful Apollo. A shocked sideways glance from the girl disturbed his rhythmic gyrations. There were no gestures from him, no instinctive pulling up of trousers, followed by the immortal line of 'It's not what it seems!' Instead, his face carried an expression of melancholic justification. It was the waitress's inexcusable nervous giggles that prompted Charmaine to seize hold of a large plastic bottle of mayonnaise standing on the nearest shelf. She hurled it at the wall above their heads. The container recoiled off the wall, spewing mayonnaise over their dispirited copulation – showering them both in undignified sinfulness.

Charmaine walked home. A subconscious cloud descended through her mind. As she crossed the river bridge into the village, she sang inwardly to console her shattered ego, whilst swinging her shopping bags dispiritedly. She could feel the semi-conscious thoughts fusing with her conscious awareness; they ebbed through to her soul – the deepest, most personal part of her – the only place where she felt that she had total ownership. By the time she reached Demetri's grocery stall, he was closing for the day.

"Hey Charmaine!" he chanted. "Had a nice day?" he asked, unwittingly.

"Yeah," she answered with a relaxed smile. "Actually, fucking brilliant!" Demetri, though used to her tactical replies to his smutty utterances, was stunned by her response. Holding a box of apples in front of him he stared back at her; his posture was frozen like one of those street artists who spends weeks practising complete stillness to mimic a famous statue.

He managed to mouth out a reply. "That good, eh?"

"Yup, that good!" As she began to cross the road she realised that she still had the Flintstones tie in her bag. She turned back to face him with a reflective leer. "Oh by the way," she said, "a present for you." She tossed him the tie.

"A present for me?" Demetri enquired, catching it over his arm. "What's that for?"

"Your honesty!" she shouted back.

21

Charmaine wondered how she could have let this happen; she was usually more in control. The analysis became painful. *There must be an explanation. What did I do that was wrong?* The frailties of her conscious mind had been invaded by unconscious desires. But she felt no need for tears or regret. It was just part of an unplanned journey; an interlude in the movie of life. And yet as thoughts jumped like electrons around her mind, the feeling itself was opening up; like a butterfly hovering for a more perfect place to land, an earnest comfort flooded down into her belly. A sense of restfulness streamed through her soul, washing away the stains. She could let it go. *There is a reason for everything. Someone better is waiting for me.*

Like Nathan, Charmaine had come to learn how the iceberg mind takes on a will of its own. After all, she had studied the theories. Although when the cavern of one's own yearnings plummet into the sub aqua tropics of acquiescence, our restraint can be easily shipwrecked. She knew the only way to stop it was to stay on dry land. *But that might be difficult. There is a life to live.* There was always the unexpected: the ship that sailed towards you, bringing with it the promise of the perfect island paradise. But for now she had to plan her journey carefully; it would mean building a life raft. It would also mean staying away from stormy waters.

For the deep thinker, the need for self-reflection is not just a way of analysing one's mistakes. It is a healing process; a way to decontaminate our imperfections. We could simply refer to it as soul searching. But more than that, it's a leap of faith for one's own fate.

REFLECTIONS AND PERCEPTIONS

The sales office secretary at Nathan's office phoned to ask him to meet the area manager outside one of his customer's shops in the coastal town of Scarborough. The heavy morning rain suggested an imminence of spirit-dampening. When he arrived at the music shop, there was no sign of his senior colleague. The area manager portrayed a constant depiction of formality that made Nathan feel uncomfortable. He decided to wait in the sanctity of his car for a while, awaiting the arrival of his superior with the dread of a schoolboy who had been requested to stand outside the Headmaster's office. The tones of early morning radio coupled with the battering noise of rain on metal were an unwelcome pre-med for the operation in hand. After waiting for an hour, Nathan decided to make his way into the customer's shop; he needed the pleasantries of amiable introductions to lighten the heavy expectancy. By the time his boss arrived two hours late, Nathan had already clinched the order from his satisfied customer, who had ordered six new synthesizers, five electric guitars and an assortment of accessories. His boss was eager to show his distaste at Nathan's apparent disregard for his absence. He deliberately chose not to disguise his adversity in front of the customer, by casting verbal aspersions rather than congratulatory remarks. The short-lived ecstasy of a morning's work subsided into an after effect of ego deflating enormity. His boss continued to rant at him outside the shop, his face twitching in spasms of anger.

Nathan had fallen victim to the worst sort of verbal caning: displacement, a cowardice action that deflects the animosity onto the innocent. Nathan knew he had done nothing wrong yet his boss opted for the unconscious escape route for his own repressed anger. Nathan just happened to be holding the route map. The clear skies of elation which should have been hanging over him deflated, leaving a cloud of discontentment. He grappled with the flight or fight reaction swarming through his body. Part of him wanted to crawl back into his childhood bedroom. He wanted to curl up on the bed like a boy and detest everything in the world. He battled against his sensitivity and walked back to the car with a robust step.

After parting from his boss he decided to drive along the sea front and take a walk along the pier.

"Fuck it! *Fuck it!*" He bought a large ice cream cornet with a flake. Self-reward was better than none at all. On walking back to the car he noticed a young boy who was playing on the beach by himself. The boy's mother looked on from the dry cover of the sea front shelter. Nathan was intrigued by the boy's actions; he was using a stick to etch patterns into the rain-smoothed sand. The multiples of ordered lines didn't appear to resemble anything in particular – only the overactive imagination of a child's inner mind. They were the kind of patterns that allowed you to see whatever you wanted to see. Nathan saw himself at the same age, on a similar wet day playing on the beach in Lowestoft; lost in a world of subconscious limbo, as his mother and grandmother watched from the cover of the promenade. Nathan was amazed at the accuracy and vividness of his reflections.

If he could only remember what his thoughts were back then and if they held any significance to his present life, there might be an outcome to his trials. That young boy there on the beach was him; not a dreamlike apparition of a former life but a living, breathing mass of flesh and blood, captured in the same fantasy, just another dimension of time. The boy carried that look of outer happiness, the same look that Nathan had always worn as a child. His eyes, though, disclosed an inner confusion. Nathan could tell the normal childish egocentric traits were buried even deeper than usual – just as they had been within himself as a child.

His gaze followed the boy to the incoming tide. The boy then danced around as if performing a ritual to his creation in the sand. He chanted warrior-like utterances, then immediately ran back over to his sand painting and tapped his stick on the sand as he trampled carefully around the outline.

His mission was complete and sanctified with the sea as witness. Nathan wondered exactly what the boy's actions had meant to him. He was snapped out of his trance-like state when the boy's mother called him to come out of the rain. The boy ran exuberantly back to his mum who then tweaked his baseball cap over his eyes, suggesting they treat themselves to a hotdog. Nathan climbed back into his car; the freshness of sea salt air and rain melted into an aroma of polished dashboard and air freshener. He watched the boy and woman walk hand-in-hand along the sea front. The boy never looked back at his work of art, that world where moments ago he had been lost somewhere in his own future. It was as if he had already forgotten, that is until the time in his life when he would come to climb that spiral staircase in his unconscious. Nathan had not forgotten. He was happy again… happy because he remembered that enlightenment is only a subjective thought away.

★

Charmaine came around earlier than usual.

"What's up?" Nathan asked sarcastically. "What's made you so happy?"

"No, I'm fine, it's just mum's gone down to the club again. Any sane person would keep well away after what happened, wouldn't they?"

"That's the trouble though. She's not sane is she, in the normal sense of the word. Listen, let me do the honours for a change, but it'll be pasta and salad – maybe some red wine if you're lucky, but nothing fancy."

"I feel a bit cheeky," Charmaine said apologetically, "I usually do all that. That's the deal right, why I come round?"

"So it makes a change, chill out! Sit down, watch TV and enjoy," he said, handing her the remote control. "You can even sit in my chair if you want."

"Now that is an offer."

This was the first time they had ever talked with the added ingredient of alcohol. Their conversation edged towards a more risqué domain. Charmaine had incited it by being inquisitive about Nathan's past love life. He could see another side of her beginning to emerge. The articulate manner and the coat of intellectual confidence had been slightly scratched, exposing her vulnerability. He liked this side of her – the girl with the classroom giggles and clement frigidity. It didn't undermine his perception of her, rather it reinforced his trust in her womanhood. Long after midnight and small talk, Charmaine rose delicately to her feet and offered to wash the dishes. Her gesture, whilst wholehearted and genuine, contained an amount of seduction.

"Can't get rid of you tonight then, eh?" Nathan jibed. "Go on then; I know you feel duty-bound, but remember all breakages will be docked from your wages!"

"Funny, can't remember you paying me before for my professional services." They had flowed further down the stream of their relationship and were happy to be drifted along without navigation. At least that's what they believed.

Nathan touched her lightly on the arm as he said goodnight. "Thanks for an even more than erm, wonderful, usual erm…" he stuttered nervously.

"I know what you mean, you don't have to get all

tongue-tied. Anyway I should thank you, you cooked for me remember."

As their evening was about to formally close, the sound of a man's scream boomed around Nathan's porch.

"The hell's that?" Nathan shouted.

"Don't know but it's coming from my house," Charmaine replied worriedly. Both of them instinctively raced the few doors down to Charmaine's house. Nathan decided to enter first, with some trepidation.

"Shout your mother!"

"Mum! Are you alright?" Charmaine gripped Nathan's arm firmly as they proceeded upstairs to where the continuous screams were coming from. Charmaine's mother walked casually past them, with a look of satisfaction emanating from her face. Nathan followed the shouts into her mother's bedroom. A naked man was lying on the bed, clutching his genitals, which appeared to be blazing red. An overturned kettle lay on the floor.

"Bitch! Fucking crazy bitch has scolded me balls off!" the man yelled in obvious agony.

"No more than he deserves!" Charmaine's mother declared from the safety of downstairs. The man attempted to dress himself through the pain and made for the front door, hobbling and balancing on one foot at a time as he pulled his trousers up hurriedly. Nathan couldn't help noticing that the man still had his shoes and socks on. He also couldn't help feeling amused at the bizarre scenario playing out before him. The man's socks were striped with a Dennis the Menace face and his light brown, plastic shoes looked like he had bought them from one of those 'bargain basement' shoe shops. His greasy, grey hair had a few coppery yellow strands that slicked back round his head like a fishbone. The man darted out of the door, shouting blasphemies whilst still holding his boiling loins.

27

"Fucking psycho woman!" This was a man who, three months earlier whilst in a drunken stupor, had sexually assaulted a lady with known psychological problems in the car park of the local working men's club.

Nathan drove through the rest of the week with a different outlook. From his travelling observatory the contrasting visions of millennium Britain passed before him. *Every scene could represent the social errors of modern day life. Queuing at a traffic light junction can give a person much insight into human behaviour and the state of society.* A young mother he deduced to be no more than eighteen years old pushed a buggy along, complete with infant. An older child – a girl of about three – walked solemnly behind; her head was bowed as she stomped her feet in the puddles. Nathan realised the child that was walking was dressed in a dishevelled, stained coat and shabby shoes with untied laces. The mother turned her head and shouted obscene threats at the girl then grabbed her by the collar of her coat, hauling her along the path. Such a callous act of aggression of a mother towards her own daughter shocked Nathan to the core. There was a cursory glance between Nathan and the woman; he decided there and then that her life was over, in the sense that it was not hers to savour. *Her freedom had been squandered in two decisive moments; her psyche had been left behind, somewhere in an empty glass.*

Perhaps this is why those of us who cannot realise the call from our soul become lost. This is because it is blown into the wilderness of silence; left forever to float on the ill winds that take it from here to there. The young woman's conscience had been brutalised by her own misgivings. We can never decide right from wrong according to our own morality. Hers had evaporated and ceased to be active, waiting like a volcano, for the right moment to erupt. Nathan decided it had done so twice. In the same way that magma from the volcano leaves its enduring mark, the eruption of our empty soul can also leave us with an unending legacy.

He was looking forward to meeting Eddie. Eddie's Music, as his shop was known, was the last bastion of small town music stores. Pro rata he had probably sold more guitars to budding musicians who had gone on to make it in the music business than any other shop in the north. Ed the Ted had inherited his nickname from his teen days; he was now a portly fifty-something with long, grey hair tied back in an essential ponytail. His chubby fingers would ease elegantly up and down the guitar fret-board and there wasn't a rock riff invented that he couldn't play perfectly.

Nathan held a lot of respect and affection for Eddie; he was *his* kind of person – true to himself and others. He never expected a large order; although Eddie's mutual fondness for Nathan would always guarantee an order of some kind, even if it was a couple of lower priced classical guitars.

As soon as Nathan entered the shop he became aware of the unusual atmosphere. There was no virtuoso performance of famous rock riff melodies, and no casual callers clad in leather jackets who hung around to smoke roll-up cigarettes and swap grunge gossip. Eddie's number one helper Ray drifted up from the basement on hearing the shop doorbell chime.

"Hi Nathan, how you doing? Not good news, Matey." A sullen expression leaked out through his face. "Ed's gone and had a heart attack, silly old sod."

"Oh my God. When?"

"Three days ago. He's hooked up to all them monitor things; it's not good, Matey." Ray made Nathan a strong cup of coffee as he updated him on the capers of the last few days. Nathan did not want to discuss business with him, feeling that in the circumstances it would amount to treachery. But Ray had been given instructions from Eddie to order four of the new range of semi-acoustic guitars. Nathan suggested the financial details could be sorted out at a later date.

It was an unimportant transactional activity when compared to a visit to the hospital.

The nurses in the coronary care unit told Nathan he wouldn't be able to see him. Only close family members were allowed to visit whilst Eddie was in this critical stage of recovery. Instead, Nathan bought a sun-faded get well soon card from the hospital shop. As he begun to compose what he felt would be an appropriate message, a young woman approached him.

"Excuse me, are you Nathan?" she asked him assertively.

"Yes I am," he replied with a look of surprise.

"I'm Ella, Eddie's daughter."

"Oh, right, hi, I'm sorry." Nathan was more taken aback by her appearance than anything else.

"We met once before when I was helping Dad out at the shop."

"Oh yes, I remember now." He also knew about much of her life from the many anecdotes that Eddie had revealed to him, but he was still surprised by her demeanour. Hardly the typical offspring of a wild-child ageing rock and roller; she was dressed in unfashionable corduroy trousers and hiking boots, with a tatty checked shirt half tucked in and half hanging out. As she explained her father's current status, he remembered that Eddie had once told him she lived on an organic farm complex, spending much of her spare time protesting about the destruction of tropical rainforests.

She was touched to accept Nathan's get well card.

"I'll make sure Dad gets this," Ella said, wafting it in the sterile air of the walkway. Nathan wished her and all the family well and headed back through the antiseptic corridors. He knew that one of Eddie's favourite albums of all time was 'Sheer Heart Attack' by Queen. Inside the card, he had written:

Eddie, it will take more than one sheer heart attack to rid the world of a big style rocker. See you soon for a pie and a pint (or two). Onwards and upwards, matey!
Best wishes, Nathan.

Driving home, Nathan slipped into autopilot. His thoughts were on Eddie; the fragility of life became even more obvious. By the time he reached home soil, his mood was reflective and he was forlorn.

★

Charmaine's time at the Bistro had been made easier to bear due to Toto's dismissal. The owner was a devout Roman Catholic and was against any such fraternisation between staff, especially on the premises. It turned out that Charmaine was not the only one to have had the displeasure of catching them in the act. Although she enjoyed the build-up of spare time, she was counting the days to the start of term; there had been a void created by the lack of essay deadlines and research projects. Since the genital scalding incident, her mother had been quite well. She had even taken on a new hobby of dried flower arranging. It was as if the sense of revenge had sedated her into an almost normal disposition, where the tantrums and panic attacks had been neutralised. Every so often, Charmaine would book an appointment at the nearby salon. To her this was more like a hypocratic oath to her femininity than a desire.

She left the fantasy-induced world of the hairdressers with a fresh vigour. Her long, dark hair had always been naturally curly and the hairdressers all seemed to know how to maximise its plainness without it ever looking like a Seventies perm. The ambience of the village invited her to seek new warmth. The inner sense of radiance gave her that feeling funfairs can give you at night. When she arrived

31

home, her mother was happily working away on one of her new arrangements.

"You're becoming a bit of an expert now, Mum. You'll be getting orders from your friends at the club next."

"There's a thought." The house was beginning to resemble a hotel conservatory. And, though she was happy to let her mother's brightened mood blossom, a glass of whisky never seemed too far from reach.

As Charmaine scanned the local newspaper before planning a girly bath, she noticed an advertisement for a psychic and spiritual fair that was being held at a hotel in the next village. Spontaneously, she decided to call on Nathan with the idea of enticing him into a wacky evening. As she breezed up Nathan's garden path she wondered if her request would place too much of a burden on them both. In the ten months she had known him, they had never been together outside of his house.

"Hi, good day at the office, honey?" Nathan jibed in his best fake American accent. The untimely joke busted her composure for a second.

"Swell," she equalled. "I wondered if you fancied doing something really weird tonight for a change."

"Oh okay, I'm excited already," Nathan jested with a wry gentlemanly look of innuendo to accompany his remark.

"There's this psychic fair thing going on at the Wasp's Nest Hotel in Kirkthorpe. Thought it might be a laugh to, well you know, see what it's all about." The seconds passed until Nathan replied, almost dragged into a timeless fit of regret and embarrassment.

"Psychic fair eh, okay, well like you say might be a laugh if nowt else. And who knows, you might discover your third eye," Nathan added in contrived laughter at his own joke – whilst at the same time contorting his facial expression. "Okay, let's do it… Though I usually think these sorts of events are an excuse for people to unite in a form of vacuous worship, brought about through a spiritual insecurity."

"Is that right?" Charmaine replied with a hint of sarcasm in response to his overthinking.

"Oh yes – churchgoers by default, searching for some self-indulgent deliverance into a mystical existence. And, and – a lot of them claim to have contact with the dead. Which is creepy, don't you think?"

"Yup, I just might agree with you on that, Mr B. Come on then – get ready."

It wasn't that Nathan was closed minded to all avenues of soul searching or thirst for unexplained phenomena – quite the opposite. He believed strongly in the power of the mind and the way it could be channelled outside of the normal realm, after all that is exactly what had lured him to study philosophy. He just didn't like having spiritual fulfilment promoted to him. It was a good feeling to be there with her, seeing her face alert to the animations of others.

She bore a childlike yet graceful persona as she dragged him through the malaise of psychics and palm readers.

"Didn't you once tell me your family were all Roman Catholics?" Nathan asked her curiously as they sauntered.

"Lapsed," Charmaine replied swiftly, avoiding any necessity to elaborate.

"Hey look at this," she said as a redirection from his inquisitiveness. One particular stall had caught her interest. Charmaine suggested Nathan should sit for a Kirlian Photograph.

"Now that's something I believe in, a bit anyway," he announced. "I think that's what people actually see when they believe they've seen a ghost. It's just the Kirlian aura of heat and energy that some people leave behind when they've died. I really believe that there are some people who are capable of seeing the Kirlian aura of a person without a Kirlian camera, that's all."

She giggled at his deep sense of creative perception, which uncovered another layer to his boy-like identity. After a few minutes they had a funny looking image of Nathan to laugh about.

"Wow, look at all the heat coming from your head!" Charmaine said excitedly.

"Hmm… does that mean I'm a hot head?"

"It means what I always suspected – there's a lot going on in there!" She tapped his head lightly with her finger. "What about Tarot?" Charmaine inquired.

"Definitely not! Can't be doing with all that curtain twitching stuff and the wailing voices."

After a couple of hours of roving, Charmaine could see that Nathan had just about outlived his battery life for esoteric adventure.

"Come on then, shall we call it a night?" she offered. She decided to buy a few keepsakes on the way out, one a copper bracelet and the other a simple string of rosary beads from the solitary Christian stall close to the exit. She quickly dispatched it into her handbag, though her hidden embarrassment didn't stop him from noticing her purchase. "Good for the circulation!" she explained to Nathan as they headed back to the car.

"Well that was interesting," Nathan remarked.

"Glad you thought so."

When they arrived back at Nathan's house an eerie yet comfortable silence came over them. Charmaine made some coffee whilst Nathan donned a pensive posture in his favourite chair.

"There's some of that wine left if you fancy?"

"Ok, maybe after the coffee."

"So what are you thinking?" Charmaine asked him whilst ushering in with the coffees.

"No, nothing in particular, was just drifting like you do when you've been to a psychic fair."

"Oh, you mean to say you've been evoked, after all that doubting?"

"Well I don't know. I don't believe in all of it but yeah, I mean how can you not think about what life's all about and stuff like that when you've been to one of those things?"

"So you don't just think they're all space bandits?" Charmaine jested. Nathan laughed whilst sipping meaningfully at his coffee. "Come on then, tell me what *you* believe in; everybody believes in something: God, fairies at the end of the garden or alien spacecraft." Charmaine quizzed him further.

"I don't believe in little green men that is for sure! I used to when I was about sixteen. I read some of those famous books at the time, like 'Was God an Astronaut.' Then it was like all of a sudden I had this kind of epiphany."

Charmaine laughed. "Really, Go on!"

"Well it was like when I started to study philosophy I kind of got into the idea of the existence of the soul. You know like it must be a separate thing from the rest of us – separate from our physical existence that is."

"Okay."

"Yeah, because the brain is only a lump of flesh and blood right, so I can't believe that there isn't something greater, controlling it all, how it works… if you know what I mean?"

"Interesting idea, Mr Blakemore," Charmaine replied half-sarcastically but sensing the onset of a stimulating and worthwhile discussion. "So like… it's all controlled by God, then?"

"Maybe."

"But a cognitive psychologist would say that's just how your brain processes information; thoughts and feelings are just cognitive processes. So our brains are really just like computers or processors of information, yeah?" Charmaine felt that she had presented an accomplished argument as she hugged her coffee mug with both hands.

"You realise that makes us nothing better than machines?" Nathan responded.

"Well yes, to an extent. I'm not saying that's what *I* believe."

"Oh you're provoking a philosophical argument, are you?" Nathan suggested, enjoying the implied direction of the conversation. "Well anyway, I can't accept that. There has to be more about us than that. Think about how you feel sometimes when you fall in love or feel really sad; you telling me that's just a process? And if so, does that mean robots have feelings also? I don't think so. You see my point? *We* are different. We're even different to animals if you think about it."

She was becoming intrigued by his depth of thinking. His face found new light when he was forced to discuss issues that excited him. "But aren't we just more evolved than animals?" Charmaine was expertly laying down the intellectual gauntlet. "After all, we have the same basic needs and instincts."

"Ah but that's if you believe in the actual principle of evolution."

"So you don't then?"

"Well I have no problem accepting evolution as a theory for how species adapt. But to say we evolved from something like a stick insect, who's been sitting around thinking, *Well one day in about twenty billion years I might just turn into a man, and walk down the pub for a pint.*" Charmaine giggled like a schoolgirl. "I mean that Darwin bloke, honestly; he goes to some remote island and sees a few different looking birds and because one has a yellow beak and another has orange feet or something like that, lo and behold – he gives us the theory of evolution, to explain all life." Nathan took a quick swig of his coffee. "But seriously, I just don't see it that way; we *are* special, and, we're on a very different level to animals in terms of consciousness."

"Hey, are you saying my cat's not conscious?"

"No, no I'm not saying that, but… she, she *is* a *she* right?"

Charmaine nodded. "*She* is not conscious in the same way that we are."

"Well no, because she's a cat... right!" Charmaine toasted him jovially with her coffee mug.

Nathan began to gesticulate from his armchair lectern as he sat forward.

"Ah but it's not just because she *is* a cat – if you get my meaning? Right, ok think of it this way; animals don't know they are what they are."

Charmaine laughed again almost hysterically as she sprawled out on the rug in ecstasy from the stimulus of intellectual conversation. "So, you're saying our Gitty doesn't know she's a cat? So why does she do things the other cats do then, like chasing mice?"

"No, but you're missing my point Char; she's only doing what she instinctively knows to do. You know about conditioning from psychology, right?"

"Ah, so you do believe in instincts then?"

"Yes of course but listen; what I'm saying is she does all this cat stuff but on a basic level, she doesn't walk around thinking, *Oh what a beautiful cat I am.* In other words she has no real awareness that she actually is a cat, for all she knows she could be a dog, or... a fish – she just lives and eats and sleeps. Whereas, you and me, we can think about stuff like that – like how nice or how crap we look, and what shall I do at the weekend and all that."

"But how do you know for sure? For all we know, Gitty might like how she looks. And maybe she does feel better on some days than others."

"Yes maybe that's true but, one thing's for sure, she's not capable of making long-term plans like, *Oh I think I'll build a cat house next year, or have a cat holiday with my friends from the alley.* She can't solve problems or think abstractly."

"But isn't that because of what I was saying earlier? It's

37

only because her brain's not like ours, remember? Animals are not as cognitively developed as we are; their cortex is not as developed. Anyway in psychology we learned about this experiment on apes where they put a spot on the ape's forehead to see if it can recognise itself in a mirror. That shows they have awareness. Explain that, Mr Philosopher Soul Man, ha ha!" Charmaine flipped over onto her back, punching the air in elation, feeling she was beginning to devour her conversant opponent.

"Ah I've heard about that one. That can be explained by other factors; it still doesn't mean they are conscious to anywhere near the same extent as we are. It just means…" Charmaine jumped to her feet exuberantly to get the bottle of wine from the kitchen as Nathan continued his comeback, raising his voice to ensure she heard. "It just means they can learn to recognise something different about what they see. That's it!"

He realised the curtains were still open and their conversation had taken place in darkness, apart from the watery reflection of street lights that filtered in through the bay window which housed his chair. Nathan stretched out.

"Has all this intelligent discussion tired you out?" Charmaine asked as she poured him a glass of wine.

"No, it's actually kept me awake otherwise I'd have been asleep ages ago."

"So what's our conclusion, Mr Nathan Sir, on this subject?"

"Well I think first round to me," he jested.

"No way, you didn't convince me of anything, only that we have a different level of consciousness to cats."

"So you need more convincing? I'll have to prepare my argument for round two then. Or you can just read my PhD when I ever get around to doing it. Then you'll be swayed for all time," Nathan joked, doing an impression of a mad scientist.

"Hmm PhD eh, that is big league. And what title will you give to this revered offering to humanity?"

"Not sure yet, but it has to be something about consciousness, I guess."

"The consciousness of cats!" Charmaine proposed followed by a hearty laugh. "That's what you should call it!"

"I'll drink to that," Nathan said, holding out his glass out to clink hers. "The consciousness of cats!"

THE PROBLEM WITH INSIGHT

Nathan woke up with that surprise of a man who was floored by a few extra glasses of two-day-old wine. It was nine o'clock on Saturday morning and the stiff-neck effect of falling asleep in his armchair was already urging him to go back to bed for more quality sleep. Charmaine had let herself out; true to form she had conscientiously washed all the cups and glasses. A note was placed thoughtfully on the kitchen table.

Thanks for the great convo; we must do it again soon. C X.

He muffled a laugh, remembering she had been full of sparkle the night before; the Charmaine he had come to know had introduced a previously hidden persona. He felt invigorated by the previous night's events so decided he would go out for a jog – though not before a welcome power nap.

Nathan didn't always know how to play it with women; he was the kind of man most women loved to have as a friend. His outward demeanour suggested he understood their feminine psyche, which made them feel comfortable in his company; they were not threatened by the possibility of him making the wrong kind of advances. Nathan had always told his male friends that he never came on to women, even when he found them attractive. Instead he preferred to hand them the task of steering around the traffic cones of seduction. In any case he always felt like he needed permission before he was allowed to express his desires in any way. His theory was that women knew immediately and exactly what they wanted from a man, be that friendship only, sex, love or in rare cases all three – where pure, unblemished love flows – this set the tone for the entirety of any relationship. Nathan certainly liked Charmaine on all of those levels but because she was a decade or so younger than him, he was unsure of how she would view the potential of their relationship. It would be safer to auto-cruise along in the platonic friend mode rather than attempt any suggestive gamble. Despite his almost clinical rationale for dating women, he was a romantic dreamer. What he really desired was the real deal, full-on, unashamed love; Gene Kelly love with all its glittering edges and blue sky happiness. This was what he wanted with Charmaine; a wish-fulfilled fantasy love story. How to get it was another matter. He recognised that he and Charmaine had shared some fairly intimate hours through their intellectual bonding. Though moving beyond the classification of mutual friends was something just outside his aversion to risk taking.

I was sure that Nathan's real troubles lay in his confidence. He'd said to me on a few occasions that there is nothing worse than having to live with the notion that a woman knocked you back by refuting your romantic advances. To him this was as bad as being accused of a crime you didn't commit and having to live with the shame. But here was a woman who touched his very soul. This was not like one of those prospective relationships that you can fall into like a soft job; only realising some months later that it's not at all like you expected because it doesn't fulfil you to the marrow. This was The One. Charmaine had left an indelible mark on him, somewhere inside his previously unaccessed mortality. All he had to do now was find a way to preserve it.

Nathan stocked up on snacks and red wine and cleaned the whole house with the spiritual exhilaration of a newly-ordained priest leading his first mass. Whilst the house bore some expectancy of seduction he didn't want to broadcast the hint of sexual agenda, so he decided against dressing up or wearing perfume. When Charmaine arrived on time, he was just in the process of taking a pizza out of the oven.

"Smells good."

"Yes it's one of those…"

His pause was interrupted by Charmaine's observation. "I can smell cleaning," Charmaine interjected.

"Well I felt it was needed, it's kind of cathartic in a way, to clean. A psychologist like your good self should know the reasons why."

"Don't tell me, because your mind just drifts aimlessly and subconsciously and all that, yeah? Anyway, you'll put me out of business."

"Yes I know. I'll just have to advertise in the local Observer."

"Can I help with the interviews?" Charmaine jested.

"You can do them – after all you have the experience, you're the executive house manager, ha ha." Holding on to his façade, Nathan retreated into the lounge.

"What's up? You seem a little different, edgy?" Charmaine asked.

"No I'm fine, I'm okay honestly. I've just been in one of those strange moods today."

"Like when you can't decide if you're happy or sad?"

"Something like that, yeah."

"You want to talk about it?" Charmaine probed.

"Hmm, not sure. We'll see," Nathan replied, realising that even though he'd been subconsciously rumbled, it had at least created a more comfortable direction to the evening's proceedings.

An hour or so passed with each of them making shallow jibes at the trashy horror movie on TV.

"So anyway," Charmaine said, breaking the silence. "What do you think about it all?"

"All what?" Nathan responded with a poor impersonation of pretending he didn't know what she was talking about.

"Us!" The word hung with expectation in the way a match point hangs in a tennis match. Nathan did his utmost to display an exterior coolness, though the pangs of anxiety started to pump gently from his chest. It all had to unravel; in these next few instants that crystalized into timelessness, his future would unfurl. His heart raced and he could feel the hot flush of anticipation commanding his body to reach out to her.

Nathan offered a response. "Well I think we've become even closer than we were, over the last few weeks or so."

"And... is that it?" Charmaine asked with a headshake.

"I'm just a little bit..."

"A little bit what?"

"Scared!"

"Of what, the commitment thing?"

"No it's not that. It's more like being scared of..." Nathan became pensive again, finding it almost impossible to finish a sentence without stammering into a verbal void. "Well for me it's like I get scared of the things that might go wrong. It's almost like I have a preconceived notion of how relationships go. I also don't want to make a prat of myself by... well you know what I mean, don't you?"

"Nathan, I do understand what you mean. It's also hard for me, maybe even harder in some ways. I agree about the impossibility of romantic relationships. But maybe overcoming the fear is half the battle," Charmaine stated assertively. She sat beside him on the sofa. Casting him a tilted sideways glance she placed her hand lightly on top of his. "Look Nathan, we know we both like each other; truth is I've always had a crush on you, but lately I guess it's developed into something much more than that."

"Okay."

"You are really shy for your age, Mr Blakemore. Don't be so scared." She moved gently closer to him and kissed him on the cheek; as Nathan turned his head towards her the exchange of nervous glances preceded a first kiss that imprinted itself onto their embodiment. They lay together for the rest of the evening; that kiss and the subsequent body language signified their exit from the friendship zone. Nathan knew their world had changed forever.

At this point I feel we should take stock and accept that no sex took place between them that evening. In fact unlike most new relationships, sex was not an impending certainty. Instead their love appeared to take on a less physical form; it *spiritually* conjoined them in a way that is almost unimaginable. Thus we have two people who were reaching out to each other yet cautious, not because of fear, but because of a greater yearning inside. 'Souls entwined' is a song lyric through the ages, an overused and trite expression of lovers falling in love. However in the context of our story it is a fitting analogy; this is because the tentacles of their souls could not fail to interweave as they grappled for a recognisable life source to cling to. But let us also remember both Nathan and Charmaine ride a different train of thought than most normal individuals. Most couples faced with a similar situation would simply board the train and see where the journey led them. Our couple is on the platform; they both want to jump onto the footboard. Yet, they have a synchronised tendency to pour lead into their legs, re-balancing the gravity of their situation.

Hence we shall afford them a proper perspective of their developing feelings. The neurochemistry in their brains is playing havoc. We know that Nathan believes that his mind is greater than mere flesh and blood; Charmaine knows the mind is capable of witnessing great love – yet with deception at the same time. The inertia of eternal love might be the source of our inspirations, pain and sin.

Should they then stay rooted to the platform, or should they jump onto the carriage to face the pain? I don't believe either of them knew the answer to this conundrum at this time. I was sure about one thing; Nathan was ready to jump onto that train and leave the world behind – even if he didn't realise it himself. All it would take was a sign from her: a packed suitcase, a plan or a ticket to anywhere – as long as *anywhere* didn't have icebergs.

★

The onset of a typical British autumn was not going to cast a shadow over the sunlight inside Nathan's world. Their togetherness was decreed, spiritually and wholly. Even the wettest summers had their benefits. Nathan was predestined to organise the statutory week away somewhere. He knew Charmaine had finished university for the holiday period and he had some well-earned holidays from work due. He had also finished teaching at the college until the coming September. Thumbing through piles of glossy holiday brochures did nothing to entice him into spending a week in Cyprus or Greece. They had both worn that T-shirt; the typical British sun-seeking crowds were not the kind of escapism they craved. Nathan wanted it to be something more serene. He'd just about given up for the night when he decided to check the news on TV. He recoiled his finger pressure on the channel three button just as an advertisement for the Scottish tourist board grabbed his attention. The word 'eureka' only escaped his lips because of its corniness. Tomorrow, he would spend the day at home. He could use his weekly paperwork as an excuse; he would plan the whole trip.

By the time Charmaine had made herself comfortable in Nathan's chair the following day, his eyes hinted towards a pile of brochures spread aptly on the coffee table.

"So I thought we'd go to Scotland," he announced casually as they buried themselves into the sofa.

"Wow! Really? I always wanted to go but never had the chance. You lovely man!" She exhaled, hugging him.

"So you're happy with my choice then."

"Happy? I'm ecstatic! Wow. I can't wait."

"Well in that case, you better pack tonight."

"Tonight? Oh, my life."

"Yup, we leave tomorrow, but not until tea time, so we can take it steady. Anyway it will be nice to drive up with the sun setting."

"You old romantic you," Charmaine said.

"Well you know it."

"So where in Scotland are you taking me, Mr Blakemore? In fact you know what, I don't care. It will be wonderful."

"I thought you'd prefer to go to the less obvious places; so yes in a way it will be a bit of a magical mystery tour. De ye ken?"

The drive took them about five hours. Nathan had been happy to let Charmaine choose all the music during the journey. She had flitted between classic radio and the assortment of CDs in the glove compartment. However, the multitude of conversations had dulled much of their awareness of any pre-selected tunes. Charmaine often sat sideways in the passenger seat, watching him like a love-struck teenager.

"What?" Nathan said shyly the first time he noticed her staring.

"I just like to watch you sometimes – your facial mannerisms whilst you're driving. You're sweet."

"Well at least the roads up here are far less stressful to drive on. I mean how many cars have we seen coming the other way?"

"I don't know," she said. "I'm not looking for other cars."
He placed his hand on her knee gently and smiled contentedly.

"You happy?"

"Very."

They spent the last few miles of the journey in a mutual contentment. Nathan had opted for the less populist village of Luss, on the quieter banks of Loch Lomond. The Highlander was a stone built, three star hotel with a quintessential gravel driveway. Even the landlady fitted the imagined scenario perfectly: a sky blue apron draped over her wool cardigan and checked skirt with soft shoes. Mrs Abernathy afforded them a warm, hearty welcome. She offered politely to bring sandwiches up to the room for them, which they were both happy to accept. Although countryside darkness had now set in, Charmaine wanted to keep the curtains open. She lit one of the fake, battery-operated candles in the bay window and flopped onto the cushioned window seat. Mrs Abernathy brought a selection of ham and cheese sandwiches with a pot of tea for two.

"There you go," she said in her fine Scottish brogue. "Enjoy your supper. Would you like a wake-up call in the morning?"

"No thanks," they both chanted together. "We'll be fine. Thank you for the sandwiches."

"You're welcome, are they okay for you?"

"They're perfect," Nathan said. He sat on the bed looking across at Charmaine. "You have that look again," he said.

"What's that?" she asked softly.

"That look of serenity. It's very spiritual."

She stood up and walked over to the bed and climbed gently up to his side. "Hi."

"Hello you." They sat holding hands, staring out into the night as the candles flickered flawlessly. "Real candles would have been better," Nathan joked.

"Fire hazard."

"Oh yes I keep forgetting, the way of the world now."

"I wonder what's out there," Charmaine pondered.

"Or who," Nathan teased playfully as he rib-tickled her.

"Well they can't get to us in here. Like our own portion of paradise, separated from the outside world and all its troubles." Nathan noticed their reflection in the window. He recognised a soothing scenario for two souls who just wanted to find something – who deserved to find something – a peace, a longing and a reason to be. The blackbirds offered up their mandatory dawn chorus as Nathan cricked his neck away from Charmaine's shoulder. Charmaine mustered a slight groan. The sunlight bathed the room in a cosy dust and traditional breakfast smells hovered outside the room.

"Oh dear, we never even got changed." Nathan said.

"No," Charmaine replied as her arm felt around for his. "I think I slept for England," she said.

"You mean Scotland?"

"No, definitely for England – in Scotland."

"Ah you mean you slept on behalf of England in Scotland?"

"Something like that," she replied, throwing one of the flattened pillows at him.

"Well there's a whole day to be had," Nathan suggested enthusiastically.

"Okay okay, chill out Mr!"

"Shower and breakfast, or is it breakfast and shower?" Nathan knew his own preferred routine but sought approval on his decision.

"Whatever."

A relaxed breakfast in the dining room set them up for a day of fresh air. They decided to walk without a plan, to just meander and see where the day led them. On that, they were both in agreement. Hillside pathways wound upwards and beyond; every twist was an exploration of their togetherness. The stiff breeze took the slight heat out of the persevering sun. Walking and talking, they rejoiced in the immaculacy of the morning. Their conversations swung from the state of the world to the variety of wildlife they witnessed. This was the first time they had broken free from the chains of insecurity and the hold placed on them by the past. The environment lavished upon them a backdrop of splendour. Nathan sucked in every moment as if trying to hold it in his breath forever. *What could be more perfect?*

They sat down on a well-positioned country bench overlooking the more quiet stretch of the loch. Their deliberate pact to stay away from villages had meant they had only seen about a dozen people all day. The choppiness of the loch caused an alloy-like shine to skim off the surface, glinting into their eyes. They held hands and gazed, looked at each other, then gazed some more.

"What?" Nathan asked as if pre-empting Charmaine's thoughts.

"No, nothing," she replied.

"You sure? You looked like you were about to say something. You know, like something profound."

"Nathan?" she uttered.

"No. No," Nathan intervened calmly.

"Maybe we shouldn't say anything. Sometimes people say things at times like this, almost as if there's an obligation to. What really matters is what you're feeling right now, or what we're both feeling right now... just being here. You know, feeling alive." Charmaine smiled and clasped his hand as if using it to confirm her underlying emotions.

"Yeah, words are easy to, well you know, use," he added. "But what we really want is so deep inside – words alone can't always explain."

"Hmm I'm not sure about that," Charmaine said finally, breaking her period of silence.

"What about all the poetry that's been inspired by places like this? It might be just words but how else can you let out your feelings, then?"

"Well I don't know if I have the answer to that, but."

"But?"

"Well like, all those poets are just writing about how wonderful all this is. You know? Like, they come here and think about love and write some romantic notions and everyone thinks *wow, yes this is what it's all about.*"

"What's wrong with that? Isn't that why we're here?" she said, nudging him.

"Yes but… what if it's not real?"

"Oh, I see what you're doing. You're being all philosophical again. But a bit philosophically negative don't you think Mr B?"

Nathan turned his body slightly towards her and smiled. "My point is – yes, it's beautiful. But what I mean is that, well it's just a backdrop. Why can't it be like this without all this stuff?"

"What, you mean love?"

"Yes, love – and life."

"Maybe sometimes Nathan, you think about some things too much. Maybe people don't need all this stuff, but it's still wonderful to see. Especially when all we have to look at is a garden shed and brick wall."

"It's true that sometimes I don't know why I'm thinking what I'm thinking. Why can't I just accept?"

"Maybe you're just frightened by it all."

"You think?"

"Yes I do. You're frightened by the illusion of love, not the view," Charmaine suggested.

Nathan looked at her and kissed her head. "You're not an illusion, that's for sure! Come on, I'm starving."

"Oh and how do you know I'm not an illusion?" she said, pretending to run away.

"Because someone like you could never be," he said, catching up with her. He held her forearm and she turned to face him. The long smiles shaped into a different expression. He kissed her in a way he had never done before. Their exchange became frantic. His fingers pushed through her tied back hair, coming to a clasp at the back of her head. Nathan was embarrassed by his own bodily reaction. She could feel him through his jeans. His shy pull away from her caused a slight discomfiture. She smiled at him and they continued to walk back across the hills in silence.

A nervous expectancy awaited them as they walked pensively into their room. The bedding looked as though it had been aligned with a crisp aura of anticipation. A simultaneous tension overcame them for the first time; then slight to-ing and fro-ing of who would shower first evaded any preconceived notion of enforced sex. Charmaine came out of the shower with her hair still wet.

"Oh I'm so tired," she said. "Must be all that walking."

"Yes, that'll do it every time," Nathan said. "Fresh air and hills."

She lay on the bed with her back towards him. "Okay I'll take my shower now." Nathan was desperate to fight off his erection in the shower. His whole body urged to be let loose on her. By the time he stepped out of the shower in his bathrobe he still felt conscious of his semi-hardness. Disguising his posture he climbed carefully onto the bed, trying to conceal his needs. He lay on his back, staring at the spiralled chandelier surround. Nathan thought that their reciprocal stillness was impeccable. All he could hear was a shallow breathing through a raised alertness.

"You okay, Char?" Nathan asked.

"Yes," she replied, "just resting. You?"

"Yes." Nathan turned his head towards her carefully as if trying not to make her aware of his movement.

"I feel you," she said.

"What?" he asked through a disguised smile.

"You're moving."

"Well we've both been so still for the last hour or so."

"Yes," she answered with an intentional vagueness.

He finally decided to turn towards her, deliberately leaving a few inches between them. "Char."

"Yes?" An obvious tension broke through her voice.

"How do you feel?"

"Nervous," she replied.

"Why?"

"You know why."

"Well I think I do but I can be wrong about these things. Can you say it – just so I know?"

"Because I know what we both want."

"Okay. So there's a 'but', yes?"

"Yes."

"Come on Char, after what we have become to each other surely you can tell me anything that's on your mind."

"You're not the only one who gets scared. I'm scared, Nathe."

"What of? I hope not me."

"No… of me."

"Can you be a bit more crystal? I know we like our conversations to be intellectual and all that, but that's a bit too abstract, even for me."

After a thoughtful pause Charmaine turned over to face him. "I love you," she breathed softly, touching his face with the back of her hand.

"I love you too."

"And I do really want you," she added, "but I somehow feel everything is different with us. Like there's a kind of purity between us that sex would spoil."

"Oddly enough I know what you mean," Nathan replied.

"Really? You really feel the same?"

"Well maybe not exactly the same but I think I understand what you mean when you say that."

Charmaine rolled over onto her back. "I know we've

come close to making love before. But something happened to me as we were becoming closer."

"Really?" Nathan asked with an intrigued roll of the head towards her. He turned his body to face her again, using his lower hand to prop up his head.

"Yes," Charmaine continued. "When I could feel myself falling in love with you, the more cherished I wanted it to be. It's like a contradiction of my feelings — and urges."

"Do you mind me asking? Is it because you don't find me attractive, you know — in that way?"

"No it's not that at all. I really do. This is not one of those 'it's not you, it's me' situations. In fact I used to go home after being with you and dream about us being together in a different life. I wondered what it would be like to make love to you. My body felt ready."

"And your mind?" Nathan interjected.

"My mind was also ready. I think. But my soul Nathan, something was pulling me away from anything impure."

"That's quite deep, Char. And there's definitely not anyone else? Because if there is, despite the fact it will hurt, you know I'm not the type to try and stop you — I would give you up decently — with dignity."

"No," Charmaine replied with an intense honesty ringing through the tone of her voice. Nathan stood up and paced around the room, looking out of the window at the dusk laden hills.

"Why did it have to happen to us, or to me? I just thought we had found something here."

"We did."

Nathan turned from the window and sat in the window seat facing her. "So what is this thing that's somehow managed to pull you away from us?"

Charmaine rose steadily to her feet. Smiling, she walked

over towards him, kneeling and placing her hands on his knees. "It's not easy to say."

"Can you try?" He asked, taking hold of her hands. "Don't tell me, you've joined a religious cult and they've guaranteed you a place in heaven!"

She sat down on his lap and parted his hair with her fingers. "In time, my love. I'm just trying to piece everything together slowly. But it's definitely not a religious cult," she laughed. "I'm not going to be the seventh wife of someone claiming to be the returning Messiah. But, you have a right to know."

"Well I don't know that I have a right, but if it was me I would feel an obligation to be truthful with you."

"I promise, Mr Blakemore, as soon as I work everything out in my mind, you will be the first to know."

"Swear on it. Raise your right hand please," he added jokingly.

"Okay. Come on let's eat, Mrs Abernathy will be wondering why we've not yet sat down for dinner." On their last day in the Highlands they drove for almost two hours on narrow country lanes. The roads seemed to fade into the hills without intention. They came to a small village with a sloping, cobbled square at its centre.

"This looks nice," Nathan suggested.

"Perfect," Charmaine answered. The village looked like it had been taken from a tin of shortbread biscuits, decorated with tiny shops selling crafts and textiles. Jolly looking residents smiled and bid them good morning as they walked along a street that time seemed to have snubbed. Charmaine carried a joyous expression, taking in the whole view like it was hers alone to savour.

To her it was. This was a stepping stone towards her wish; she wondered if this was one final deed of self-indulgence in the closeness of the man she loved until providence summoned her.

"Nathe, we've got to eat something really Scottish before we go," she announced elatedly.

"We have. What do you think Mrs Abernathy has been feeding us for the past few nights? She'd be well upset if you tried telling her it wasn't Scottish."

"I know but I mean something like that!" She pointed at a haggis outside a small delicatessen.

"No way, sorry, I've never fancied stuffing myself with something that comes out of an animal's stomach."

"Come on! Where's your sense of adventure? Go on, for me!" Charmaine tugged at him knowing he would have to succumb. "Anyway, you eat eggs don't you?"

Nathan raised his eyebrows and pulled his chin into his chest. "I must be mad… but okay."

He thanked her sarcastically for coaxing him into breaking his rigid dining habits.

A further stroll to digest their meal brought them to an old church. The arched gateway led to a cobbled pathway that sauntered invitingly up to an open door. Choral voices wafted soothingly from the ambient vestibule.

"There's a service of some kind," said Nathan.

"It's a funeral mass."

"Oh, in that case we shouldn't…"

Charmaine gently tugged him towards the open door. "Come on," she whispered.

"But it's a private thing."

"Shush, we are just paying our respects." They stood in anonymous profile at the back of the church as the priest gave his blessings to the laity. The small cortege slowly made its way outside to the rear of the church where a pre-prepared resting place waited for the dearly departed.

As a few of the lingering mourners lit candles and knelt in prayer, Nathan turned to see Charmaine walking to the front of the church. A ray of sunlight angled in through one of the side windows. It glanced angelically off her hair. Enchanted by her outline, he stood in silent reverie. His stare fixed on the woman he had come to love like no other. An old lady huddled past him, her face breaking into a tender smile as she passed him. He smiled back until his eyes followed the layout of the church before returning to Charmaine, who was lighting a candle to the side of the altar.

She stood facing a statue of Christ, and appeared to be praying. An unrobed priest treaded softly up the aisle, acknowledging the last few mourners. A few scattered worshippers began to make their way out of a side door. Nathan watched her for a few more seconds then walked outside into the garden. He had never witnessed her in such a righteous poise. Knowing he would have to conceal his intrigue, he sank onto a bench, which provided him with a view of the continuing funeral service.

Nathan's gaze shifted from the church entrance to the ongoing funeral. A few minutes later, Charmaine walked up the side of the church, towards him. As she walked, he noticed her head was partially bowed. A mutual smile was all they needed to reunite them.

"Okay?" Nathan asked.

"Yes," Charmaine responded softly. A saintly smile etched its way across her face as she took his hand.

It was not what Nathan had envisaged for a last night in the Highlands with the woman he had come to adore. Though, he was pleasantly surprised at how his urges had been replaced by a more meaningful sensuality. They lay on the bed in a spooning position; Nathan behind, soaking up her scent. The pendulum of the hallway grandmother clock swung unapologetically. Nathan's attention drifted between the quarterly hour chimes and the vast unknown of unrequited love. He could not decide if the surge within him was fear of losing her or absolute joy in having the time he had with her. The space between their fingers was interlocked in a timeless vacuum. Charmaine sighed with contentment, her body expanding to accommodate his. Nathan smiled and gently kissed the nape of her neck; a tear tried its best to force its way from the corner of his eye.

The drive home was a solemn comparison to the jollity of their outward journey. It wasn't that a new-found tension had seeped between them. To Nathan it felt like an expectation of loss. His soul was being drained of the one thing that completed it; the one person whose own soul had impressed itself on his. Occasional glances of consideration replaced the mutual appreciation of musical whims that played remorsefully; eye contact was a little more conceited and conversation less precocious. Nathan's heart felt like it would leap out from his ribs and clutch desperately onto the ventricles of Charmaine's. *Why am I thinking like this? She hasn't said we won't be together. Why does it feel to me like this is already ending?* Charmaine drifted into pockets of sleep as Nathan followed the bends in the road unconsciously – whilst looking across to her at every opportune moment to gaze upon her face. That face, which had been nurtured in his psyche; the face of a friend, the face of a beautiful woman, the face of a soulmate; the face that had given him a reason to dare to hope.

PART TWO

THE STRIVE FOR EQUILIBRIUM

Nathan was not looking forward to the three hour drive south but it was something he needed to do in order to secure an order from one of the company's biggest customers. He would at least receive a decent commission from the order, an outcome that made it easier to bear. XTS was a large music store on the outskirts of London; the manager had always respected Nathan as he had lived a similar previous life on the verges of the music business, albeit he had been much more fortunate with the financial rewards.

Terry Naylor was a very smoothly dressed character for someone who ran one of the most successful music stores in the country. He wouldn't have looked out of place in the pages of a mail order catalogue; a throwback of his initial success in the music business as the manager of a famous boy band in the late 80s, who had a few hit records in the UK and Europe before failing to crack the market in America which would have catapulted them into mega-stardom. Terry had also recorded a couple of his own throw away pop tunes which also sold a few thousand records, despite being the type of songs most credible-minded musicians and fans love to hate. However, the success had allowed him to invest in quite a few related businesses, such as tour bus hire for well-known acts, as well as the music store.

After the formalities of the order, which was even more lucrative than Nathan initially expected, Terry invited him for lunch at his favourite Chinese restaurant. Terry always broke customer protocol by offering to pay for lunch and Nathan would always accept graciously. As he listened wilfully to

Terry he couldn't help sending a thought in Eddie's direction. He subconsciously tried to vindicate success and failure; here was Terry who despite being a decent guy was fairly talentless yet had capitalised almost effortlessly from the music business, whereas poor old Eddie with all that skill at his fingertips had barely scraped a living for the last twenty-five years in the same industry. Was it luck or insight, being in the right place at the right time, or who you know? *Too many variables and not enough integrity* was the line playing through Nathan's head. As Nathan came back to the conversation, Terry was still talking about his new venture into music publishing; it seemed Terry would just get richer and richer; instead of owning a boat on the Thames he would soon own a yacht in Marbella, whilst Eddie would be lucky if he could afford to replace his five year old van anytime soon. Nathan was glad to do business with Terry but even more happy when it was time to leave. He certainly didn't dislike him – there was nothing *to* dislike – but he was never at his most comfortable when having to digest the fiscal accomplishments of others. Nathan was glad to be back in the car heading north, to the grinding reality of working class Nirvana. He was quite joyful as he calculated the commission in his head, so decided he needed the right kind of audio stimulus. As he fingered through his pre-selected radio stations for the appropriate tune of the day, the chorus of 'Can't Buy Me Love' by the Beatles sounded through the car radio speakers.

Nathan sang along through his own laughter.

"It's so fucking true." *There is justice in the world!* Suddenly he felt at ease with himself again. The ice inside his soul had begun to melt; he could now drive home in a lukewarm comfort. *Can't wait to see her.*

When he arrived home there was a sense of Charmaine's presence. Some of her folders and textbooks were lying on the floor in uncharacteristic disarray. Charmaine was usually much more organised, at least with her academic belongings. Judging by the opened textbook and research notes on social psychology, he decided she must have come over to do some work at his place where she could progress without being disturbed. It seemed odd that she would just leave everything in this way, yet he assumed she must have had to dash for some domestic chore back home; after all she hadn't officially left home to move in with him; it was still a 'transitional issue' according to her.

Nathan had planned to cook a curry but after the Chinese lunch he didn't feel his stomach was up to an extra helping of spice in one day. Besides, he had a rule, or two rules regarding eating habits: *if you eat a big lunch then you have to have a smaller dinner;* and *never eat more than one type of cultural dish in any one day.* This meant if you had had a pizza for lunch you couldn't eat Indian or Mexican later in the day, instead you had to go for something plain like a baked potato and salad. Nathan believed this was equilibrium for digestive capabilities. To his friends this was just another one of his quirky concepts he may have read in an overpriced men's health magazine. He also needed to go jogging. The second rule – that after a heavy lunch you had to justify dinner by doing some form of physical exercise beforehand. It was because of these idiosyncrasies that some of his mates aptly referred to him as Nathan Quirkmoor; a nickname he was proud to have received one night in the Dog and Gun.

A skittish idiosyncratic was a character description Nathan had come to live with; he only had to look in the mirror and although he was capable of accepting his apparent cuteness, with sandy brown hair and boyish looks, he could also see the susceptibility radiating from deep down. Though he didn't like it, he had learned to live with it even though there was a period of reflective doubt every day which consumed him like a tidal wave of discomposure. He often wondered if the fine layer of confidence which coated his exterior would crack once and for all, exposing him as a frail excuse for a man. Having said that, if there were awards for overthinking things, Nathan would probably have an Oscar, a Grammy and a Pulitzer all rolled into one.

As evening drew in, Nathan sat in his bay window chair drinking his second cup of tea when the phone rang.

"Hi, it's me." Nathan was alarmed at the lack of usual zest in Charmaine's voice.

"Hi," he replied. "Are you okay? I've been worried about you."

"I'm ok."

"You sure? You sound a little down. Where are you?"

Charmaine answered his question with another question. "Did you call at my mother's?"

"No, you know I don't always like going, though I was getting close to it. All your books and other college stuff are here. Char, are you sure you're ok?"

"I'm fine, really I am. I just need some headspace to think things through."

"What things? Look if it's about us you don't need to worry; if you're not ready for us then it's not a problem, we just go back to how it was."

"It's not that, Nathe. I've just been thinking about things on a different level and I needed to do something."

"Something?" Nathan questioned. "You really do sound strange. Please, you are definitely okay yeah?"

"I will be in touch in a few days. Please don't worry," she said calmly.

"A few days?" The receiver went dead. Nathan stared at it, believing that somehow the answer to Charmaine's inexplicable behaviour would come leaping out of the mouthpiece. He paced up and down the stairs; then he walked into every room of the house as if by doing so it would conjure up a clue as to her whereabouts or unfamiliar conduct.

Although it was against his will, he felt the urge to call at her mother's house. Nathan could see the lounge light filtering through to the unlit front porch. Through his apprehension, he knocked tentatively on the coloured glass pain. Charmaine's mother padded up to the unlocked door.

"Hi," Nathan said before she could get a word out, "can I come in?" Her mother strolled back into the lounge leaving Nathan to follow on and close the doors behind him.

"Would you like some tea, dear?" she asked.

"No, no thanks."

"What about a whisky or brandy?"

"No honestly, nothing thanks," Nathan suggested, wanting to get on with his routine questioning. "I'm worried about Char – Charmaine. I've just had a phone call from her but she seemed a little distressed and wouldn't say where she was. Have you heard from her?"

"Well I wouldn't worry dear," Charmaine's mother replied, seemingly unruffled by the news as she poured herself a whisky. "Sure you won't join me, dear?"

"No, please no," Nathan replied with a vigorous shake of the head and hand. "So she's not been in touch. Any idea where she might have gone?"

"She's done this before you know." Nathan watched as she sat comfortably back into her patterned chair. He noticed the action of a police drama on the television; the volume was hardly loud enough to hear, like it was on for companionship rather than entertainment. He couldn't help thinking about a TV advertisement in the Eighties for Shackleton High Seat Chairs: an elderly lady sits back contentedly whilst stroking the arm rests as if the chair was a much-loved pet. "In fact she used to do it when she was a child. She'd just go missing for a few days then waltz back in as if everything was normal. We would be beside ourselves – me and Auntie Norma, that is. We called the police a few times but they just told us to keep better control of her. Mind you in them days kids did go off more, not like now."

Nathan didn't interject but rather took on the mantle of intrigued listener as Charmaine's mother scuttled up to the old fashioned sideboard and unravelled an old photo album from the top drawer.

She began a commentary on Charmaine's escapades since she was a child, resting briefly to pass Nathan the odd photograph. Nathan was fascinated; many of the photos of Charmaine showed her in various guises: like the ones from her time in the Brownies and some from special events such as PDSA collection days which the school had organised. Charmaine posed proudly, decked out in rosettes and badges. Nathan rummaged through the photos, occasionally hesitating to focus on one that caught his attention.

"Odd," he mused. "How come there isn't any of Charmaine with her Father?" Nathan added inquisitively. Charmaine's mother raised her eyebrows slightly but didn't answer his question.

"Who's this then?" Nathan queried handing a photo back to her; it showed Charmaine standing next to some old guy in a dark suit.

"Oh that was Father Michael, I think," she said, holding the photo to her screwed up eyeball.

"Father Michael," Nathan retorted. "You mean a priest?"

"The vicar, dear, from St Bede's Church of England down the road." Nathan gazed with intensity. "He was always coming around, like vicars used to in them days. You know, to try and get us all to go to church. Well that's their job isn't it?"

"So did she ever go?"

"I think she went once with two of her friends then decided it wasn't for her. She joined the Brownies instead."

Charmaine's mother rested her head back and used the arm rest to take the weight of her glass.

"I thought she told me you were Catholics."

"Did she? Well it's true her father was but my family are all C of E. Charmaine was christened in the Church of England. But it's true she always did want to know more about her father's faith and what not."

"Why do you think she never went again, to church?"

Charmaine's mother sipped thoughtfully at her whisky. "I remember what she said when I asked her that same question once. What was it now? Ah yes, she said, 'I don't think God lives in that church.' When I asked her why she thought that, she said, 'because you can tell it feels empty.' I remember saying to her that the church was always quite full, especially on Sundays. Then she said something really clever for a ten year old."

"Oh, what was that?"

"She said, 'no I don't mean the people, I mean it's just a building with no soul, I don't think God would want to live there.'"

Nathan sank back into the chair. His thoughts were running amok. "How weird," Nathan said randomly.

"What's that, love?" Charmaine's mum asked.

"No, it's just I'm trying to piece together all the stuff that must be going on with her. It's like she has a part of her life that's a secret."

"She's always been a bit like that."

Nathan had become so caught up by learning of Charmaine's past that he'd almost forgotten his reason for calling in the first place. He shook his shoulders to bring himself back to the state of affairs.

"Anyway, I just wanted to know where she is and if she's alright. But it seems none of us know!"

"I'm sure she will be okay dear. Just you watch, she'll be

67

there making you a cup of coffee when you get home from work tomorrow, just like nothing happened."

"Thanks for showing me the photographs," Nathan said as he rose to his feet, all the time eyeing every corner of the lounge for one last hint.

"Ok dear, please can you lock the door on your way out and put the key through the letterbox, I'm too tired to get up now." Nathan climbed into bed and turned on his portable TV with the remote; he was surfing through channels like each press of the channel button would bring about the answer to where she might be. As the midnight movie climaxed he drifted off to sleep.

Nathan couldn't face work the following morning, so decided to call in sick. As he offered up his reason to the office secretary, he thought about something he'd recently read in the Sunday papers. Apparently about twenty million man hours are lost to fake illness each year in the UK; people phone in sick with hangovers after international football matches, or because they have broken up with a partner. Some companies even offer what are classed as duvet days: days for just staying at home when you don't feel like working, or because your pet hamster has died, leaving you in a state of depression. He anointed the day to be a duvet day for milling about; for lying on the sofa carefree whilst switching between the radio and countless TV channels; for drinking copious amounts of coffee and tea.

Nathan became fascinated by a programme on one of the wildlife channels, about meerkats. He found their movements and body language almost hypnotic. Their alertness was enviable, their mannerisms hilarious. But most of all he believed they had a hidden, alien-like intelligence that was untapped by man. *If only she was here now we could have a brilliant debate about the consciousness of meerkats.*

An old Humphrey Bogart movie was halfway through

on one channel. *Key Largo* was one of his favourite Bogart movies. The main character was a war hero who was reluctant to react violently towards the hoods who had taken over the local hotel. Instead he chose to bide his time, using his guile to defeat them and win over the heroine, who was played by Lauren Bacall. Nathan admired that type of character trait in people. If only he could be like that; or be faced with a scenario where he could save someone. He would be seen as a hero. He would then live forever. The day had stretched out accordingly. The afternoon brightness turned selfishly to eventide grey; Nathan decided enough was enough.

The following morning brought the zesty sound of breakfast TV that woke him from a troubled sleep. Treading cautiously down the stairs in his sleeping attire he could hear the sound of clanking dishes. Charmaine stood at the sink, humming softly with an air of contentment; her curly black hair was tied back.

"Good morning!" Nathan gestured with purpose.

"Hi you," Charmaine replied softly as she turned her head inoffensively. "Coffee?" Charmaine offered him his favourite mug, full.

"So how was your day yesterday?" Nathan enquired in a manner that was a cross between slight cynicism and casual sarcasm.

"Nice, in fact wonderful," she replied.

"You want to talk about it?"

"There's no need."

"Don't you think it's a bit odd, that kind of behaviour, just disappearing for two nights without letting anyone know?" Charmaine's only response was to look away with an unprovocative smile. "Come on Char, I'm trying to ask you where you went; surely in any relationship a person just doesn't decide to go AWOL without saying anything?"

"I called you, remember?" she responded.

"Yes you did, but you were very cloak and dagger about everything. It all sounded a bit, well cagey. I was worried."

Charmaine finished washing the dishes and stood staring out of the kitchen window. "I'm sorry, it's just something I do sometimes."

"Can I ask where it is you go?"

Charmaine rested against the table tops in the kitchen and folded her arms unthreateningly. "Could I say no? It's just somewhere I have that's for me. Somewhere and something I need as a kind of... insurance."

"Oh well that really throws light on it then," Nathan said sarcastically. He ventured back upstairs to get ready for work, taking his coffee with him. By the time he had showered and dressed Charmaine had left; he noticed all her books and work folders were now neatly stacked underneath the coffee table.

Nathan's day coasted into one of those days that only sales reps recognise. His one-time mentor and former manager used to call them DEAD days (Driving Endlessly and Aimlessly Days). In classic sales rep mantra he had invented the acronym to explain why sales reps sometimes drive without any real aim or direction; an unplanned journey into pointlessness without any calls or appointments. Fortunately, it was easy to hide DEAD days in any so-called diary or schedule. One could easily manufacture a few cold calls or re-visits to regular customers for one's call sheet. Nathan's mind had certainly been elsewhere. Whilst he had learned that this was *something she did*, the way in which it had all unfolded: the disregarded college books and folders, the casual explanation from her mother, and that vague phone call, brought about a lack of security in Nathan's mind. Suddenly the much longed for relationship was very unsafe; the problem was Nathan's parachute-like mind was not working normally – parts of it were closing and the expected fall could be distressing. How would he feel when she did it again? What if next time she was gone even longer? The questions ate away at him like a hyena of the mind. He could sense his unconditional love for her evolving into an agonising finale. At least he had half-expected the possibility of it going wrong since the holiday in Scotland.

Thursday evening would at least bring him some mental diversion through his philosophy class. Nathan enjoyed teaching adults who were looking to stimulate their lives through taking on an academic discipline. However, he also disliked the armchair philosophers. Those with airy-fairy ideas but they couldn't back them up through the application of proper philosophical concepts.

They were the types who assumed that if they just managed to turn up to class they could pass an exam within one week. They failed to appreciate that academic success requires a discipline and training of the mind, as well as weeks of practise to be able to express concepts in written format, whilst sticking rigidly to the relevance of a specific question. Because of this, many of them fell away disillusioned after a week or two, leaving only the genuine seekers of knowledge left to complete the full course. Ironically for Nathan, the topic for his lecture was Freud; it seemed everything found a link back to Charmaine. He had prepared a lecture on Freud's explanation for religion; the notion that God was merely an illusion and father figure that man had created through a sense of wish-fulfilment. According to Freud, it was the desire and nature of human beings to seek salvation; religion offered that salvation, though Freud believed psychotherapy was the only real way of finding it.

Nathan had asked his class the previous week to research philosophical arguments against Freud, so he was hoping for some worthy contributions from the group, based on philosophers who were classed as apologists. Nathan loved to provoke debate in his class; for him that was what philosophy was all about; and nothing was better to stir up those philosophical ideas than the philosophy of religion. The ingredients: a small but multi-racial group of adults aged between twenty-two and sixty. Whisk them up into a frenzy of scholarly wisdom, toss in a couple of thought-evoking theories and then stir in a little personal promulgation whilst you leave to simmer – and there you have it – the objectives of the lesson are underway.

"Freud is right because if you think about it we do create things in our own mind, so why not create God as someone to look up to?" one young student called Beth in her mid-twenties offered from the back of the class. The oldest student in the class was called David. He had recently retired and was doing the course to keep himself occupied; he challenged the statement.

"So, you believe that just because this guy came up with a theory that sounds intellectual, then it kind of explains away God?" Nathan leant back on the front wall of the classroom pensively, one hand on his forearm and the other moulded to his chin, with one finger over his closed lips. The comments kept on coming – firing across the classroom bows.

"Who said Freud is right, anyhow? Didn't he take lots of coke or something? Sounds like Sigmund might have been off his head coming up with all these wacked out theories if you ask me!" one of the younger male students argued – raising a laugh from some of the younger students in the class.

"But surely he's just explaining why some people believe in God! After all not everyone on planet earth does!"

"Some great ideas you're all expressing folks," Nathan commented, with a keenness to show that he was listening.

"Yeah because there's no proof anyway right, that God exists?" another student shouted out.

Then, Lizzy who was normally one of the less vocal ones in the group, retorted.

"Well there's no proof that Freud is right! It's just *his* theory after all."

And so the debate continued as Nathan paced around the classroom, still with one hand cupping his chin, fascinated by the depth of the observations.

"What do you think, Nathan?" one of the students asked him.

"Well you've all made some really valid comments; as for what I think, well Lizzy you just made a statement about proof, right?" He stared in her direction. "But the thing is, what is proof? What can we actually prove in the world? To be honest, not that much when you actually think about it." Nathan got into his flow. "You see, science works on the principle of testing a hypothesis yes; establishing cause and effect. But how many scientific experiments can find the truth unequivocally – one-hundred percent? Remember that philosophy is not science!" He now had his audience in a captive gaze. "Okay so we know for certain that gravity exists; that is absolutely and categorically true yes – if you're not convinced try floating out of the window just now. But what else do we know for sure?"

"Smoking causes cancer!" someone shouted.

"No!" Nathan responded, assertively. "We know that there is a possible link between smoking and cancer; we could even say there is a high probability that it does, but can we say for sure without argument that it always does? I bet all of you know someone who's smoked for most of their lives and never got cancer. I certainly do; my Gran smoked all her life and died at eighty of heart failure but she never got cancer. You get my point? Proof is about possibility and probability so we could say there is a possibility that if you smoke too much you might get cancer, or we might even say if you smoke all your life for fifty years or more, then there is even a probability that you will get cancer. But we can't say that is proof; proof would have to mean it's without question, one-hundred percent the truth – that every single person on the planet who smokes will get lung cancer!" Nathan was almost breaking into a sweat from his commitment to the debate. He could feel his heart rate increasing from the excitement. The whole class were absorbed by his command of philosophical ideas. One or two of them scribbled notes as others stared ahead in unfathomable thought. "Okay folks, well that's just about a rap! Great lesson; well done, everyone. Next week we will look more at possibilities and probabilities, inductive and deductive reasoning, nothing less. For next week make sure you can explain the difference between the two and relate that to the idea of creation! There are some reading references on my desk, so be sure to collect them on your way out."

Whilst Nathan was packing away his resources he noticed one of the students still loitering. He looked up to find it was Lizzy.

"You okay, Liz?" he asked her.

"Don't you think that there are some truths we're not meant to find out?" she asked as they both made for the door. He could sense she wanted to extend the discussion, or the time in his company.

"That's a good point," Nathan replied, "maybe not."

"Like maybe God only wants us to find out some things but not others."

"Hmm... maybe."

They continued to talk as they made their way out of the building.

"There are so many laws of the universe, and it's like God has set them in place so that we can work some of them out," Liz added to her suggestion.

"Indeed," Nathan replied, looking at his watch at the same time.

"I have an unfinished bottle of white wine in the fridge if you'd care to join me," she offered.

Nathan's heart raced as he visualised sharing laughter on her sofa; the conversation moving into flirtatious territory; her leaning over him to kiss him where upon she tells him how much she had fantasised about this moment.

"That sounds great Liz, but I have to get back."

"No worries, maybe another time."

"Yes, maybe another time."

"Goodnight Nathan, see you next week yeah."

"Night Liz, take care." He watched her walk along the road a few paces, then turned to continue his own walk home. Any lingering thoughts of regret at not accepting her offer, he threw into the gutter.

During his walk, the leftovers of the class debate scoured his consciousness. He thought about those complicated theories for truths: deductive versus inductive reasoning; then he thought back to the ideas Lizzy was proposing. *It is good that others think about stuff like this. If only more people did – and more often.* A notion occurred to him... *Plato really had it right all that time ago; surely the soul is a higher reality than the body; the soul wants to travel into heavenly realms; the soul is trying to steer the mind towards these heavenly spheres.* For once he felt the clarity of his thinking was helping him to make a decision.

The whole concept of understanding life to the philosopher is in part to prepare for death.

Death will come eventually in whatever guise we believe it to be. Just as our physicality will cease, so shall our dreams if we do not keep them alive. Nathan wanted to keep his dreams alive. His only way to making certain of doing so was to face them head on. It was no use holding them in a cloud somewhere above his head. He had an urge to discuss something in particular with Charmaine. He just had to put the question to her, but only at the right moment.

★

Charmaine's graduation was preconceived in the mind of her mother and Auntie Norma even before she had decided to go to university. Not that her mother was always in tune with Charmaine's aspirations; in fact she didn't have the mental stability to be the doting mother. But to her, Charmaine was like a beacon that would shine brightly through the rough seas of a traumatic family history. Nevertheless, on the actual day of her graduation the whole neighbourhood was only too willing to pay their compliments to a much loved member of the local community. The small but genial celebration at her mother's house became a constant stream of well-wishers. Even Toto had sent her a bunch of flowers with a note attached: 'Congratulations Charmaine, you deserve all your success and long may it continue'; of course it also contained the statutory line at the end which read – '*I still think of you*'. However Charmaine hardly even noticed it. Any thoughts of Toto still carrying a candle for her had not only been forgotten with motivation, but truly lost in the inner-space and time of her implicit memory.

Nathan was honoured to be part of the party and reflected deeply about his own graduation. As a mature student he had raptured in the reality of what had seemed for many years an unlikely scenario. He had dressed smartly for the occasion in a new, dark blue suit, though preferred to wear an open neck shirt rather than going for the option of a tie. In his mind this was his way of ensuring he felt appropriately dressed for the presentation at the university but also not too overdressed back at the house where most of the casual callers were dressed down. Nathan always gave much thought to such decisions, whereas most people would not even ponder on such unimportant aftermaths.

Their first real moment of togetherness was only transitory. Demetri ushered towards them through the front porch.

"Hey Charmaine, congratulations love," he said, hugging

her for all he was worth. "She's very talented and gifted you know."

"Yes, I know," Nathan replied.

"Here my dear, a graduation present just for you." Demetri handed her a wicker basket full of exotic fresh fruit: pineapple, strawberries, bananas, watermelon and kiwi fruits all centred by a bottle of champagne. "You try not to eat everything at once eh, and you watch her after she drinks the champagne because she will become as fresh as the fruit," he jokingly warned Nathan.

"Thanks, I will," Nathan replied with unoffended scrutiny.

The party started to dwindle as Nathan and Charmaine sat on the wall of the front garden. Charmaine was still dressed in her graduation gown though her mortar board hat was now being tossed around like a frisbee by the kids from next door.

"So what's next then Miss Laffe?"

"A nice hot bath then bed I think."

"You know that's not what I meant."

Charmaine looked down at the ground, planning her official response. "I don't know. I would like to carry straight on with my Master's but I've been thinking about things a little differently lately."

"I've noticed."

"Hey, Mr Sarcastic," she replied, nudging him and half-spilling her champagne over his trousers.

"Hey watch the trousers, not C&A material this."

"Really, Calvin Klein is it, or maybe Hugo Boss?"

"Now who's been sarcy?" A brief moon daydream gave him just the right amount of time to pose the question. "Char. You ever thought of doing something really different; you know something that's out of the ordinary?"

"Well I thought about bungee jumping once."

"Ah, you know what I mean."

"Yes I do know what you mean. And of course, but didn't you hear me? I've been thinking about things differently a lot recently. Things that are anything but ordinary."

"Okay so, what's in your mind then? I'd love to know — after all I've been trying to find out for the last few months."

"Well let's say I'm open to ideas. I do have one of my own but I need to keep that under lock and key for a bit longer."

"Okay Mrs Secretive. Well I've been thinking about handing my notice in at work and going off to Africa or somewhere like that. I've been checking out the options with VOA, you know the Voluntary Overseas Aid."

"I know what it stands for, Mr B."

"Well, don't you think it would be really uplifting to go work in a Third World country for a while, helping them to build mud huts or water wells? I don't know, to me it would be kind of like setting my soul free; really tapping into my altruistic nature." Nathan's face was alive with a craving for trying to convince her that this was a fantastic idea; though the onset of anxiety was let loose through his body. "Would you come with me?" That was it, he'd said it. There was no going back now. The question to launch a thousand possibilities had been asked. Charmaine held his hand lightly and rested her head on his shoulder.

"Oh my goodness me! It's been a long day. Can I think about it?"

"Of course, take your time." Nathan looked around at the kids who were now using Charmaine's Mortar board as a table top to place their cakes and juice on. "Have you made a decision yet?" he jested. Charmaine nudged him even harder than last time.

The coolness of the evening descended upon the celebrations; those untidy endings of party closure began to thread their way through to the stragglers and tired children. Charmaine's mother had fallen asleep in her chair, although her hand clutched at the half-empty bottle of scotch like a terrier's jaw locks onto a catch. Party poppers and leftover cake were strewn around the house. The mix of lighting was typically working class suburbia, with an assortment of pink and yellow shades absorbing the leftover light before complete darkness drew in. Nathan kissed her goodnight.

"I know you'll want to sleep here tonight, it's okay, I'll see you later." He scuffled home the few hundred yards, all the time contemplating his predicament.

"What now?" He asked out loud to anyone who might be listening as he unlocked the door. His inner voice hacked away at him... *What now indeed?*

The brochures that he received from the VOA highlighted some very interesting parts of the world where much needed help was required. For some reason it was the Philippines that caught his eye, as perhaps in his mind it posed a safer option than India, Pakistan or beleaguered African countries. The roles sought were labourers and project managers for house building, water irrigation and people with his particular skills could also teach English. The very smell, look and feel of the brochure infused the philanthropist in him; his belief in the idea was becoming cemented into his thinking. This was what he had to do; it was the only soulful thing left.

His only worry was how to persuade Charmaine that this was a great idea. *It would be like a mutual rebirth for both of us.* He knew her recent state of mind had been slightly erratic; a possible reflection of a family history of varying psychological problems. He wondered if she really had the emotional rigour and more importantly the same yearning that he had for such an adventure.

A rainy summer of going through the motions was all part of Nathan's preparation. Charmaine's plight was somewhat different; she had already alluded to the idea of starting her MSc and Nathan was having a difficult time trying to sway her to go with him.

He felt a deeper bonding beginning to materialise as they spent most nights huddled together like new-born kittens on the sofa, as the night rain splattered the bay window with aesthetic mien. Times like this would make it even harder for him to leave. He spent a couple of nights each week down at the local pub as a way of trying to gradually detach himself from her. It was as if nothing had changed: the same faces, the same type of jokes and the same commentaries on the local talent. On one particular night an old school friend came in. Chris had been one of the only males that he felt comfortable to confide in. This had come about when Chris had entrusted Nathan with a personal issue two years after leaving school. Chris had revealed to him that he was gay. At the time, it was a brave move to announce one's sexuality to a friend; men especially, in the late Seventies, still held fairly homophobic attitudes, at least in the drinking houses of working class suburbia in the north of England. Nathan's advice at the time was not to worry too much, suggesting that there wasn't enough love in the world as it was, so whatever love you have to offer had to be a bonus to mankind. Though it might have been a vague statement for consoling a friend, Chris had never forgotten the moral support Nathan had given him, from then on. At Chris' request Nathan also kept the information to himself – until his eventual decision to publicly out himself in the local community a few years later.

They sat in their old place at a small, round table beside the fireplace; they had chosen it back then because it was within easy reach of the jukebox. Nowadays, the jukebox had been relocated to the wall. After the catch-up on how each of their lives had mapped out, Nathan told Chris of his dilemma.

"It's a kind of no brainer," Chris remarked after a long stint of listening. "You would regret it if you never went to do something like that."

"I know what you mean," Nathan replied, "but you know what love can do, right?"

"Yes, but from what you've said it doesn't seem like Charmaine is one-hundred percent about going."

"That's the problem – I'm not even sure she's fifty percent the way there."

"Sometimes you have to do what you've got to do, if you know what I mean?" Chris urged.

Nathan looked into his empty glass, then around the pub at the local drinkers propping up the bar. "You might be right my friend, you might be right; another beer?"

Nathan decisively handed in his notice at work, so only had to serve out the formalities before embarking on his quest. The college had given him an unofficial yet welcomed sabbatical in the hope of re-employing him in the future. Nathan's boss had decided to throw a meagre lunchtime leaving party which included the office and warehouse staff. Nathan's most cringeworthy moment came when his boss decided to give an impromptu speech declaring Nathan to be 'a trier who never gave up and loved his job immensely'. Nathan's reluctant acceptance of the leaving present was followed by a few lame claps and well wishes. He decided this would be the last time he would be drunk for almost a year and so embraced the afternoon soiree with a little more conviction than he expected. He felt quite ill on the way home in the taxi – a mixture of the alcohol and toxicity from his job seeping out from his pores. None of the streets looked familiar; he might as well have been in a different town for all he knew. The taxi driver traversed around a roundabout, waiting for Nathan to decide which exit was the right one. Nathan tried his best to focus his eyes on the road; only after the third time around did he point the driver in what he hoped was the right direction. Nathan was not used to being out of control; sure he could get drunk but somehow always managed to keep an element of self-composure, even if that was his own distorted perception. When he finally managed to reach the house he fumbled his way into the side entrance. His usual routine was to make tea and toast and sit in front of the TV until he had to drag himself to bed. It never happened. He woke up lying face down on the sofa; the dryness in his mouth and rattling ball bearing headache was a memory of days gone by. He more or less crawled off the sofa and up the stairs to shower before trying to assert himself on the day.

Nathan spent two days semi-tidying the house and garden. He then made a flying visit to see his mother for one night only. When he returned, Charmaine was not in the house. He had sensed this lack of presence before; where the house is not just empty but composed of a deliberate hollowness. She had gone again. No trace, no romantic note in a scented lavender envelope on the mantelpiece; just an eerie calm. He had no idea how long she would be gone this time; two or three days, maybe a week. He could only wait and wonder. For the first time he thought more deeply about her looks; her dark hair that fell gently onto her perfect cheeks; her Cleopatra eyes and enchanting face. He had a longing for her that he had not recognised before. If only she was here now. He could reach out and touch her polished skin, thread his fingers through her wavy hair and pull her head to his chest; he would kiss her forehead and tell her how much he needed her.

Three days later, she arrived. It was six o' clock in the evening whilst Nathan was watching the news. Charmaine walked around the sofa that Nathan had converted into a semi-permanent annexe and kissed him on the head. She sat down beside him with her weekend bag on her lap.

"What's happening in the world?" she asked, gazing across at the TV news.

"Oh you know, the usual; floods in Thailand, unrest in the Middle East and political scandals at Number 10."

"Really? The world doesn't change." Nathan noticed that something about her was very different, though he couldn't quite work out what it was. There was a smell he didn't recognise; a subtle aroma of muskiness clung to her. She even looked slightly different. Her hair had a little more delicacy to the waves and curves; instead of falling mysteriously to her shoulders it now forked its way into her neckline. There was little conversation between them. It was almost like a replay of days gone by when she used to simply come over just to be there. But now everything was different. That was before any physical contact. Before that first kiss and before the passionate embraces; that was before their souls had collided and spun them into an orbit of no return. Over the next few days Nathan was torn between total bemusement and disinterest. As usual, Charmaine carried on as if nothing had happened. The expectant conversation loomed over them.

It was one rainless night when she decided to tell him. He had to be in his chair when she broke the news; that would at least be a comfort zone for him. She came into the lounge and sat on the sofa.

"Nathan," she said softly. He had pre-empted this moment for the last few days; days that dragged like a six-month winter. "I can't go with you. I'm sorry but, I just can't."

Nathan's expression formed immediate reflection. "I can't say I wasn't half expecting this," Nathan replied. "But I really think I deserve an explanation after all we've been through. Don't you?" he asked.

"I can't give you one, my love." she said. '*My love*'… the two words shot into his stomach, causing his inner body to solidify. She had never used those words before; *why now did she choose to use them?* She was about to bring down a sledgehammer of disappointment; crashing it down on his sculpture of optimism and smashing it to smithereens. "Nathe, you know I want to do my Master's this year. And there is the other thing."

"Oh yes of course, the other thing. The *other* thing that you keep safely to yourself. The other thing that no one has a chance of finding out what it actually is. What happened here, Char?" Nathan asked solemnly. "You used to just turn up and stay. Then you decided to tell me that you had a crush on me and we started a relationship. Or did we?" He paused and sat forward. "Because I'm not exactly sure if we did, technically," he added.

"Come on Nathe, you're more intelligent than that. You know full well we have something much deeper than the average relationship, something much more real than silk sheets and French windows."

"I know that but," Nathan snapped, "it's been eating me up; ever since you did your first disappearing act. I've tried to ask myself if I'm expecting too much from you."

"No Nathe, not at all. This is a mutual relationship, remember. It's just I found out that there's a part of me I just can't give to you."

"Could I ask you this then?" He stood up and looked down at her as she shrank deeper into the sofa.

"What?" she asked quietly.

"Could you give it to someone else?"

Charmaine's eyes moved upwards to meet his. "In a way, yes."

"So there is someone else."

"Kind of."

"What the hell does that mean, Char, 'kind of',"

"It means what it means. There is kind of someone else. But you and I have something special."

"You mean we *had* something special." Charmaine burst into tears and ran upstairs. Nathan soon ran up after her. She was staring out of the bedroom window towards her own house.

"I'm sorry," Nathan said.

"It's okay. I know you needed to say that."

"Is there a chance for us?" Nathan asked.

"Maybe, just a chance," she replied.

Nathan walked over towards her and put his arms around her from behind. "Well a chance is better than nothing, right?"

"Yes, better than nothing."

Even the DJs on the radio introduced a daily patter about the endless rains that washed out the summer. Nathan decided to go for a drive anyway; he thought a change of scenery would bring about a refreshed outlook. He noticed how huddled all the pedestrians were, hurrying to avoid the pitiless deluge. They walked briskly with arched backs and inflicted gait. Pulling away from the town, he smiled to himself when he saw the signpost for Kirkthorpe. He was tempted to revisit the place of the psychic fair, but instead decided to turn right into the small village centre. He remembered there was a coffee shop at the end of the high street so turned into the open carpark opposite.

Reversing into his preferred position, he caught sight of her. She stood there chatting merrily to a man right outside the coffee shop. They were sharing the same umbrella. The man looked to be in his late forties, with greying hair and a Mediterranean tan. His clothing was dark and inoffensive. They stood face to face laughing, oblivious to anyone. Charmaine urgently interlocked her arm with the man's and they darted into the coffee house. Nathan had a clear view through the large window; he watched as she shook her wet hair and placed her umbrella in the corner. The man took off his thin, dark coat and held it over his arm and brushed his tanned fingers through his shorn hair. They stood at the counter in whimsical stature before ordering their chosen delights. Charmaine went to sit in a seat near the window; the man followed on shortly afterwards with the tray of drinks. She stared out of the window and up at the sky. The man appeared to make a comment then they both glanced outside at people splashing their way along the flooded pavement. Nathan knew she couldn't see him; his windscreen was too distorted by the rain – and besides he knew Charmaine had no idea about the makes and models of cars.

No words came into his mind; all he could feel was the adrenaline flushing upwards as it passed his heart somewhere in the middle, which was descending to the entrails of his gut. His fingertips tingled and his heart raced. He clutched onto the steering wheel as if holding onto a lifeline.

He hung his head before raking his neck to make sure it was definitely her. He knew it was, even though he wanted to deny it. Taking one last stare, he witnessed the man take hold of Charmaine's hand. He held it there for a moment before pulling it away to pour the tea from a white, porcelain teapot. *So this is the other person? He looks like he's rich enough to own a villa in Marbella. Maybe she was seeking a surrogate father figure all this time so she opted for someone even older, with enough money to offer her a real escape. Maybe all she ever wanted was someone who could give her security. All we had was a fairy-tale, a platonic ideal. That's no competition for something real.*

Nathan drove off; he had no idea which direction he was going in. The wiper blades rubbed tauntingly to the image playing in his mind. He imagined her on top of the man, controlling her hips to gain maximum pleasure. The man looked up at her, caressing her breasts with one hand whilst placing the other on her cheek. The eroticism came to a climax as Charmaine leaned forward, resting her hands heavily onto the man's silver haired chest. Her face contorted in ecstasy.

She has found in him what she couldn't find in me: sexual joy; orgasms and erotic gratification in all the right places. She has found a way to love through mind, body and soul. I guess that's what she craved for; what we all crave for.

★

The thirteen-hour flight gave Nathan plenty of time to reflect on the plane. The selection of second-rate movies and music was not enough to divert his thoughts. Every song or drama pointed his compass towards Charmaine. Though he had already made his decision to leave, with or without her, what he saw through the coffee house window was all he needed to ratify it as being the right one. What he hoped was that she would be waiting when he got back; sitting in the lounge waiting to tell him that she had been stupid and that all she wanted was for them to be together as one. *Maybe it was a fling – something she needed to get out of her system. She'll soon find out that the man was a lothario with a string of women spread across the continent; a Latino lover who knows how to woo women but is incapable of practicing monogamy. I can forgive her if she gives herself to me wholly.*

"Ladies and gentlemen we will soon be starting our decent into Manila." Nathan flipped back into the real world once again. He rubbed his hands and prepared himself for touchdown. As he did, one last thought about her came into his mind. The old adage, often preached by his mother and grandmother: 'absence makes the heart grow fonder'. Gazing out at the sun-kissed jungle archipelagos, he smiled. *It just might.*

ANOTHER LIFE

Two weeks into his assignment in the Philippines, Nathan became ill. The flu-like symptoms lasted for just twenty-four hours then he was almost ready to get back to work after another day of rest. He was proud to have been given the job as Project Manager for a team of volunteers; their aim was to build fencing and pathways along the riverbank, in a fishing village close to the town of San Fernando in Pampanga, the northern part of Luzon – north of the capital, Manila. His fellow volunteer workers were made up of British people and other Europeans, New Zealanders, Americans and Australians. There was also representation from the local community. Nathan's co-workers had joked about his illness saying it was jungle fever; a process of adaptation to the sometimes hostile tropical climate. It was a staggering contrast to the cooler climes of northern England. The humidity took no prisoners; within minutes of stepping into the fresh air it would leave you to marinate until the next shower.

Nathan surprised himself by not sparing a thought about his life back in the UK. He had done a sterling job of compartmentalising his life back home; here he was, someone different from the complex Nathan Blakemore who thought deeply about everything from the origins of life and faith, to the reason for human existence. There was no headspace for that type of thinking here; life was much simpler. Nobody gave a second thought to the process of thinking itself; here it was about survival. For many of the locals the task of feeding themselves and their families on a staple diet of rice and small fish was an undertaking beyond the realms of comprehension to Nathan. That was until he witnessed the day-to-day slog of people scraping a living by fishing or hacking coconuts from trees. Others taxied commuters in the local town, from six o' clock in the morning to seven o' clock at night on pedi-cabs: a bicycle complete with welded-on sidecar; all for a salary which in the UK would be less than a child's pocket money. This was what he wanted for now; the sweat and the toil of honest work. This was his new reality. He absorbed the smoky coconut fires and constant sticky skin with a feeling of immunity. These were the very sensations he hoped would become the anaesthetic he needed. He also wondered how long it would be before he started to think about someone who was a few thousand miles away.

A ten-week stint with almost no respite had earned the team a much-needed break. With the help of local guides they embarked on a mountain trek with the aim of spending a couple of days walking and camping up Mount Pinatubo – a volcanic mountain an hour or so north of the camp. The guide for the trek had even negotiated safe passage with the National People's Army, known locally as the NPA, who were embedded into the terrain of the mountain that served as their hideaway. Their organisation, though fairly benign in recent history, could still be intimidating to people, especially foreigners who were unaware of their plight. However, in exchange for some supplies and food they were willing accomplices for any groups or parties who wished to explore the mountain area. Nathan felt like he was in one of those 1960s movies where intrepid explorers would set off on their mission to an unknown world. It excited him; the danger of poisonous snakes and bandits who camouflaged themselves into the background. All that was missing was the irreproachable femme fatale.

During the second day of hiking, one hour of heavy rainfall forced the party into taking refuge in some empty shacks that were strewn deliberately along the trek. When the sun broke through, the party leader called for them to move out; a sultry figure fell in line immediately in front of him.

She glanced back at him with a warm smile.

"Hi," she introduced herself. "I'm Amelia."

"Nathan," he replied.

"It's hot, yes?" Amelia said.

"You can say that again, hot and wet."

"I have an extra towel if you need one. You're sweating, or is it the rain?" she asked, smiling politely.

"Probably both," Nathan said. He thanked her for the towel and as they continued the steady climb he gazed guiltily at her tanned legs, which were moistened perfectly by the rain. Her hair was tied back, revealing glistening gold shoulders; her ponytail was just long enough to sit tightly between her shoulder blades; its end, dampened by the sweat and rain, snaked down to the rib of her combat vest. Nathan thought her to be strikingly attractive. Despite the task and environment she somehow still managed to give off a sweet scent of freshness. She kept turning around to check on Nathan, all the time her smile becoming more evocative and her eyes more sincere. Nathan suddenly became oblivious to his tiredness. Higher up the climb she slipped slightly backwards on some uneven stones. Nathan instinctively put one arm out which he pressed into the small of her back. He wanted to keep his hand there for longer; the warm dampness filtered onto his hand as his other caught hers in order to stop her slipping back. Her hand gripped his tightly and she regained her balance.

"Woah, you okay?"

"I'm okay thanks." He counted the steps they took before their hands slid apart in reluctant release. Her embarrassment was tainted by the direction of her glance, and her innocent smile failed to disguise an inner longing.

Near the top of the mountain, the group leaders planned

camping arrangements for the night. As the organisational frenzy got under way Nathan tried to refrain from making his stares towards Amelia obvious. She had now re-joined her Filipino colleagues but almost apologetically glimpsed across at him in-between making small talk and preparing her tent. Nathan decided to ignore social graces and walked slowly over to her.

"I believe we're having dinner," he said humorously.

"Yes Lechon, I'm one of the cooks."

"Wonderful," he replied, "I look forward to it very much. That's pig, right?"

"*Di ba,*" she replied in her native Tagalog. Nathan was astonished to see the trek leaders unveil a dead pig from a large sack. He was just glad it had already been disembowelled as the thought of having to watch such an event left him in a state of semi-disgust. Although vegetarianism was never on his agenda, neither did he ever feel the need to witness the violence of slaughter, albeit he accepted the cultural relevance. No one would have guessed they were one-thousand feet up a mountain as two of the Europeans from the party performed a version of John Denver's 'Take Me Home, Country Roads', all the time encouraging the rest of the group to join in. By the time they got onto 'Bridge over Troubled Water', Nathan was only too willing to lend his dulcet tones to the harmonies. When the applause came he was delighted to see that Amelia was leading it with a standing ovation. After some ruffling and clicking of portable equipment the Filipino group announced it was their turn to offer a slot. The music rang out and they immediately formed into a well-drilled, traditional dance group. Amelia smiled constantly as she joined in whilst Nathan looked on, spellbound. Their eyes never actually met as she tried hard to focus on anyone but him. Once again, applause rang out as Filipino-brewed San Miguel beer was offered in plastic cups. Though it was warm it offered a refreshing kick to the proceedings. A freedom of spirit drenched him; he soaked it up willingly, drinking and breathing every molecule.

During a quiet moment, Amelia padded over towards him and sat opposite him on a well-placed rock.

"So you like to sing!" she said.

"Well like to try, more like," he replied modestly.

"We Filipino people love to sing."

"But your dancing is very impressive," Nathan complimented.

"*Salamat po*," she replied.

"You're welcome, or should I say *walang anuman*?"

"Ah, you learned some Tagalog, impressive!"

"A little, from the locals helping at the river project."

"Oh yes, I've seen you there," she stated. "But I don't think you ever noticed me."

"I'm sorry for that," he excused. "I'm not sure why, probably because I'm always so busy."

"Well you did wave at me once."

"Really?"

"I'm the one who comes in the white van. I'm the supply coordinator for the project."

"Oh, now I'm embarrassed," Nathan said.

"You don't have to be, anyway I normally see Cedric who orders all the supplies."

"Ah yes Cedric, the Filipino project manager from the community. You beep the horn when you come yes?"

"Yes," Amelia replied. "It's a Filipino thing. We do that!"

"In England you can get in trouble for that unless you have a good reason."

"Really? I will try to remember that if I ever drive there." The background noise continued to provide a decoy for their conversation.

"So you've never been to the UK?"

"No, it's not easy for us to get a visa to go there."

"Unless you get married to someone from there, *di ba*," Nathan added, introducing the new word he had just learned from her. Amelia tilted her head in approval.

"Yes, if we marry anyone from UK then we can go." Their conversation flowed into the early hours until Amelia suggested she needed to sleep. Nathan felt disappointed that the discussion had to end, even though they had been talking for about two hours.

The next day the party reached the summit of the mountain. Their aim had been accomplished and Nathan felt pride in his achievement, though it wasn't a real climb in the true sense – more like an amble up a hill, albeit a very steep and at times treacherous one. All they had to do now was make their way back to the camp before dark. A few more hours of toil and sweat before the best cold shower ever.

The project workers would have one day of leisure before returning to hard labour. Nathan intended to spend most of it sat on his bed in the camp writing letters home, reading and listening to music. As he unpacked his rucksack a quiet knock on the open door of his hut turned his gaze upwards.

"Hi, sorry to disturb you," Amelia said. "Are you busy tomorrow?"

"Oh, not really, why?" Nathan asked.

"I wondered if you would like to see a bit more of the culture in the Philippines. It is my village fiesta tomorrow. I would like to invite you as my guest."

"Wow! That sounds great. I would, yes – thank you."

"Okay great, I will come get you at eleven."

"In the white van?" Nathan joked.

"Yes," she said laughing, "in the white van, but I will not beep the horn."

Nathan couldn't sleep. Something ate away at his conscience. He knew exactly what it was though he tried worthlessly to repress the thought. *After all, she isn't here with me. It was her decision not to come. Why should I have any feelings of guilt? And besides, why should my intentions be anything other than strictly honourable?* Nathan tossed and turned in his camp bed. His small electric fan blew at him, a judgmental din. He sat on the edge of the bed with his elbows on his knees and his hands clasped over his nose. His bottle of water on the bedside cabinet was warm and almost empty. Loud coughing from the next bunk hut flipped him back to real time. He sat in the small, wooden chair in the corner of the hut and reached over to turn on his battery lamp. A mosquito flew at him in kamikaze-like fashion, as if it sensed that he was outside the jurisdiction of his mosquito net. He clapped it into his palms with rehearsed care.

"*Patay!*" He flicked the deceased insect off his hand with a gladiatorial satisfaction. He would go tomorrow. He had earned the company of another woman, though he knew he was culpable. Something was urging him; he had felt this before many years ago, in a quiet corner of Paris. The tremors in his stomach signalled a warning. A warning that those primitive urges will surface, even when we try to smother them with our conscience; the command to deny ourselves is overwhelmed. The sin is committed in our minds long before the flesh succumbs. It is another aspect of our human frailty – guilt versus morality. Nathan's only consolation would be to manipulate the consequences to fit his own rationality.

The following morning had a holiday feel about it. Many of the project workers sat on makeshift sun loungers drinking ice-cold drinks and reading shabby paperbacks. Some preferred to stay in the shade of the communal social huts or sit under trees. Western pop music floated across the camp as the Filipino contingent sat in a huddle, smoking and playing cards. Occasionally some of them would sing along enthusiastically to songs they recognised. By half-past ten, Nathan had already showered but decided it was too hot to change into his clothes; instead he lay on the bed in his boxer shorts, flipping through some week-old British newspapers that had been shipped in for the UK workers.

At ten fifty he decided to put his clothes on; carefully thought out attire of plain khaki combat trousers with a loose, white T-shirt and white pumps. Amelia arrived at seven minutes past eleven. Nathan waved from his hut and after locking the door, hopped across the track to the waiting white van.

"Morning," Amelia shouted. "Sorry if I am late. I had to take my mother to the market."

"No problem," Nathan gestured.

"Please don't mind but it's a forty minute drive and sometimes bumpy," she announced.

Nathan gestured with his open arms to convey it was not a problem.

"Okay then," she added. "Shall we go?"

By the time they arrived at the small town of Santo Nino, the main street was already thick with people. Stalls selling everything from second hand clothes to local foods lined the side roads up to the church. A mass was already underway; people were lined along the outside, desperate to be part of the service as others fanned themselves intermittently in-between paying mild attention to the words of the priest. Amelia was dressed in thin, beige jeans and white sandals, which matched her blouse. Her hair hung loose; she had emphasised her cheekbones with a subtle tone of make-up and the gold crucifix around her neck rested uncompromisingly on the flat of her chest. Nathan thought she looked even more stunning than she had on the mountain. There was a softer edge to her beauty. The lack of exposed flesh draped her in a distilled sensuality. After a few hours of strolling and sampling small delicacies a friend of Amelia's shouted over to her. It was customary to offer food on Fiesta Day so Amelia suggested to

Nathan that it would be polite to accept. Nathan had become accustomed to the Pinoy diet of rice, chicken, pork, fish and the necessary coconut wine affectionately known as *tuba*. A dessert of rice in coconut juice and locally baked cake called *puto* followed; their glasses were constantly refilled with *tuba*. Two hours later Nathan began to feel a little lightheaded. Amelia recognised this and decided to use this as a reason for them to leave. Nathan tried his best to mumble a thank you in Tagalog. Everyone laughed but only with polite respect at his effort and genuine acknowledgment of their hospitality.

"I think you need to rest, Nathan," she said assertively.

"Maybe, I'm okay but that *tuba* stuff. Wow! It's strong."

"That's because you are not used to it," she replied. "Okay well my house is not far, we can rest there for a while." Amelia's family home was a robust but basic house of unpainted concrete. She introduced Nathan to her parents and siblings then after a few minutes of pleasantries excused them both.

"Oh, I thought we were going to rest?" Nathan asked.

"We are, but in my house. That's the home of my parents and brothers and sisters. That's my house." She pointed to a beautiful cane and bamboo shack that was inset about one hundred metres deeper into the jungle. Nathan could see that despite its ethnic simplicity, it had been built with the skill and guile of someone who cared about their home. "I had this built two years ago," she said.

"It's remarkable. Sorry, what a rubbish word. It's great, fantastic!" Nathan declared as they came up to the front.

"My uncle built it for me." Two lights adorned the front elevation, which formed a terrace that led up to the door. Two dogs came bounding from behind the house, which startled him.

"Don't worry, they will not bite you." Amelia commanded them to go. "We all have them here, for safety," she added.

"Well that's good to know," Nathan said. Inside, the house

was laden with furniture made from bamboo and polished coconut tree wood. A TV and stereo system sat on a glass cabinet which contrasted with the plainness of the interior.

"Please sit here," she gestured. Nathan rocked back in a comfortable chair complete with foam seat. "Would you like to drink anything?"

"I'd really love a coffee, but you probably don't have that."

"I do," she said. "Some of us do drink it. But it's mainly for guests. It's Nescafe."

"Great!" Their restful conversation was like an antidote to the earlier hubbub. They took turns to talk about their lives. Nathan held back inner disappointment when he learned that Amelia had initially built the house for her and her fiancé; they were to be married until he jumped ship after a fling with a teenager resulted in an unexpected pregnancy. Thus, being the expected culture in the Philippines, he had no choice but to marry her. When the inevitable was raised, Nathan had to compose himself and retreat further back into his chair.

"I can tell," Amelia said, "there is someone. You have a girlfriend or wife," she added with a giggle.

"I don't know anymore. And I'm not trying to do the 'oh I'll pretend I don't know if I have a girlfriend or not' thing just to be cool." Nathan paused in realisation that he was almost putting himself out there. "Sorry I'm babbling," he said.

"I don't know what is babbling," Amelia said. "Sometimes I cannot understand English people when they speak too fast, you eat your words," she said, laughing.

"Sorry, I should understand," he returned apologetically.

"But you do have someone special yes?"

"I did have, yes. But something went wrong," he stated, sitting forward and staring around her room forlornly. Before his intended further explanation, Amelia walked over to him. She stood in from of him.

"It's okay," she said. She reached out and stroked his head, gently. He leaned forward and wrapped his arms around her waist. The side of his faced grazed her blouse. She pulled him closer until he could feel the contours of her midriff underneath the warm cottoned fabric. "It's okay," she repeated. Nathan's heart began to pump violently; he pulled his face slowly away from her diaphragm and looked up at her. She was beautiful; she gazed down at him in like she was the angel of empathy for the whole of his life. He stood up and placed a fatherly kiss on her forehead. He then kissed her cheek, until she sought his lips. He sat back down, still clinging to her waist.

He kissed her slightly exposed naval and slowly undid the buttons on her blouse. As he did so he planted his lips on her stomach in an upward motion. Thankfully, she saved him from the clumsy undressing scenario.

"Come," she led him into her bedroom. Nathan's eyes were suddenly drawn to the crucifix above her bed. A surge of contrition held him back until she realised his impasse. Again the simple words, "It's okay." Amelia undressed without embarrassment and lay before him on the bed. Nathan felt that he was about to explode; her breasts were now exposed like hidden treasures and her vagina hid behind a delicately shaped forest of pubic hair. By the time he undressed, his erection was intense. Laying carefully over her he kissed her all over her body. She tried to turn him over to do the same but he held her hands down strongly, though without aggression, and entered her. Her moans turned to gasps and then to light screaming. He hadn't felt this for a long time. Letting go of her hands he brushed one hand across her face and the other clasped around her breast, sucking lustfully at her nipple. He writhed into her until he came viciously. He continued to lay inside her for a while still semi-erect, such had been his need for sexual gratification. Amelia stroked his hair as she lay, fulfilled.

"Everything is okay," she said.

"Yes," he said, "everything is okay." Nathan's head fell

next to hers on the pillow. He fought desperately to alleviate himself from any guilt. Amelia was a beautiful woman with the warmest of hearts. Clutching on to this exquisite lady, his eyelids managed to pull themselves open to catch a glimpse of the high moon. A tear crawled out of the corner of his eye, blurring the clear unpolluted skies; someone far away might be looking up at that same daylight moon, wondering about something weird – like the consciousness of cats.

★

The pain of living with her decision to not join Nathan on the VOA project was only lessened by her growing love for someone else. Her life plan was actually now on course; the Master's degree seemed to be going well and she had found a suitable evening job with an excellent salary at the local call centre to finance her needs. Whilst it did have its moments of stress through the odd caller who became verbally aggressive, unlike her work at the Bistro the offending person was remote. Her mother had started to drink heavily again at home and Auntie Norma had virtually moved back in. Charmaine was content to have her old room back. She had created a safe haven for herself once again; it provided anchorage in contrast to semi-cohabiting with Nathan, which although she found to be wonderful, had opened up doors that she needed to keep closed.

The forceful yet soothing pull that was leading her life in another direction became ever-present as the weeks passed. She began to have doubts that she could complete her degree and started to miss the occasional lecture. This was something she had never done before; in her previous years of study her attendance had always been commended. Nathan was far from some kind of stop gap. She had gone from a schoolgirl crush to unquestionable love, far greater than she had experienced in the past. After all, he had been both her pillar and her sanctity. She never thought that Nathan would have a contender for her unconditional love; neither had she sought it. She sensed the onset of impending conflict; she would have to summon all the courage she could in order to survive this battle.

At this point in our story I should probably state the obvious: we cannot always choose who we love, and the process of love itself in the climate of a relationship throws up many challenges. Some people fall out of love; yet let us remember that Nathan and Charmaine at this juncture have allowed their love to surface. Therefore, the anguish borne out through external factors lays heavily on their minds. Love is sometimes like the wind; it blows wherever it wishes; it takes on its own life force. But, there *can* be a rationalisation to love, especially when it comes from the depths of the person's soul. Because that is when love is truest of all – it is not aesthetic or cloaked, it is not a persona driven by unconscious desires – it carries a pureness. However, for whom or for what that love is for is uncontrollable, because purity is only reached when control is removed. I have always listened to Nathan with serenity, though there are also times when I have felt the need to articulate my opinion about his thoughts with candour. Nonetheless, our two lovers will not find it easy to choose the right path; the brain does not always follow what the soul desires. This then, is their predicament. It was my hope that they would follow their souls to purity, whatever the external outcome for the both of them.

★

The rainy season was intent on starting earlier than usual and threatened to halt the completion of the project. This extended the final few weeks of his stay in San Fernando. Nathan liked Amelia very much. He might have even loved her though he seemed happy to maintain the slightest distance between them. This gave him some control – something he didn't have with Charmaine; with her it was an all-consuming intensity in the pit of his stomach. He hoped the delayed departure would give him the opportunity to find equilibrium with Amelia. At that moment he had no idea if he wanted to be with her, or to leave her with only memories for both of them to savour. Luminosity had filled their lives for the past months and they had not even tried to keep their relationship secret. In fact their openness was almost infectious as other associations between project workers and locals, or between other workers surfaced without embarrassment or judgement. Nathan's only question now was the durability of the relationship; he would soon be leaving for another island in the Philippines. Would it peter out into photographs of yesterday or could he foresee something longer lasting? Perhaps he knew that something or someone else might have a bearing on his decision.

He spent his last night in the Pampanga region with Amelia. Nathan didn't have the stomach for a goodbye scenario. Instead, they both behaved as if this was a temporary break. After all, why should it end? There was an element of mutual love even if it was at the shallow end. Their feigned acceptance of the possible outcome was packed away, along with Nathan's luggage bag. It was there but it didn't need further inspection or discussion; perhaps only on reopening would they realise what was inside.

"I have something for you," Nathan said.

"Really?" she replied, with widening eyes. He jumped up from the bed like a ten-year-old on Christmas morning. Thumbing through his wallet he pulled out an old black and white photograph.

"I want you to have this. It's a photo of me and my grandfather on holiday when I was eight years old." Amelia smiled and looked over the photograph. It was a world that was a million miles away from hers. She could see his grandfather standing behind him, resting his hands on Nathan's shoulders; such small, perfect shoulders. Nathan was dressed in a white sweater with checked shorts, white socks and sandals. His hair was von Trapp blond; in the background she could make out the ponies walking up the beach carrying young children, and older couples walking together, eating ice cream. Amelia started to cry.

"What's wrong, hon?" he asked, touching her cheek.

"Nothing, it's just your smile looks so…" she didn't finish her sentence.

"So what?"

"Incomplete."

"What, you mean like the person who took the picture didn't give us chance to smile properly?" Nathan somehow realised that was not what she meant, though he couldn't quite perceive her train of thought.

"No. I mean it's like you look happy, yes. But it's, how do you say this one?" She tried to find the right words in English. "It's like something inside you can see into the future and you don't like it."

"Really, you see all that? I've never noticed before."

"And the smile of your grandfather is the same… like, not a full smile."

"He became ill after that holiday."

"Oh I'm sorry. Did he…?"

"He didn't die," Nathan interjected. "In fact he lived longer than we all expected, until I was seventeen. My mother said it was his will to see me grow up."

"That's a nice story," Amelia said.

"Well I wanted you to have it. It's a special photograph for me. I've never wanted to give it away," Nathan said.

"So why now, and why me? Does this mean I am special to you?" Amelia asked, still wiping runaway tears that slid down her perfect cheekbone.

"Yes. That's exactly it. You are very special so I want you to have part of me that's also very special."

"Thank you Nathan, thank you. I will treasure it," she said. "please take care of yourself," she added.

"I will. And you also." Nathan wasn't quite sure why he had chosen to give her the photograph. It was a genuine act, but he couldn't decide if it was an act of cowardice, or a symbol of his legitimate intent. They held each other all through the night. Their love-making took on a more tender tone, as if their delicacy might cause them to shatter into a thousand pieces. Each piece might fade into dust before they could be put back together.

A one-week holiday of island hopping was all he needed before joining his second sixth month assignment in the Philippines. The project in Puerto Princesa on Palawan Island meant that Nathan had a similar role, though in addition he was to teach English to some of the local children who were not in formal education at school. Nathan buried himself in the project. He worked tirelessly, embracing every problem or challenge with a zest even he did not recognise. He had already soaked up the culture in Pampanga; not that it had deterred him from doing his job properly, but only now did he choose to have no respite from full-on commitment to his work. Perhaps it was his way of repressing any unwanted thoughts or desires that might serve to divert him; Nathan wasn't the kind of man who liked too many doors to be open. There were plentiful opportunities for relationships but this time he didn't feel he needed the stimulus of sexual pleasure or the tension of so-called platonic friendships with beautiful women. He spent most of his free time writing in his notebook or listening to music on his headphones. He also enjoyed riding the motorcycle. It gave him the chance to explore the villages and small towns; he grew accustomed to the stares and shouts of '*Hey Jo*', which was a throwback from the American

GI years. It seemed that every white foreigner must be an American; no other country existed in the parochial minds of some of the villagers.

He did become very friendly with a family who lived near to the camp: Menting and Corazon, a middle-aged married couple with no less than nine children with ages ranging from eight to twenty-five. One of their younger boys called Guti became ill with a chest infection and the family couldn't afford to pay for any kind of treatment. There was the free local clinic, but that was ten kilometres away and they had no transport. Also, the clinic was staffed by nurses who could only offer limited treatment. They had however suggested that the boy needed to see a doctor. Nathan had no choice but to help and so he took the boy to the hospital. The doctors said Guti needed to stay in hospital for three days on a drip as his lungs were in danger of becoming infected. Nathan paid for all the treatment. From that time onwards, Kuya Menting and Ate Corazon – as he came affectionately to refer to them, were eternally grateful. Nathan reciprocated the shared fondness by frequently visiting their modest shack. He would always take them a sack of rice, some bread and fruit.

Nathan sometimes woke early enough to see Kuya setting out to sea to catch crabs. Nathan would watch him through his small cabin window as the dawn sunlight forced its way through the morning haze. As he sipped at his strong coffee Kuya's silky figure would row doggedly to his catch. Just a few crabs would bring enough pesos to buy rice for the day. Meat or vegetables would be a bonus. He was inspired by Kuya Menting's unwavering defiance to feed his clan. And yet, never did he see them unhappy or envious because of their predicament; rather they clung onto faith, hope and love with an enviable tautness. Nathan tried to imagine them fitting into his world. He wondered what they would make of microwaves, leather sofas, king size beds and hot, running water, and what they would think about being able to walk through a supermarket with a trolley full of groceries. Would they even be comfortable? Perhaps it was all part of the geographical accident that plagued our world. *At what point did our seed generate into who we become and into whose womb we are planted?* He repeatedly asked himself these kinds of questions. *Why do I have to think so deeply about everything? No one else does! While the rest of the world ticks away blowing itself to bits – why? Does it even matter?* That was the problem – to Nathan it all did. The deep thinking was back with a vengeance.

With one month of the project to go, Nathan became ill again. It all happened one day whilst he was helping with the well construction. One of his colleagues told him to sit down in the shade because he looked like a ghost. Some of the other workers became aware of his state and suggested he should visit the camp doctor. As they helped him to his feet his eyes began to roll and the muscles in his face started to twitch uncontrollably. Two of his co-workers threw one arm each over their shoulders and attempted to escort him to his cabin. Nathan's legs didn't appear to be responding; his feet dragged along the dirt track like those of a fallen soldier being carried to safety from the battlefield. The two workers kept shouting his name whilst splashing water onto his face. The project doctor was urgently alerted and drove the short distance to Nathan's cabin. He looked over at him and immediately shouted instructions to the co-workers to call the hospital to warn them of an imminent arrival. The doctor checked all Nathan's vitals but knew he was losing consciousness rapidly. He decided to drive him to the hospital himself with the aid of the two co-workers.

The hospital was a ten kilometre ride away. Nathan was laid across the back seat of the four-wheeler with one of his colleagues holding his head in her lap and another at his feet. Inga was a Norwegian girl of about twenty-seven; she had worked quite closely with Nathan as his deputy supervisor though they had hardly spoken on personal terms since the beginning of the project. Luka was a Belgian and had shared the odd night-time beer with him but only in the confines of the social area in the camp. Such had been Nathan's low profile on a social level this time around, it was almost like they were escorting a stranger. Nathan regained consciousness intermittently. Inga did her best to keep him conscious on the advice of the doctor. Her hard Scandinavian tones and flaxen hair gained Nathan's attention for a few flickering seconds. By the time they reached the hospital Nathan was almost fully conscious again though his confusion was obvious to all.

"Where are we?"

"It's okay Nathan," Inga uttered, "just try to stay awake."

"I need to go to Newcastle tomorrow," he said.

"Well you need to rest first," Inga replied appropriately, knowing full well Newcastle was a city in England. Two doctors and two nurses teemed around Nathan as the camp doctor explained his symptoms. He was placed immediately on a drip, which made him become anxious.

"What's going on? Why do I need this?" he shouted, with alarm in his fading voice.

"Everything will be okay Nathan," one of the Filipino doctors assured him, "we will take care of you, don't worry."

"What's wrong with me?"

"You just have a sickness, but you will be fine soon." As the nurses tried to help him into a bed, Nathan's facial twitching manifested into a full-blown seizure. His co-workers were ushered out of the ward immediately and the doctors rushed him into a private room as others came running to join them. The commotion that followed took on the look of a TV hospital emergency drama. Inga, Luka and the doctor from the camp could only withdraw with concerned expressions.

★

The end to the academic year brought about a deep relief in Charmaine. It had been fraught with diversions and desires for something else. She had somehow managed to stumble through the first year of her Master's degree with a lesser feeling of accomplishment than all her previous scholastic achievements. There would be no celebration, or night out with peers. In fact she had hardly befriended anyone during the year. She hadn't even made token appearances at group or club meetings, which in the past was something she was always keen to do. She had been thinking about Nathan. Walks in the park and along the canal bank made her smile reflectively about some of the times they had spent together. However, she wore her seclusion with a comfort that she never anticipated.

Even her mother's deterioration failed to lure her into any feelings of panic. Instead, she was the one who brought a sense of calmness to the household. She had many open discussions with Auntie Norma as her mother slept off another booze-filled day. The unfashionable Formica table had turned into a place of pilgrimage. Auntie Norma was always quick to express her concern at the sorry state of Charmaine's mother. Her usual steadfastness in dealing with her own sister had been reduced to a quiet alarm.

"I don't know what to do anymore," was the persistent remark she made across the table. "Maybe we should take her to AA."

"It's okay Auntie," Charmaine replied with a restful tone after hearing the announcement one too many times. "We are the best people to help her."

"But you're not always here, and what if you decide to go off again for a week like you did at Easter?"

"I know you will be okay," Charmaine said reassuringly. "I've seen how you take care of Mum. No one could do as much as you have done. You can't do any more than that, so please don't worry. Mum is how she is. I'm not sure if we can change her now. Just be there for her."

An uncharacteristic tear welled up in Auntie Norma's eyes. The stalwart hardiness had begun to crumble. "I just feel that she will drink herself to death one day soon."

"I know," Charmaine said. "I've also thought about that. But in some way, if that's what brings her to peace then, so be it."

Auntie Norma wore an expression of shock on her lined face. "But you don't want her to die, surely?"

"No of course I don't Auntie," Charmaine replied, still airing a calm exterior, "but I just feel it will be like torture to put her through some kind of rehabilitation treatment program. Mum hasn't got the strength for it. Mum has always been a tragedy, as long as I can remember. But in her own sweet way, that's kind of who she is."

"But she wasn't always like that Charmaine, love," Auntie Norma stated sentimentally. "It all started when your father left."

"Yes I know. That's my point. It's almost as if he took the best part of her with him. But I'd rather her be whole, that little part she has left, rather than break up into more pieces. That's what rehab would do to her because she has no fight left."

"Well maybe you are right, love. I just think it's all such a shame. She was really clever and talented you know, when she was younger. Her teachers said she could become a dancer. She was also really good at making things, you know like clothes and curtains, stuff like that."

"That's more like it Auntie," Charmaine said with smiling eyes, "and that's the way we should always remember her." Charmaine reached over to hug her Auntie Norma. They hung onto each other for a while before Charmaine broke away. "I'll make some more tea. Maybe Mum would like some too."

The pale, grey trim-phone that hung on the wall woke Charmaine like an alarm bell. She trod briskly down the patterned carpet staircase in her bare feet.

"Hello, could I speak to Miss Charmaine Laffe please?" the authoritative voice requested on the other end of the line.

"Yes, that's me speaking, who's calling please?"

"My name is Michael Burrows. I'm one of the project directors for the VOA in the Philippines." Charmaine knew immediately that the conversation was going to be about Nathan.

"I'm afraid I have some news," the caller uttered.

"Yes, about Nathan, Nathan Blakemore?" she affirmed.

"Yes that's right," he said. Charmaine remained unruffled as she jotted down notes on the telephone message pad. "You are the only other contact we have apart from his next of kin which is his mother. But we can't seem to contact her. The number we have is unobtainable," the caller stressed.

"Oh I see," Charmaine replied formally, "I know his mother has moved house now but I'm not sure if she's on the phone yet." Auntie Norma appeared at the top of the stairs in a supportive stance. She could sense the seriousness of the conversation though was also aware that Charmaine was coping with the news with a quiet self-assurance that she was becoming accustomed to. "Okay Mr Burrows, thank you for your help," Charmaine said into the mouthpiece as she gazed up at her auntie. "I have to go to the Philippines," she said. Auntie Norma's closed smile and almost unnoticeable nod of the head was all she needed as approval.

★

It was Charmaine's turn to ponder on the plane; the 'what ifs' fired through her thoughts like arrows shot from a troupe of archers. She had gone through some personal changes and

109

adopted a more serene face for all to see, but it was more difficult to bury the feelings she still held for Nathan. Though she had come to accept that there was no more possibility of romantic love between them, love didn't end like the spool of an old movie reel – it faded like an etching through the years. But her love for Nathan couldn't fade so easily and the remnants of a different type of love still lingered intensely. She knew this would always be the way it would be; her best hope was a congenial repression of how she used to feel. There would always be that place, but access had to be refused. However, her love for him had transcended into something otherworldly. After landing in Manila she had instructions to take a short ride in an airport taxi to a hotel close to the terminal building; she was also booked on a domestic flight to Puerto Princesa the following day.

Michael Burrows stood at the back of the grotty airport arrival hall with a handwritten sign pulled into his chest. Charmaine could hardly recognise her name, which was misspelt and looked as though it had been written by a ten-year-old. She strode towards him as his eyes looked ruefully towards her.

"Hi I'm Charmaine, Charmaine Laffe," she said.

"Michael Burrows," he announced formally. "How was your flight?"

"Fine, thank you."

"I have a car waiting, please let me help you with your luggage." During their telephone conversation Mr Burrows had offered Charmaine a room close to the hospital for as long as she needed. The length of her stay was to some extent out of her control. Charmaine was surprised to see a large four wheel drive car waiting for them. The Filipino driver vigilantly opened the rear passenger door for her and smiled. Mr Burrows put her small bag in the boot and jumped briskly into the front passenger seat.

"It's just a thirty minute drive," he said, raking his neck around to address Charmaine. "A few bumps on the way but nothing to worry about. Philippine roads are not so great in the provinces," he added as he and the driver exchanged mutual smiles.

Despite the arduous nature of her journey she couldn't help paying attention to the obvious Christian nature of the country. Churches and chapels lined the roads and sun-bleached posters of Roman Catholic saints adorned makeshift billboards. Her preconceived notion was that Buddhism was the major religion in all of South East Asia. Despite her academic intelligence, geography and worldly knowledge had never been her strong point; a musing that brought a short smile to her face. She didn't expect to smile again on this particular trip. Mr Burrows told the driver to wait for them, then escorted Charmaine to the entrance of the dishevelled building. A smattering of worn out, maroon coloured, leather chairs adorned the foyer.

"I'll wait here for you. I think you would like to see him on your own," Michael Burrows suggested. Charmaine could hear footsteps padding along the red and grey tiled floor, which looked like it had been laid in the 1970s. A refined-looking Filipina lady appeared in a smock that matched the colour of the sofas. She carried a document wallet under one arm.

"Hello Ma'am, welcome to St Teresa's," she said in a formal but polite manner. "I will take you now to see Mr Blakemore."

When she first looked upon Nathan the tightness in her throat forced her to gasp for air.

"Are you okay, Ma'am?" The essential presence of oxygen masks and electronic monitoring equipment sterilised the moment. Her eyes never left his face as she ambled forward rigidly before reaching out for his right hand. She thought it odd how at times of duress such as this, irrelevancies become noticeable: like the mint green paint on all the woodwork and the murky white walls with a print of the Holy Family that hung at an ill-corresponding angle to the ceiling. The jug of water on his bedside locker looked tepid and the air conditioning unit struggled to carry out its duty. The windows looked more like that of a jail than a hospital – small with leaded squares. His head and face were swollen and his eyes sunk back into their sockets. Through the vapour of tear-loaded eyes she tried to read the label on the drip bag that invaded his other hand. She read the label feeding the drip. *Mannitol,* which the doctor later explained was a drug used to treat Japanese Encephalitis.

The disease came from mosquitos. Although it was quite rare and not always so serious, Nathan's immune system had apparently triggered an allergic reaction to an infected mosquito bite.

The doctor and one of the nurses stood opposite Charmaine in the corner of Nathan's room.

She was given the prognosis as they gestured her to sit on a white plastic chair just a few feet away from him; the only man who had tapped into her unconscious without deceit… the man who had fired her soul into life.

"He's going to do a PhD," she announced with unexpected randomness. The nurse and doctor both smiled and looked at each other before turning their gaze back to Charmaine.

"Ma'am, we think Nathan might have suffered some brain damage, though we cannot be certain yet. The neurologist will be making his assessment in the next forty-eight hours." The very phrase 'brain damage' rang out with hollowness. She smiled with a soft gasp and looked across at him.

"What if he can hear us?" Charmaine said.

"We don't think so, Ma'am. He is unconscious at the moment," the doctor replied politely.

She immediately remembered those heady discussions in

Nathan's living room. "How can you be sure?" Charmaine asked inquisitively.

The doctor smiled at her with caution. "We don't think so, Ma'am."

"Do you know about consciousness?" Charmaine asked them, still looking at Nathan sorrowfully.

"Sorry Ma'am," the doctor asked. "I'm not sure I understand."

"Consciousness – it doesn't die. Did you know that?" Charmaine walked out of the room, unable to hide her distress, which at last overcame her dignified self-control. The nurse followed and graciously ushered her into a quiet room. She offered to bring Charmaine some coffee and give her time to gather her thoughts. After some time had passed the nurse walked courteously back into the room.

"Are you okay Ma'am?" she asked.

"Yes. Yes I'm much better thanks, thank you." Charmaine replied. "I've never heard of Japanese Encephalitis."

"It's quite rare, Ma'am," the nurse replied, confidently.

"Will he wake up – I mean soon?" Charmaine asked, immediately reflecting some regret in her question.

"I'm not sure, Ma'am. Do you want me to ask the doctor to come and discuss it with you?"

"Yes please, that would be nice, thank you." Charmaine looked up at the crucifix above the door as the doctor and nurse reappeared. The nurse was about to leave but Charmaine asked her to stay. The doctor was able to give some assurance. He told her that he had experienced two cases before where one woman had made a slow but almost complete recovery with minimal brain damage. When Charmaine asked what minimal brain damage meant he responded by telling her that the woman's short-term memory was affected but this didn't disable her from returning to work and carrying out normal day-to-day activities.

"What about the other person?" Charmaine asked.

"Unfortunately I believe the gentlemen is still in a coma. As far as we know. He was transferred back to a hospital in America."

"So that's like a fifty–fifty chance then?"

"Well only for the cases I've known Ma'am," he replied professionally.

Charmaine stood up. "Could I see him again please?"

"Yes of course Ma'am, Nurse Jane will take care of you, please excuse me."

"Thank you doctor, you have been very helpful."

Charmaine hesitated before walking back up to Nathan's bedside. She looked up at the tilted picture of the young Jesus, Mary and Joseph and then down at Nathan. She knelt down by his bed and took hold of his hand.

"Nathan, I know for sure I have to leave now," she began solemnly, "but I will always be with you, please believe me. You will get better, I know." Charmaine looked up at his face one more time. Still holding his hand she rose to her feet. "I love you," she whispered. She pressed her cheek against his cold hand then eased it back down onto the bed. The nurse walked her back to the place of the tattered maroon chairs. Mr Burrows rose with efficiency. Charmaine turned to thank the nurse.

"Our pleasure Ma'am, with God's help Mr Blakemore will make full recovery," she said with a confident smile. Charmaine looked across at the crucifix on the wall one last time.

"Yes, indeed," she said, "with God's will."

★

The helicopter fan hovered to a standstill and a wave of fresh air swept over his face. His eyes scrutinised the space above him. Muted voices fused with the pulsations of automated paraphernalia. *Charmaine must have brought friends home.* Twisting his head tugged something inside his throat. *What the..?*

"Hello Nathan!" a voice bellowed. "Can you hear me? You're awake, Nathan." An unrecognisable yet angelic face stared down at him.

"Mr Blakemore, it's nice to see you," she said. Soon, more people were in the room adorning white coats. He knew this was no dream; he had always been able to distinguish between his dreams and vivid reality. *Where the hell am I and what's going on?* One of the men in a white coat stood beside him.

"Nathan, any second now I will pull this small tube from your mouth. I want you to try and blow out as hard as you can at the same time. I will count to three. Please nod your head slowly if you understand." Nathan did understand and prepared for the countdown. "One, two, three, okay excellent, well done Nathan." A sharp intake of breath was followed by dryness like he had never experienced, not since he had his tonsils removed at the age of ten. *So this is a hospital. Okay, so these people are doctors and nurses. Something's happened to me. Wait, I know my name: Nathan John Blakemore, I know where I'm from: Leeds, I know I used to sell musical equipment and taught philosophy part-time. I know all the people in my life: Charmaine. Charmaine! My mum is retired and lives in Blackpool. I know I came to work in the Philippines; this looks like it's the Philippines; these people look Filipino. See, I'm definitely not crazy or dreaming. I know myself. But something doesn't feel right. It doesn't feel like me, but I know it is me. Jesus is on the wall, with his mother and father. I know him.*

"Nathan, how are you feeling? Can you remember what happened to you?" one of the doctors asked caringly.

"No. I just know I came here to work with the VOA on a project," Nathan replied, struggling to voice his words clearly.

"Here, drink some water, but only small sips," the doctor ordered. "Nathan, my name is Doctor Rodriguez. Me and my colleagues here," he gestured towards two nurses and another younger looking doctor, "have been looking after you since you arrived here."

"Thank you," Nathan answered intuitively.

"Nathan, please try to tell me as much about yourself as you can remember."

Nathan began a short biography of his life. It felt like he was been interviewed for a job, though he was happy to go through the motions as a sign of reassurance for his own existence.

"Okay, good. Can you remember who the Prime Minister is in your country?"

"Mrs Thatcher, I think," he answered. The doctor didn't seem too keen to affirm.

"Can you remember my name, Nathan?"

"I think so, yes. It's erm…" He stuttered slightly and clocked the room, "Doctor Ramirez," he said. "Yes, I remember – like a Spanish-sounding name."

"Thank you Nathan." Again, no confirmation came. "Nathan, please don't mind me calling you by your Christian name. In our culture we prefer to use the formal address – Mr Blakemore or Sir, especially in a professional setting. However we understand in this situation you will feel more comfortable if we use your given Christian name."

"Thank you Doctor, Doctor Ramirez. I prefer that."

"Nathan," Dr Rodriguez began again, "you suffered a small infection due to a mosquito bite. This unfortunately made your brain swell slightly and we had to incubate you so that you could breathe."

"You're joking – all this because of a mosquito?" Nathan jibed. "So I've had Malaria?"

"No, not Malaria," the doctor replied. "It's something called Japanese Encephalitis."

"Sounds scary."

"Well it can be but not always."

Nathan suddenly became a little more attentive. "And?" he asked, inquisitively trying desperately to read everyone's expression in the room.

"Nathan, I'm not sure when is the right time to tell you but we believe you have experienced some slight damage to the brain." Nathan was silent. His eyes moved in saccades before focussing on a small lizard on the wall. "Are you okay?" Dr Rodriguez asked him.

Nathan laughed sarcastically. "Well that's not an easy question to answer, Doctor. I've just woken up and now you tell me I have brain damage. How the fuck can I be okay?"

"I tell you what – we can discuss this later – you get some rest just now." Doctor Rodriguez told Nathan he would leave him for a while and that the nurses would be on hand for anything he needed.

Nurse Rosita introduced herself and checked all of Nathan's vitals. She also used the time to console him and provide a listening ear.

"That explains why I feel so weird."

"It's normal," nurse Rosita said as she rechecked his pulse. "Would you like anything to eat or drink?"

"Yes please, a pork pie and a pint."

"Sorry," she answered confusedly. "I don't know that one."

"No it's okay, I was joking."

"That's good," she said. "Good that your sense of humour is strong."

"What choice do I have?"

"We have chicken and rice, and I can get for you some tea or cold drink."

Nathan turned onto his other side stiffly. "That's not what I mean, my sense of humour – never mind."

"Oh okay," she replied. "I'll be back soon, please ring

this if you need anything." She handed him a small, white porcelain bell.

"I see you have all the mod cons here."

Can you fucking believe it! What the fuck happened? It could only happen to me! Japanese what? Shit! Bollocks!"

One exact week from waking was the time that Nathan spent in that same room. The many discussions with doctors were accompanied by frequent visits to the physiotherapy room.

Michael Burrows became a frequent visitor along with a host of other very formal looking people who were not always Filipino nationals. Nathan found quite a lot of the discussions confusing.

In one particular discussion with Mr Burrows, Dr Rodriguez and two other people he didn't know, he began to get frustrated. A tittle-tattle of words came out of Nathan's mouth that made little sense to him or anyone else.

"What insurance? I'm not signing anything! Why do I have to go back? Why the fuck can't I carry on here? I'm okay now! You all stand there talking about me. I'm right here! Right fucking here!" Nathan could only attend a little information at a time. His frustration could quickly turn to anger in an uncharacteristic flash. In a further conversation with the nurses he became irate because he felt they were ignoring him. He started shouting as they left the room, hurling his water jug in their direction and kicking his bedside locker against the wall. "Don't fucking come back!" Nathan yelled. Thirty minutes later he was in tears; thirty minutes after that he was laughing at a Filipino daytime TV show. One of the auxiliaries came in to clean up the mess.

"Hello Sir," she said quietly.

"Hi," Nathan replied happily. "Come in, do you like this programme?" he asked her.

"Yes Sir, I watch it sometimes."

"Watch, come sit here," he gestured to the empty visitor seat. "Sorry about the mess," he said.

"Oh that's okay Sir, I can clean, no problem."

"Have you got a cigarette?" Nathan asked her.

"No Sir I'm sorry, I don't have." She stood and watched the TV for a while, mop still in hand, then continued to clean up. He hardly noticed her leaving the room; his behaviour had succumbed to stimulus-bound immediacy. Anything beyond that decayed into another lost memory.

Nathan was unhappy about being moved to another room. Although it was much larger with bigger windows, there were three other patients. Some days he would totally ignore them yet on others he would entice them all to play childish games such as 'shag, shoot or marry' – something he would normally have found tedious and inapt. The boredom would sometimes kick in with remorselessness. His need for constant inducement was growing like an addiction. He had taken up smoking – at least ten cigarettes every day – and constantly requesting ice cream or milkshakes, which was hard to come by in the Philippines. His lowest ebb came during a rowdy card game with the other three male patients. When one of the younger nurses came in to do her routine patient check, Nathan made an inappropriate remark.

"This one is gorgeous," he said, loudly enough for her to hear. "She's got real cock lips."

An uncomfortable silence encased the room. "What?" Nathan said staring at them all in disbelief. "Don't you agree? Are you all fucking gay?" he said, angrily throwing the cards all over the room.

"Nathan, calm down, there is no need for that," one of the other patients said.

"You calm down!" he retorted. "I'm sick of you all anyway, you're all fucking boring and stupid! You don't know anything, just sit there staring at the window or playing this dumb fucking game!" He paced off into the gardens, clutching at his crushed cigarette packet. Halfway through his seventh smoke of the day, Doctor Rodriguez trod cautiously over towards him. Nathan saw him coming out of the corner of his eye.

"Good afternoon Nathan, how are you today?"

"Not so good," he answered, gazing down at the burnt dried grass. "I'm tired and I don't know what's what anymore. It's like my head feels like it doesn't belong to me, like it's not mine, you know?"

"I do understand Nathan, believe me. Perhaps it would be good if we can talk some more about your situation. Maybe this will help you?"

"Sure, that would be good, thank you Doctor…" Nathan tried but couldn't quite summon up his name.

"Rodriguez," the doctor interceded, "Dr Rodriguez."

"Yes, sorry, Doctor Rodriguez."

"Okay we will have this conversation, but not now. Tomorrow when you might feel a little better, yes?"

"Okay Sir," Nathan said, smiling as he docked his cigarette in the makeshift coconut shell ashtray. "Thanks for everything. I know you are all helping me. I just feel confused and angry a lot of the time."

"Believe it or not Nathan that is very normal for what you have experienced; it will take time. Anyway, we will talk more tomorrow, okay Sir?" He said jokingly as he eyed Nathan's facial response. Nathan smiled like a man who still had enough insight to understand the pertinence of the jest.

Nathan was over one hour late for his scheduled meeting with Dr Rodriguez and the visiting neurologist. His awareness of time had become somewhat hampered.

"Good afternoon Nathan," Dr Rodriguez said. "This is Dr Samonte, our visiting neurologist."

"Nice to see you again Nathan," Dr Samonte announced. "It's good to see you are making a recovery."

"Good afternoon Doctor and Doctor," Nathan replied,

shaking their hands in turn. Dr Rodriguez explained the purpose of the meeting. He deliberately paused at certain points in his speech to ask if Nathan could understand everything that was been said to him.

"Please feel free to ask us as many questions as you like."

Dr Samonte pulled a large slide out of a brown envelope and placed it onto a backlight on the wall.

"Nathan, this is a scan of your brain after the infection." He said, pointing with his hand. Sliding a ballpoint pen out from the pocket of his shirt he pointed to a particular area of the scan.

"This here is where the damage occurred. This part of the brain is known as the frontal cortex." Nathan found it unnerving to be staring at a photograph of his own brain. "This small section here," he said, circling his pen in a small grey shadow, "is exactly where the tissue has been damaged. We are thankful that it is only minimal, though you will still experience some unusual symptoms."

"I can't remember anything about what happened," Nathan remarked.

"This is quite normal. Your long-term memory for everything up until the illness should not be affected. However, you may have some short-term memory problems," Dr Samonte informed.

The neurologist continued. "Damage like this to the brain usually results in something we call dysexecutive syndrome. What this means Nathan, is that you will find that some things are very different to how they used to be."

"What do you mean?" Nathan asked, still staring intently at the scan of his brain on the wall.

"Well, your behaviour can change."

"Ah, you mean like I will become a raving lunatic!" Nathan joked.

"Well not exactly Nathan, although have you noticed anything different about yourself?" he asked.

"Well I eat a lot more than I used to," Nathan answered. "Oh yes and I'm smoking now."

"This can be a result of impulsive behaviour," Dr Samonte stated. "It can also be easier to get angry at small things. You might also find it more difficult to make plans or be organised, or do things that you did very easily before."

"Wait, so are you saying I've kind of lost my mind?"

"No Sir, not at all. In fact your intelligence will not really be any different. It's just the day-to-day things that you might find have become harder to do."

"Such as?"

Dr Samonte tucked his pen back into his shirt pocket and thought carefully before speaking. "Such as remembering to take a shower in the morning, or planning a journey. You might also find it difficult to motivate yourself on some days."

"You mean I'll become lazy?"

"No, Nathan we know you are not lazy. This is just how the brain can be affected with this kind of incident. It's a symptom called abulia."

"So it is just a fancy word for being lazy then?" The two doctors smiled at his continuing desire to jest. "What was it again – that did all this?" Nathan asked them sharply.

"You mean, what caused the damage?" Nathan nodded. "It's called Japanese Encephalitis. It is caused by an infected mosquito bite."

"Oh well at least it's the Japanese type, that's not so bad then is it?" Nathan jested. The two doctors smiled deferentially at each other.

"Nathan, in the UK there are many support groups and organisations for this type of condition," Dr Samonte proposed.

"You have done your research, Doctor." Nathan replied keeping his mood jovial.

"We want to help you as much as possible, Nathan."

"The point is Nathan," Dr Rodriguez interjected, "what

we want you to understand is that you can still lead a fairly normal life. If you get the support you need back in the UK you will eventually be able to manage the symptoms."

"What Dr Rodriguez is saying is absolutely correct Nathan," Dr Samonte reaffirmed. "Because the damage is minimal, in two or three years' time you may not even realise that you have these symptoms. There will of course be a period of adjustment." He continued, "The key thing is self-awareness," he added with assuredness.

"What, you mean like being aware of who I am?"

"In some ways yes, but more like having an awareness of your symptoms. Recognising your…" the doctor struggled to find his preferred words to use in English.

"Limitations," Nathan interjected.

"Well okay, if you like. This will help you to cope with any of the continuing side effects."

"How?"

"Because there are methods you can use, and you will learn to compensate for those difficulties. The UK is very advanced in treating and rehabilitating this type of condition."

"A lot more advanced than we are here in the Philippines," Dr Rodriguez added.

"Like anger management classes. Hugging sessions and all that?" Nathan jibed.

"That is one example, yes." Both doctors smiled again, considerately.

"I guess I can also buy some of those books to read with the yellow and black covers." Both of the doctors adopted a puzzled yet inquisitive expression. "I can't remember exactly. Like learning a new language – French for dummies, that kind of thing. The kind of books that are written for… ah it doesn't matter anyway, what the hell."

★

I felt it important that I should speak with Nathan before he returned to the UK. Unfortunately, he had developed a tendency for what neuropsychologists call confabulation; a fusion of his thoughts could come out like a verbal conundrum. *He* as well as the rest of us, could not always be sure which thoughts were real and which were false. One afternoon he began to talk about Charmaine.

"We're so in love," he began. "She's going to University to get a degree in Law, or then become a lawyer? She used to work in a bar. That's where we met. She was going to come here with me but couldn't because she was working on a special case." I listened patiently. "Besides – the sex was fantastic! In fact I'm sure the minute I arrive home she'll have the whole house draped in sunshine and smiles; we will get married in summer. But I have to finish my job here first. I'm building a bridge. You know – like the one over the River Kwai – a great big fucking bridge! It will probably be on the news."

His prowess with articulation had not been affected, though I could tell that his memories had been contaminated. From the conversation, I gathered there was also a significant other who had left an indelible mark on his libido. I knew this would be a minefield for him but he had the nous and grit to come out on the other side, intact. The hospital had done a fantastic job in taking care of Nathan. The VOA people had arranged for him to fly back to the UK within weeks. Though I was a little concerned about his readiness to integrate back into a life he had left behind, I believed he had the intellectual capacity and will to get through it.

Much had been done behind the scenes to make his transition as easy as possible: the VOA and hospital personnel had been in touch with the social services in Nathan's local area in order to prepare him for a return to his local community. Whilst he was making an excellent recovery, he was not yet capable of negotiating complex arrangements. One of his co-workers had been assigned to travel back with him and stay over for the first few nights. Just before boarding the plane he spoke to me with a quiet eloquence. A shard of his former self came to the fore.

"You know I wouldn't change anything about what happened," he said. "This is the life. I'm not scared of what will happen anymore. After all, I've seen what's ahead for all of us. Believe me I saw it all." He then smiled without once looking back at the jungle backdrop just yards from the runway.

It is for such circumstances that people like Nathan are born. Not because their predicament is pre-ordained in time, but because as our story implies, through the thought processes of people like him, we can understand the coherence of the soul. Therefore when part of the mind becomes damaged we can expect the soul to immerse itself on another if not a greater plane. Thus we gain hope; Nathan's mental abilities are distinct from the material substance of brain matter. Swinburne composed the idea of property dualism, which addresses this very conundrum. Just as dynamite is a distinct event from the explosion it causes, our thoughts and consciousness are distinct from the materialistic nature of our brain. The wish for our main character then, is that he can find his way out of the material, into the non-corporeal – that he will find the way to his soul even if a small part of his mind has been lost.

And so, I believe at this point it is fitting for Nathan to take up the story. Indeed, that was his wish.

PART THREE

MY SOUL, MYSELF AND I - *WHEREVER I MAY FIND THEM*

The strangest feeling for me was the actual feeling itself. Even now I find it hard to explain but it was like my head belonged to someone else, it had just been fixed onto my body. I had been assigned a community support worker from the social services called Emma. She was a thick-set young lady with an almost permanent smile attached to her full face. Her thick, strawberry blonde hair was layered and flashed with a ray of chocolate. She came to visit me every day just to make sure I was doing the normal things that one should do, such as showering, eating properly and keeping the house clean.

For the first couple of months or so I slipped into a fairly boring routine: I'd make breakfast then sit in my trusty armchair in the bay window until lunchtime. It seemed quite natural for me to turn the chair towards the window. Although I didn't realise at the time, it was also good for retraining my memory. The community rehearsals were certainly interesting to observe. The post-woman would traipse up the garden path at about eight thirty; then followed the recoil of the letterbox flap, followed by a splodge of mail falling onto the hallway floor. About ten minutes later the man across the street would reverse his white van out of the driveway then leave his engine running whilst he jumped out to close his gates. I could hear the unoiled iron hinges moan like a ship's door. Round about eight fifty, the girl in the blue coat would walk past; she had a slight crouch to her stride, possibly due to the beefy rucksack she carried on her back. I often wondered what she had inside it. She was most likely a student, which meant it was full of books and papers. In my mind, it was full of secret ideas that she wanted to unveil to the world one day.

Apart from a few random passers-by and the odd car, the next timed event was the elderly man who lived next door but one, called Pat. He would venture out at ten o' clock every morning. Without fail his mannerisms never changed; first he would close the gate behind him as he looked back to wave at the old lady who lived between us; he would then set off walking, shrugging his shoulders and zipping up his jacket as he passed my house. If anyone was coming in the opposite direction he would do a polite shimmy to one side, as if giving way to someone more important. His thin, grey hair was always combed smartly back; he would quickly sweep it back across his head if the breeze blew it forward. Then it was the turn of the dog woman at ten thirty. She was a short, plump lady who always wore a pink sweatshirt. Her two little dogs, which I think were a kind of Jack Russell cross, would tug relentlessly as she repeatedly shouted at them to 'stop pulling'. Even from the distance of my window I could see her badly-applied makeup and the dark roots of her bottle-blonde hair. I could remember this sequence of events without writing it all down. Strange though it may seem, I had more trouble remembering what I had just been doing should I walk into another room in the house. Or, remembering what I *had* to do was even more challenging. It was all about patterns and repetition.

Emma would come at eleven thirty. Her small, black car would always pull up from the opposite side of the road; it was probably her way of trying to look unpredictable. I had gotten used to her coming so would unlock the side door in preparation.

"Morning Nathan," she would bellow as she clambered in. Predictably, she would shout through to me. "I see you're still in your chair then."

"Yes," I would reply. "I like it here. It's the perfect goldfish bowl."

"Five empty cups as usual," she announced, with a tone of disappointment in her voice.

"Well that way I don't have to wash up as often," I answered.

"So how are we this morning?"

"Okay I guess, the same, one day's pretty much the same as the next."

"Well they will be if you don't try to do anything different, won't they?" I could sense that she was a little frustrated because I'd been sat vegetating in my chair again. It was a kind of comfort to let the world pass by. It gave me the chance to allow the jumbled thoughts and pictures in my head to gradually find a way of assembling some sense of perspective, however distorted or irrelevant they may have seemed. "So have you any plans today?" Emma asked me politely.

"Yes, I'm doing them now," I replied.

"What, sitting in the chair? You can't do that forever Nathan, life has to go on you know."

"Well I don't know that it has to Emma, though it certainly does."

"One thing's for sure, you haven't lost your sense of humour or sarcasm."

"Thanks."

Emma pulled up a dining chair and sat adjacent to me. I anticipated a lecture from her.

"Well we do need to chat about your progress," she said.

"Okay."

"I'm really pleased in some ways," she uttered. "You've done really well in getting out of bed every morning rather than just lying there."

"Well I'm tired by nine thirty so I go to bed early."

"And that's great!" Emma suggested supportively. "But

maybe now you need to think about working on your motivation to…" she paused purposefully mid-sentence. "Well trying to do a bit more during the daytime. Do you think?" she suggested jovially, though with some assertiveness in her tone.

I just nodded at her, realising she was right. "I just don't know what I can do, or what I feel like doing."

"Well that's normal but then that's why I'm here to help you try to make those decisions."

They may have told me that my injury wasn't as serious as some acquired brain injuries, but the thoughts in my head were almost uncontrollable. So many snippets of information kept drip-feeding into my mind. It was hard for me to decipher and contextualise them. It's funny, looking back at the kind of thoughts that invaded my consciousness. One day I was listening to the radio and a song by David Bowie came on. I remember how someone at school had once told me that during the 1970s he used to write lyrics in a rather bizarre way; he would apparently write down the lyrics of a particular song on paper then cut them up; he would then jumble them up and place them in a fairly random order until he had a completed song he liked. This is just how my thoughts and memories were – like a random activation synthesis of jumbled up messages. I felt that if I was ever going to get back to some sense of normality I had to somehow unravel the labyrinth in my mind. In spite of this plethora of arbitrary thoughts I needed to join the dots, or at least some of them.

Where is she? Why hasn't she come over to see me? It isn't like her. She was always there before, but not a sign. I'm not going to go round there and beg. I mulled over the possibility that she had maybe gone to the Philippines after hearing about my illness. Of course all I needed to do was walk down the street, knock on the door and she would be there with that beguiling smile she saved just for me. I wasn't sure why I was finding it difficult to simply walk a few doors down the road. Whether or not my pride had become more concrete due to the illness, or whether it was a force beyond my control holding me back, I just didn't know. The truth is that I believed that she *would* come; even if it took her weeks, surely she would come. But then I would have bad thoughts in the night. Maybe she had finally decided. Having heard what had happened she couldn't spend a life with someone who might not be the same as before.

One time I woke up in the middle of the night and went downstairs. I made coffee, sat in my chair and opened the curtains; no one could see I was there as I didn't turn the lights on. The wind made shapes with the shadows; they smuggled into my front room then into my eyes. I tried desperately to remember some of the wonderful times we had spent together. Closing my eyes restfully, I thought back to a time when we walked through the park, or at least that's what I recalled. My thoughts drifted against my will and a vision of rain-splashed palm trees and a beautiful candlelit face forced their way into my mind. *But this was not her.*

The next day, Emma had planned for me to go with her to the town centre. She said it would be beneficial to my rehabilitation; it would also be the first time she had supported me outside of my fortress. I had a few things on my daily planner – one of many new so-called intervention techniques I had at my disposal – others being a weekly planner and a target sheet. My main target was to call at the post office before meeting Emma; I had to re-apply for my driving licence and needed to complete some forms.

The small, hard-looking woman in the Post Office told me I needed to come back with two proofs of my address. The lady also told me that the DVLA would probably have to give me an assessment to test if I was still capable of driving. I walked back home spiritedly, trying not to let myself get too annoyed by the protocols of life. After all, it seemed reasonable enough that someone who had recently had a mosquito messing with their brain *should* have to reapply to drive. I completed all the necessary forms carefully at the kitchen table. Then I grabbed my passport and put it in the same envelope as my driving licence. Emma wanted me to complete all these tasks on my own, as a kind of test to see how I coped. I got back to the post office with my bag full of stuff for the day. When my turn came to be ushered forward I smiled smugly.

"Hi, I've got it," I said, confirming my achievement.

The woman unfolded my documents and looked up at me through her half-spectacles. "I still need another proof of address."

"It's on my driving licence," I retorted.

"Yes but I need an additional proof; something like a utility bill. Do you have that with you?"

I could feel the blood rising through my veins and reaching boiling point in my head. "No, I fucking don't!" I shouted. "What do you think that is on there?" I slapped my driving licence against the counter window, causing the whole place to shudder. "That is my fucking address – it's proof right, because it's on *my* fucking licence!"

The manager appeared from a door stage left.

"Sir, we cannot have that type of abuse of staff here."

"But she's asking for something and I've brought proof! My licence is proof, yes?"

"Yes sir, but we also need to have something that proves you are *still at* that address."

"Piss off! I'm telling you I'm still at my fucking address. You think I'm lying?"

"Sir, I didn't say you were lying…" I interrupted the manager.

"Well I'm telling you both to piss off!" In my rage I stuffed my documents into my bag and barged my way out of the post office. My face felt like it was on fire and my heart was thudding away at the wall of my chest. The embarrassment made me feel faint. I sat on the wall outside and reached for a cigarette. I lit it with contempt and began to puff on it vigorously.

I never went to meet Emma. My day ended right there in a flash; the fury had consumed me and left me dead to the working world. I don't remember the walk home. I can however, remember getting in through the front door, throwing my bag across the room and kicking the pouffe into the air, smashing the corner lampshade. I was hopeless to stop the rage, punching and kicking the sofa as if it was the woman in the post office. I was also kicking that mosquito; *that little fuck who fucked up my head. So this is how it's to be? Bastard hell fire!* The verbal skirmish and subsequent wrath had drained me. I lay on the sofa on my stomach, my left leg and left arm dangling over the side, limp and lifeless, like my head… *like my life.*

Three whole months of rehabilitation time passed with me hardly noticing. Apart from the shouting incident I had apparently been a model patient, or 'client' as I was referred to. Though I still felt a little tightly wrapped and incomplete I could sense a return of my old self chiselling away the plaster cast that overlay my consciousness after the illness. My mother, though quite fragile herself, had travelled from Blackpool to stay for a while. She brought an old photo album which she placed innocently on the coffee table. We spent one rainy morning in the autumn musing over some of my childhood antics.

"You remember this boy, Nathan?" she asked, holding up a photo of one of my first friends.

"Yes, that's Leslie Bartle," I uttered.

"He used to always pick on you and bully you, but you were always a good friend to him nevertheless." Fingering through the old black and white photographs I scooped up a couple of old photos of me at school.

"It's funny," I said. "I can actually name every single one of my classmates on this photo. But I can't remember much at all about the Philippines, or even what I did this morning."

"Well don't worry love, it will come back to you if you want it to," my mother insisted.

"Well you're probably right, Mum." Mum was a very well-educated lady, an ex-English teacher who couldn't help correcting my verbal grammatical errors. She wore a fairly taciturn exterior although it only needed a little tweak to reveal a genuine congeniality inside.

She was the kind of lady who would gladly help anyone in need – like the time she offered a complete stranger in our neighbourhood a three-course meal one afternoon. I was eleven or twelve at the time. It was one long, hot summer day when I had been playing cricket all day long with mates. On making our usual thirsty walk back from the fields, we came across a man sleeping against one of the old, wooden telegraph poles at the end of our street. I remember feeling a little bit scared by his bedraggled state. One of my friends, Wayne Hallam, kicked at his feet.

"Hey wake up, Mister!"

"Stop," I urged. "He might be a mad man."

"Well what's he gonna do?" Wayne replied, confidently.

"What's wrong?" The man woke up, startled.

"You've been sleeping, Mister," Wayne told him.

"Are you drunk?" one of the other lads asked which teased a laugh from the rest of us.

"No, I'm not drunk. I wasn't feeling well so decided to rest for a while."

"Maybe you've had a heart attack!" Wayne insisted.

"I hope not, I'm a long way from home," he replied. I noticed his tie was crooked and his face gave off a white, sickly essence.

"Do you want some water?" I asked him.

"Yes please," he answered, wiping his forehead with an old handkerchief that he pulled from his damp shirt pocket. I noticed the man was clasping onto a shiny, old, brown leather briefcase as if it was full of stolen money. I was fascinated by the fact that he wore odd socks; one was grey and pulled all the way up over his brown trousers, whilst the other was a blue tartan check, which was rolled down exposing his smooth, insipid white shin. I ran down the street and charged into the house.

"Good Lord!" my mother shrieked. "Where's the fire?"

"There's a man, Mum, at the end of the street. He's collapsed!" My mother followed on with a long glass of water. I can't quite recall how the conversation went but I do remember that he was one of those door-to-door salesmen. As it turned out he had become very dehydrated due to the hot weather. It was his first day doing the job and he was nervous about knocking on doors all over the neighbourhood. My mum gave him about three cups of tea and two glasses of orange juice; she also made him sit at the table to eat quiche and chips with salad.

I sat and watched as he ate everything my mum offered up. He was like a man washed ashore on a desert island – eager to try everything on the table. His name was Ken. About half an hour after he finished his main course my mum ordered me,

"Take Ken some cake, Nathan." I served it up to him subserviently, feeling this was my Good Samaritan deed for the week.

"Oh thank you," he said politely then gorged greedily on the biggest piece of sponge cake I'd ever seen my mum cut. I asked him if he wanted to watch TV. He said he did, so I flicked through the three channels we had at that time. He hummed along merrily to the tunes on the afternoon pop programme for kids. Ken hardly said a word during his three or four hours at our house. However this was also due to Mum lecturing him on why he should prepare for the day better – and to make sure he always carried a bottle of water or juice with him. That was typical of my mum; she was so helpful and considerate but felt she wasn't doing a good service to anyone unless she could offer some sound advice.

Ken seemed happy to just sit there, nod and politely say yes to everything she said. Before he left, something dawned on me about him: this was my vivid imagination even at such a young age. Ken told my mum that he was a door-to-door salesman, but he never tried to sell us anything. Perhaps it was because he didn't want to devalue my mother's kindness. Or, maybe he wasn't really a salesman at all. My fictitious scenario was that he had stolen the case from work or some nearby office; inside was one-thousand pounds. He had run all the way from the industrial estate just up the road from us. Because it was so hot and he was so unfit he started to pass out, so decided to turn up our street just in case the police were looking for him on the main road. His wife had actually left him and that's why he needed to steal the money; this would mean he could buy her anything she wanted (one thousand pounds in those days was a lot of money) so she would decide to go back to him. The reason he was happy to stay all afternoon with us was because it gave him a place to hide for a few hours. We never saw Ken after that day; maybe he went to jail or escaped to Spain with all the money. His wife probably met another man who had two-thousand pounds. What was actually funny about reflecting on the story was that my juvenile powers of invention were once again just as apparent; another symptom of my mosquito incident.

My mother must have made us both ten cups of tea each, every single day. I didn't ask her how long she would stay though I hoped it wasn't too long. It was nice to have her company and help for a while but after more than a few days she would start to grate on me. Two days before she left, she threw an unexpected question at me.

"What happened to that girl you were seeing from around here?" she asked. "What's her name?" I'd never really got to the point of telling her much about our relationship. I had mentioned in passing during some of our long-distance telephone conversations that Charmaine used to come over all the time.

"She still comes round," I said, "though not as often as she used to."

"Oh, it's a shame, it would be nice for you to have someone in your life."

"Yes, Mum. It would; I'm working on it."

My mum had never been a deeply inquisitive person, especially with matters regarding my love life. It was kind of like an unwritten rule we had as a family. But I could sense that she wanted to know a little more about what was in my mind, although she obviously couldn't bring herself to ask.

Instead, she opted to talk a bit about my father.

"Well since we lost your dad when you were little, I know what it's like not to have someone," she announced with a tinge of sadness. She had never told me the whole truth about him; all I knew is that he was in the military. He was killed in Northern Ireland when I was seven. The house was not the kind of house to be adorned with proud photos and memorabilia; the only remnant of his existence was their marriage photo on my mother's bedside locker. It always seemed to me like it was placed there with some element of duty or necessity rather than out of sincere love and affection. Neither was I curious to learn about him with any quest for closure. I was content to accept his actuality as a distant figure who belonged to my mother more than he did me.

When my mother eventually left I decided to try and get back to the self-discipline of planning my days and week.

Emma had trained me well in the skill of using my diary and to do list effectively. I slipped into the groove of checking my routine every night before I went to bed. *Nothing much for tomorrow. Ah, swimming with some other members of the support group at the local pool. 'Meet Emma at 11am at sports centre'. Surely, she will come soon now. I can't quite understand why she's staying away so long.*

One thing I've always been very good at is organising and planning in the motivational sense; not even the disease had managed to wipe that ability from my brain, at least not completely. I was aware of the benefit of planning whilst my progressive memory was in disarray. I was up at nine o' clock for breakfast and was the first to arrive at the sports centre. I was quite excited about the prospect of going swimming, a dichotomy of sorts because it was actually the one sport I was not very good at; in fact I'd always hated it. However, I believed that this was the kick-start I needed to re-activate my body.

As I waited in the reception area of the sports centre for the others, a beautiful woman who I judged to be in her forties walked in majestically. She paid for a swim and smiled as she walked past me into the changing rooms. I could barely make eye contact. This was another facet of my dysfunction, which stemmed from the paranoia that people could read my thoughts. Emma soon arrived with three other members of the group: Ray who was recovering from a stroke, Jean who was keen to express to all of us that she was recovering from a pulmonary embolism – or a blood clot in her brain. The third person, Gretchen, was a mere teenager who had crashed his car into a ditch, as a result suffering a traumatic brain injury. They all seemed to be as enthusiastic as I was about the prospect of a morning at the pool. Perhaps like me they had also been condemned to sitting around the house for the last few months.

What is odd to me now and certainly would have been before my illness was how thrilled I seemed about something so relatively mundane. But then, my perception of mundaneness had been changed. I had suffered this horrible infection that had played havoc with my personality, yet I suddenly felt an appreciation of the simplicity in something quite banal. I found changing into my swimming shorts in front of Ray and Gretchen a little uncomfortable; even though we were separated by cubicles it was too easy to look down over the low cubicle wall. Perhaps it was another kind of paranoid or suspicious thinking on my behalf.

I had not forgotten the awkwardness brought on by a visit to the swimming pool: the sudden wetness of the changing area and the chlorine-scented tunnel that led through to the pool. I sat on the edge for a while then casually lowered myself in; I noticed Emma was already in the pool, watching me dutifully. Everyone in the group was smiling at each other like we were children at the seaside. I decided to swim gently up and down the length of the pool rather than just stand there splashing aimlessly around. Luckily it was fairly quiet so I was able to swim a couple of lengths before my arms began to feel like they were made of iron. Jean was also swimming up and down the length of the pool very rhythmically, whilst Ray tended to jitter his way across the breadth. Gretchen was happiest trying to do handstands in the shallow end, or pretend he was inventing a new type of aqua exercise. I clung onto the side of the pool, gasping to regain my breath; it felt like my lungs were about to burst.

"You okay, Nathan?" Emma enquired, swimming towards me.

"Yes thanks, it's just I feel like I've swam a mile!" I answered, gasping for every nanosecond of air.

"Well you've got to remember you've not done much activity for a while, I'd be the same."

"True," I replied. "And the smoking's not helping," I

admitted gallantly. Emma smiled, raising her eyebrows, her tongue pressing her top lip outwards in agreement.

After I regained some breath I decided to set off again along the length of the pool, this time trying to follow a similar rhythm to Jean. As I tried diligently to find my tempo I couldn't help noticing who was swimming towards me in the opposite direction. It was the beautiful lady. She smiled again as we crossed. My pathetic attempt to smile and exhale at the same time caused me to lose my buoyancy in the water and in panic, I swam to the edge. I was coughing up the pool water and the stab of chlorine in my throat caused me to wretch. I tried to hide it before the others witnessed my comedy of errors, though I noticed the lady had turned her head to see if I was okay. Jean soon arrived at my side unaware of my moment of embarrassment, or if she did notice she politely chose to ignore it.

"How are you finding it?" she asked.

"Well okay, though I've nearly drowned a couple of times already," I suggested.

She laughed. "I'm sure you haven't; it's not easy getting back into physical activity," she said considerately.

"Tell me about it!" Within a few minutes both Emma and Ray had made their way up to our end of the pool. Gretchen was still making up an exercise routine in the shallow end. We all hung there with our arms lodged over the pool edge, watching all the other fun swimmers.

"Come on then, we shouldn't all get too lazy," Emma said as she broke away from the edge.

"Slave driver!" Ray joked. I continued to wade gently through the water, dodging a mother and her children patting a plastic ball around. As I approached the other end of the pool I could see the beautiful lady sitting on the side of the pool. At first I swam right to the shallow end, then with my heart pounding, I somehow breaststroked my way back towards her.

"Hi," she said courteously.

"Hi," I replied, rather surprised at her willingness to chat. "I'm sorry if I nearly collided with you earlier, I'm not used to swimming these days," I excused.

"No harm done," she replied. "I was more worried I had caused you to go under." Her legs were draped over the side of the pool and her hands rested on the pool edge close to her thighs. Her short hair was now welded to her head from the chlorine. She had a smallish brown mole on her left cheek, which perfectly matched one on her right shoulder. She also had a red blemish just above her left knee. Her black swimsuit hugged her slim but voluptuous figure and her damp skin harboured invitational warmth. Her eyes and lips, flushed with the pool water made her appear imminently permissive.

We talked for a few minutes then I asked her what the blemish was. She told me it had always been there since birth. I don't know what came over me, but I leaned over and kissed it gently.

"It's lovely," I said. She immediately retracted away from me.

"What you doing?" she shouted. I felt embarrassed as her voice reverberated around the arena. Many of the swimmers looked on. She walked briskly along the poolside, making her way across to the shallow end. I saw her approach one of the pool attendants. Suddenly, my whole stomach churned as I felt an audience of eyes glaring in my direction. The pool attendant walked around the pool edge with a look of disgust and duty on his face.

"Excuse me sir," he bellowed in my direction. "Could you get out of the pool please?" I felt the thrust of distress as I lifted myself shamefully out of the pool. "I'm sorry," he continued, "but there's been a complaint."

"What about?" I asked anxiously.

"Can we discuss it in the office?" the pool attended said. I sensed a burden of heavy shame wafting over me. Emma came over to ask what had happened whilst innocent bathers eyeballed me from the safety of the pool. The humiliation of the whole situation took a grip on me, so I instinctively headed for the security of the changing rooms. I hurriedly grabbed my clothes from the locker and half-dried myself, before throwing my clothes on then scurrying out of the sports centre like a frightened child.

I felt like a guilty man as I walked all the way home. I locked the door and turned on the TV and radio to create a sound wall of distraction. I sat upstairs on the bed trying to replay the situation in my mind. *What was it I did wrong?* An hour or so later I could hear the doorbell ringing, but decided to ignore it. I couldn't face anyone after such a scornful incident. *What if it's the police? Maybe they've come to arrest me for molestation or something.* I sat there, rigid with trepidation until the anxiety in my whole body shrunk me into a foetal attempt to sleep. *She seemed to like me; she smiled at me twice before we chatted and she asked me things about myself. She was sitting on the edge of the pool talking to me in her swimsuit. How many men would dare to show such affection?* My disturbed sleep was irritating. The rerun of the incident in my head was driving me to insanity.

I had to get out of bed and walk around the house. *This is your fucking fault! Why aren't you here with me? If you had been here this would never have happened!*

I decided there and then to confront her. I quickly dressed and marched over to her house. The porch light was not on like it used to be. I knocked violently at the door.

"Charmaine!" I shouted, surprising myself for uttering her name for the first time in ages. "Charmaine please, answer the door! It's me, Nathan!"

The next-door neighbour stuck her head out of the bedroom window.

"Do you know it's three in the morning?"

"Yes, I mean no, I'm sorry. I just need to see Charmaine."

"Where've you been for the last few months?" the woman asked brazenly. "They've moved!"

"Moved, where to?"

"It's late, go home!" My state of confusion and anxiety was now heightened as I trampled my way home. It felt like the conjoined part of my soul had been ripped from me. The one tie I had to her – our conscious amalgamation of purpose, sense and reason – had been severed, just like the neurons in my brain. I screamed at the walls and ceiling as I pushed open the front door. I cried out to my dead grandmother for help. The weight of everything was crushing my head like a vice and I wept uncontrollably. I began to look for tablets in the bathroom cabinet; unwanted thoughts were rising to the surface of my awareness. *The train would be too painful. I'm not brave enough for that but going to sleep quietly would be more my way.*

I woke up the next morning unexpectedly, to the sound of the doorbell. Emma peered through the glass as I trundled self-consciously across the lounge to let her in. I made coffee for both of us without speaking a word. I could sense Emma wasn't quite sure how or when to begin the pre-empted discussion, so when I sat down opposite her I decided to make it easy for her.

"I tried… I felt like killing myself last night." Emma didn't respond – instead allowing me to express my feelings openly. "I don't know what I did wrong. I thought I was been honest and affectionate to a girl who liked me." Emma continued her thoughtful gaze. "If I'd have found some tablets last night I'd be happily dead now."

Emma spoke out for the first time. "Well let's be thankful that you didn't then, shall we?"

She was sitting on the edge of the sofa; her body language was thoughtful, her hands clasped over her crossed knees, sitting at a slight angle to me which took some edge off the seriousness of the moment. "Can I say something Nathan?" she asked empathetically.

"Please do."

"Well, I know you must be feeling many different things right now. Like, embarrassment, maybe even angry. But in a way that's good because you have reflected on what happened. It *was* wrong what you did, Nathan. Do you know why?"

"Not exactly. Maybe she didn't like me as much as I thought she did," I concluded.

"No, it's not that. It's just… it's inappropriate behaviour. Because even when we do like someone we have to be careful about how we behave with them. Kissing someone, especially on their legs or other parts of the body in that situation, is not appropriate. It shocked her, Nathan."

I sipped at my coffee, trying to make sense of Emma's comments. She also reached for her coffee as if to drink in solidarity. "You see it would be fine to do that to a girlfriend but it's not something you do to someone you've only just met. It's just part of your learning to adjust again to social situations," she said.

I reached for a cigarette, but wanted to show her I was taking her words on board so maintained eye contact with her.

"What you also have to remember is that you have become a bit more disinhibited. It doesn't make you a raving lunatic or mad man, but it just means you find it a bit more difficult to read some social situations. You understand, Nathan?"

I paused before responding. "Well I think so but, it's not like I groped her or anything. I couldn't help myself; I wanted to show her what I was feeling – sensitive."

"That's just your impulsivity," Emma proposed. "Do you remember what the doctors in the Philippines told you? It might take you a while before you adjust properly. In some ways you have to re-learn how to behave. But that's why you have me to work with."

"So will I be arrested or something?" I enquired, half joking yet genuinely worried.

"No," Emma responded again, smiling. "It's okay, but I have to tell you that I had to go and talk to the pool attendant and the manager of the sports centre. They are aware of your condition now."

"Like you had to make excuses for me; that's fucking embarrassing! Sorry," I said, realising my anger had flown outwards again all too easily.

"It's not an excuse Nathan. It's an explanation, which is different."

"So instead of apologising for me you told them all my head was fucked by a mosquito?"

"No, I didn't have to go into all that. But I did need to explain the reason why you acted well… inappropriately. Otherwise…" she paused.

"Otherwise what? I'd be in the shit, right!"

"Well it's not really serious but maybe it could be classed as sexual harassment. But as I said, it's all okay. Even the lady is okay about everything now."

"Well that makes it alright then." Emma sensed my sarcasm so remained quiet for a while. "All part of my rehabilitation, right?" I stated, taking the last puff on my cigarette.

"That's right. Spot on!" Emma insisted, smiling even wider as she sat forward and tilted her head towards me in agreement. I decided not to tell her about my other antics at the post office. Instead I insisted that we go to the sports centre so that I could apologise to the pool attendant and manager face to face. Emma thought this was a very honourable and honest way to deal with the predicament. For me it came out of a sense of social duty; besides, I never liked awkwardness. I hated rough edges; I always felt the need to smooth things out; that was another trait the mosquito had not robbed me of.

Sometimes we are thrown a lifeline. That's how it felt

after I had made my apologies to the manager and the pool attendant. They were both very understanding and shook my hand boldly. Then, as if fate itself had intervened, who should be there when we walked out of the door. Before I had the time to summon up the courage to offer my apology, she obviously recognised Emma. But it was me she walked towards.

"Hello Nathan," she said in a friendly tone.

"Hello," I replied bashfully.

"It's okay. Please don't worry," she continued. "I'm sorry for causing you any distress or embarrassment. I didn't know that…" She stopped dead. Like most people who feel uneasy on learning about my head injury, she struggled to explain herself.

"You didn't know about my brain injury. I never used to do things like that. It's made me impulsive."

"Yes," she agreed, "but as I said honestly, everything is okay. I understand."

"Thank you," I said to her softly.

"Thank you," she retorted. As Emma and I walked out from the sports centre, the notion came to me. Looking at myself through the smoked glass panels of the building, it was clear: with some people you can tell that they have a physical or a mental disability, like Gretchen who had a dent in one side of his head, but for people like me, there was no visible sign that my brain had any damage. *Who would know just by looking? That's why she was surprised when I kissed her blemish. Ah well, all's well that ends well.* After some time I was able to make sense of the whole thing in a fairly rational manner. However, I *was* worried about acting that way again at some point in the future.

After saying my goodbyes to Emma I decided to walk home. My walking pace increased from meandering to a more strident march. I turned the corner on the main road, standing for a while as if casing a crime scene. My concentrated thought span was interrupted when Demetri came out of the front of his shop to approach some prospective customers; some of them were feeling fresh fruit outside. Then, the most deviant thought jumped into my head, like a revenge for my attempt at level-headedness. I couldn't help thinking about the way men selected their choice of melons.

It must be a sexually orientated exercise; based on one's preference of breast types. I smiled to myself as I walked over towards him, wondering if women used a similar mantra for choosing bananas. *My God, Emma's so right,* my thoughts turned aloud as I mumbled to myself, *"definitely dis-in-fucking-hibited."*

Demetri looked surprised to see me, or he was puzzled by the way I was talking to myself.

"Nathan," he shouted in his usual charming way. "My friend, how are you?"

"I'm not too bad thanks. Get the odd headache now and again but otherwise can't complain."

"Oh because I heard you had an accident in Thailand, yes?"

"Philippines," I corrected.

"Oh yes the Philippines, that's right. So you're better, yes? Happy to be back?"

"In some ways yes, in others no." Demetri's passion for charmed small talk was as strong as ever. I had hoped the conversation would at some point lead towards Charmaine; I was just surprised that I wasn't the one to instigate it.

"And how is the lovely Charmaine?" Demetri asked. Clearly my talent for insight had not been so badly affected; I knew immediately that Demetri could read the explanation for the vacant look on my face.

"Well, actually I'm... I don't know," I replied, tongue-tied. "I haven't seen her since I got back." The conversation took a welcome deflection as Demetri served a couple of customers. "I went to her house last night," I told him as he filled brown paper bags with tomatoes. "It seemed completely empty. No Charmaine, or her mother or even her auntie."

"Ah!" He exclaimed jovially, "Well I can tell you she left the house maybe two, three months ago. But I thought you would know that. So you have not seen her also?"

"No. Where did she go?"

"I don't know exactly. But wait, she came to visit you right – in the Philippines?"

"No. I wouldn't have expected her to come all that way. Did she even know what happened?"

"But I'm sure she said she was going to visit you after she found out you were in hospital there."

I tailed off the discussion and ambled towards home, feeling even more confused than I did earlier.

I decided to call at Charmaine's house again as if seeking confirmation of her lack of presence.

The house wore that look of everyone being on holiday. Peering through the back window everything looked as it should: the two-seater sofa tucked into the corner of the dining room and the old Edwardian clock on the mantelpiece, minus the pendulum swing. But there was no evidence of life going on; no magazines or newspapers lying around, nor the odd discarded cup on the coffee table. If my memory was serving me correctly, it looked far too tidy and deliberate for Charmaine's family to be living there. I would have at least expected to see a leftover whisky bottle of her mother's. It just stood like a museum set, gloating at me, offering no explanation of the recent history. By the time I reached home I began to feel ironically lost. The overwhelming realisation of the complete change to my life had now been thrust upon me absolutely and categorically. I was home but nothing was the same. *Where is she? Someone must know. But who? If only I knew where to start.*

LOST AND FOUND

The winter months came and went with leniency. I hoped the following spring would shed some much-needed light onto the more dimly lit areas of my life. Emma had more or less insisted I join a voluntary group that was made up of people going through rehabilitation after brain or spinal injuries. The seven thirty meetings on Tuesday evenings had provided me with some kinship. It was comforting to know that other people existed who were experiencing the same turbulence in their minds as I was. I was still making excellent progress in terms of my social skills and application of various compensatory aids to enhance my working memory. However, I was still finding it hard to re-establish my wholeness and sense of self.

I could walk into town, have coffee and make polite conversation with people; they would never have guessed I'd had an acquired brain injury eighteen months ago. And although some instances stretched my temper to the limit, I had learned to redirect my emotions by evading any antecedents which might stoke up my anger. It was still hard sometimes as my blood felt like it was steaming at the slightest of occurrences.

Queuing in the train station for a ticket one time, a man pushed in front of me. I stared at his red, hairy neck and looked him up and down. My *id* was coaxing me into stamping on his calf until he bent forward in agony; then I would kick him in the ribs and shout, '*you fucking ignorant prick, learn some manners you twat!*' Instead, I took a step back, breathed calmly and closed my eyes for a few seconds; I told myself it was no big deal. *I will get my ticket anyway.* I had to remind myself that these were just *sand-traps on the golf course of life – where did I get that from?* I would not always avoid them totally but there was always a way out with practise.

The evening group was aligned to a charitable organisation called Mind-Set. Between ten and fifteen of us would meet at the local community centre. It was always an open forum for people to talk about what had happened to them during the past week, or offer encouraging stories from their rehabilitation. Phil was one of the group leaders. He himself suffered a brain haemorrhage a few years back but had made an incredible recovery through the support of the charity, and of course a loving family. He was a stout man in his late forties with grey hair and a beard. He always wore green, cord trousers and a short sleeved, checked shirt. His glasses hung round his neck on a silver chain. He had a pleasant manner that suited his role as group coordinator. Every session started in the same way. Phil would place his glasses carefully onto his nose, look around at everyone then ask how everyone was. I learned quite a lot about the different ways people had acquired their different types of brain injury.

Alison was a young lady in her twenties who drove straight into the path of a wagon, rushing home to see an episode of Coronation Street. Brad was about the same age, and he had gone on holiday with his friends to Majorca. The first thing he did when they all arrived at the resort was to charge down to the beach. Brad dived straight into to the sea and woke up back in England two weeks later. He had no memory of what happened though his mates told him he crashed his head on a rock. There were a few people who had suffered from strokes and another who had encephalitis, though not the Japanese version; I was quite proud to be unique in this specialty.

I missed the last few sessions due to being over-tired from a virus. Apparently there had been an altercation between Brad, who always brought his dog called Thor, and a new member of the group called Donald. I had not seen Donald before so I needed to peer between people to spot him when he began speaking.

"Can I make a point please?" he said, raising his hand.

"Of course Donald," Phil replied. "Go ahead."

"Well I don't think he should be allowed to bring that dog here." I noticed he didn't refer to Brad by name, but as '*he*'.

"I'm not sure this is something we should discuss now, with the group. Maybe at a more appropriate time," Phil responded. I scanned around at the faces and everyone seemed politely intrigued. "Unless everyone's happy to hear this?" Phil added, looking around at everyone through his bifocals. Quite a lot of people nodded. "What about you, Brad?"

"I'm okay if everyone else is," Brad said.

"Okay then," said Phil. "Donald, would you like to tell the group why you think Brad shouldn't be allowed to bring Thor?"

"Because it's a dog," Donald replied. "Dogs shouldn't be allowed in places like this."

"You shouldn't be allowed in places like this!" Brad interjected.

"I'm telling you the fucking dog shouldn't be here. Now get him away, I told you last time!" Donald was immediately in a red-faced rage; his voice boomed around the room, off the walls and ceiling and into our faces. The whole scene had gone into meltdown in an instant. Brad stormed off with Thor. Donald bore a resemblance to Phil. Although a little older, he had the same tone of grey hair though not as floppy. However, his face was purple, possibly through the stress that had flushed his normal skin tint. *The blood vessels have probably burst a hundred times over.* A lady called Jen who sat in front of Donald did really well to calm him down.

"Come on Donald, there's no need to get so angry love," she said, and then to my surprise she burst into song. The

153

rest of the group began to smile as Donald started to sing along with her; I remembered this was the song Morecambe and Wise used to sing at the end of every show; 'Bring me Sunshine,' if only they knew it had become an instrument of therapy for people with brain injuries; the perfect de-escalation technique.

Donald's persona changed drastically from anger to one of complete jollity. It was as if the incident with Brad had never occurred, or his brain had already filtered it out as a distant memory.

Later on in the evening, I chatted to Donald and Jen during the coffee break.

I was flabbergasted to learn that despite his brain injury he was a very charming man. He loved to give quiz questions, especially on football trivia. What he didn't realise is that he often asked the same questions time and time again. I had to pretend that he had never asked me a particular question before. If anything, it taught me to become a good listener again, and allowed me to retrain my sense of diplomacy. Until my injury I had rejected the idea of such groups. But my weekly visits became a very important aspect of my recovery process.

I had exchanged telephone numbers with a couple of members of the group, although I could in no way have predicted the content of a phone call I received from Brad one evening. I assumed we might arrange to go out for a beer one time. My phone in the hallway was one of those transparent ones where all the insides lit up when it rang. One evening after my dinner I was just mooching around upstairs; I often walked through both sides of the house to gaze out of the windows. Even if there was nothing to see of note, it was in some ways a connection to the outside world. Crossing the stairway I could sense the flash of electric colour out of the corner of my eye. It was only then I could hear the phone ringing; I must have nudged the volume switch onto low by mistake. I ran down the stairs, my hands burning with the friction from trying to control my descent by clutching the banisters. I was sure it was her.

"Hello," I sighed loudly in expectancy. There was no sound for a while. "Hello?" I repeated, raising my voice in frustration.

"Hi Nathan," a man's voice mumbled.

"Who's that?"

"It's me, Brad."

"Oh, hi Brad, how are you?" I asked. Again there was silence. "Brad, you there?"

"I don't feel I've anything to live for," he said. My mind tried to juggle what he was saying though my heart was still pounding from the adrenaline caused by my dash to the phone.

"Why do you say that?" I said in a rather automated way, without thinking.

"Because life's shit," he replied. "I don't want to be part of it anymore."

"I tell you what – why don't you come over, we can watch a movie and order pizza."

"You're a good bloke Nathan, thanks." The phone went silent. I did the usual double take at the receiver just in case, but he had definitely hung up. *What am I supposed to think? Will he come over, or will he try to harm himself instead. This is not a nice position to be in.* I tried phoning him back twice but there was no answer. I sat on the steps with my hands over my face, trying to decide what to do. I had to phone Emma. I thumbed through my phone book for her number. I pressed the number buttons on the phone with extra care in case the slightest mistake might create a different outcome to my predicament. As soon as I heard her voice I began speaking.

"Hi Emma, it's…"

"Hi this is Emma. Sorry I can't come to the phone right now, but please leave your name and number and I promise to call you back."

"Shit!" I banged the phone back down on the receiver in shock and exasperation. *What's wrong with me, have I lost the confidence to leave a message on an answer phone?* I dialled again with the same precision. This time I planned my words carefully.

"Hi Emma, this is Nathan – erm sorry to bother you but I just had a phone call from Brad. He seemed very depressed and said he didn't want to live. Please can you get in touch with him because I don't…?"

"Hi Nathan, it's me." Her live voice interrupted. "Sorry I was just coming in through the door with my shopping when the phone rang. What did he say?" she asked.

"Well, he said life wasn't worth living; then he put the phone down."

"Okay. Don't worry I will go over to his house."

"Okay thanks. Will you let me know how he is?"

"Of course I will," Emma insisted, "but don't be too worried, anyway thanks Nathan; you did the right thing by letting me know." I went and turned on the TV, almost expecting Brad to come over with pizza. I imagined him stood at the door with his cheeky smile and a deep pan pizza, Thor the black Labrador sitting faithfully at his feet. My dream was vivid but intense. I was somewhere in a very hot country lying on a bed; the strange thing was, the bed was outside. It was raised from the floor on some kind of plinth. I could see the silhouettes of children playing in the background and faces kept appearing at the side of me.

Some were from the past, others I did not recognise. The next thing I knew, I was walking along a tremendous queue of people. A man in a white garment came over to me and beckoned me to come to the front.

"No, there are so many people before me," I said to him.

"It's alright, he's waiting for you."

"Who?" I asked.

"He." The man ushered me up a small flight of steps. At the top sat a man who was surrounded by a halo of silver and white light; he had piercing eyes. I was immediately filled with a peace in my soul.

"Nathan, we are proud of you," he insisted, reaching out his arm. I took hold of his hand, which felt warm and strong. Though at first it seemed odd to be holding a man's hand, I didn't want to let go. When I eventually did, I backed off and his smile sent a breath of soothing warm air through my lungs.

Over the kerfuffle of the TV I could hear the phone ringing. I sprung up from my chair, half asleep.

"Hello." It was Emma. She was calling to tell me that she had not managed to contact Brad. Either he wasn't answering the door or he wasn't in, though strangely she could see Thor sitting there. Apparently Brad never went out without Thor. This made for a worrying scenario although she assured me that he had behaved like this a few times before. It was his way of taking himself out of it for a while before getting in touch as if nothing out of the ordinary had happened. She told me I should try not to think about it too much and that she would phone me in the morning as soon as she made contact with him. I went back into the lounge and turned off the TV. I fell into bed with some relief. I couldn't sleep for thinking about that dream.

Brad did indeed turn up the next day. Emma was right – it was simply one of his blip days; he had apparently decided to visit his brother for the evening, returning home conscientiously to walk Thor early the next morning. The phone call he made to me was a cry for help – or a cry for attention.

My own experiences with depressive episodes meant that I understood his trial. Almost eighteen months after my illness, I was still learning about the psychological fallout experienced by those unfortunate enough to have suffered from any type of head injury. Brain injuries are like people – they come in different shapes and sizes with a multitude of possible consequences. There are some general symptoms, though our uniqueness as individuals seems to be reflected in the way we react to them. I had experienced the confusion, the anger, the depression, the inability to read some social scenarios and the loss of self-esteem. In addition I had fought hard to re-attain my sense of personal identity and self-motivation which had all but left me in the early weeks and months after the injury. This was all part of the package, though Emma and her colleagues had been my lifeline – my link back to the past and continuum into an unknown future.

I was beginning to find a new happiness. I still had days where I felt down, though I remember feeling like that long before I ever went to the Philippines. It was just a little harder for me to regroup on these days. However, my determination had never waned. I would use all the compensatory aids given to me with great effect; I would lay out my diary and weekly planner on the table and plan everything in detail. I had lists for everything, especially appointments and group meetings, post-it notes were stuck to every cupboard in the kitchen and my wall in the spare room. It was, after all, my progressive memory that seemed to be affected more than anything else. I started to walk everywhere. The long, hot summer gave me the chance to see my own world in a way I had never seen it before. I waved to people along the canal and greeted just about everyone who crossed my path. My rucksack was always packed up for the day with everything I needed. The mind meandering became as therapeutic as any of the group sessions. My thoughts drifted aimlessly as if my mind was protecting itself from anything unwanted or harmful.

One time, I caught the bus that skirts many of the smaller villages in the nearby countryside. As I walked along the village footpath I came to a small, unmarked crossroad. Across the road was an old church hiding behind a giant oak tree. The front door appeared to be open and soothing music filtered out into the fresh air. My memory was triggered immediately to the time that Charmaine and I came across the old church during our visit to Scotland. I was drawn inside. Church music resounded around every orifice of the stone walls. I looked to see where it was coming from and noticed a small stereo system to the side of the altar. *Quite unusual,* I thought; unorthodox in some ways yet a simple and innovative idea. I sat down in the front pew to drink in the solace. I looked around but no one else was present. I relaxed and closed my eyes. The coolness of the inside soon dried the sweat on my forehead. I opened my eyes; the crucified Christ looked down at me, filling me with a reverence I had never before experienced. In that instant I knelt down to pray. I could feel the lump in my throat swelling and the tears welling up in my eyes. I sobbed uncontrollably for what seemed like ages. My heart raced and my breathing became short. I looked up at the Christ again, his magisterium filling me with such grace that I could barely comprehend.

Then it came to me: my life had been saved. He had saved me; deciding the time to come home was not yet upon me. Whatever his reasons and wherever my faith had endured, Christ was now opening up a door and inviting me to step through. From nowhere, I heard a voice from behind me.

"Are you okay, sir?" I assumed he was the parish priest who had obviously seen me and become concerned by my state. I rose back into the pew. "Yes Father, I'm okay. I'm crying but I feel really warm inside." I said.

His smile radiated towards me. "God gives us tears for many reasons," he proposed.

"Yes Father," I replied, "I think I understand what you mean. I just didn't realise it until now."

"Well, sometimes we all need a little nudge from Him," he added, looking up to Jesus on the cross. I smiled back and nodded.

"But I'm okay Father, I really am. It's just…" I halted my sentence as he nodded back politely.

"No need to explain sir," he said. "Our Lord is truly happy that you decided to share your thoughts with Him."

"I know Father, and thank you," I said, throwing my rucksack onto my shoulder. I shook his hand and extended my left hand towards his right forearm. Just when I started to walk away I felt the longing to turn back towards him. "Father, I had a brain injury nearly two years ago. I've kind of felt a bit lost but now I feel as though I've been found again." His matte, red cheeks and soft, white hair carried the smile with even more kindness than before.

"Luke 15:11," he said.

"Sorry Father I'm not so…" I stumbled over my words and thoughts once again.

"The Parable of the Lost Son," he interjected. "It's a wonderful parable, about a son who comes back home after being away for many years. Jesus uses the words – 'he was lost but is found again'."

"I see Father. Yes, that's what I feel like. I've lost others close to me, but I feel like I've at least found myself again. It's maybe a slightly different me, but I think I've found him nevertheless."

"That's wonderful," he replied. I thanked him one more time before I left.

"Mysterious and glorious!" he voiced as I headed for the door.

I had one last look back as I left the church. "Yes Father, glorious."

Stepping back into the sunshine was like stepping back in time. For a while I was back in a quaint Scottish village, with someone beside me who completed my soul to the core. A small truck pulled into the layby on the road, bringing me back to real-time. Though I was christened into the Church of England I had never really embraced my faith. My mother had questioned my desire to visit church when I was younger; not with any disappointment at my quest but with a dubious look on her face. Since then it always felt like my faith had been placed in a store, waiting for the right time to be taken off the shelf. Though I hadn't suddenly grown into a fully-fledged Christian, I was aware that my near death experience had shown me something wondrous. I had witnessed a superlative phenomenon; I had walked through my own soul to its other side. I knew now that this numinous event had pulled me back into the physical realm. It was also the better part of me – the part which was now conscious in itself. The noetic consequences it held would be something I had to hold onto.

The depth of my thinking was still untouched. *Not bad for someone with a tropical brain disease.*

I was impressed with my ability and forethought to utilise my compensatory aids to their full extent. In a strange kind of way, I had become a much more organised person than I was before the illness. Though I have never been a disorganised person as such, the added bonus of planners, stickers and well-placed reminders in the house had allowed me to feel a little more in control of my life. My progress had been so good that Social Services had cut my support time with Emma from four to just two sessions per week.

With Emma's encouragement, I also managed to be accepted at the local charity shop for voluntary work. Two days a week gave me something else to think about and certainly played a big part in redeveloping my confidence in social situations. My duties ranged from serving in the shop to helping the van driver to deliver of some of the larger items such as tables and chairs. Having a focus re-introduced me to social responsibilities, mixed with a social freedom, I found that I was still very capable of contributing to a productive environment. Serving in the shop especially allowed me to hone my social skills. Despite the occasional urge for an impromptu verbal faux pas, I became quite adept at controlling my emotions and thoughts. If anyone did upset me or I felt the impulse to say something stupid, I would redirect my thoughts and take myself slightly away from the situation. Like the time an old lady became quite irate because we couldn't give her discount on a vase. She started to shout in the shop, accusing us of robbing her. Mandy, the shop manager, tried to calm her down by telling her the vase had already been reduced along with some other sale items. For some reason she made a beeline for me; she trundled up to me shouting,

"You're robbing me! I'm only on a pension, young man. I was in this country when the War was on!" The very sight of this wrinkled old woman, saliva drooling from her false teeth as she forced her way into my space made me want to shriek obscenities at her. Instead, I reflected decisively and said,

"Ma'am if you want to change your mind about the vase it's okay; we will take it back and give you your money back." The old lady grunted to herself and to everyone's surprise asked how much the pot cat was on the top shelf. "I'll just check for you Ma'am." I offered, already knowing it was two pounds. "Can you see the price on it?" I asked her. Straining her eyes and neck upwards, she confirmed it was two pounds. "I tell you what – you can have that for one pound fifty seeing as it's you."

"Oh go on then," she retorted, fingering through her mustard coloured purse that looked like a gift from the 1940s. In the end she left as a satisfied customer. Mandy praised me for my handling of the situation; I felt like I had passed another test in my transition back into the world of work.

There was also the time when three teenage boys came into the shop with no other intention than to try and cause trouble. I surmised that they were all about fourteen years old. One had a face full of spots and a white coloured shirt with the collar turned upwards with attitude; another was slightly smaller with a brown quiff of hair that looked too heavy for his small head; the third boy looked like an innocent bystander. He was more soberly dressed in jeans and trainers with a red bomber jacket.

"Do you sell Durex here?" the larger boy asked with the intent of invoking some kind of laugh from his two accomplices. For the life of me I wanted to take hold of him by the scruff of his stupid collar and drag him out of the shop and shout at him; *'does it look like we sell fucking Durex here you weedy little spotty fuckwit?'* Though that would have perhaps given me much gratification, I calmly replied by saying,

"Sorry we have sold out, would you like me to order some for you?" On hearing my response the boys giggled their way past some other customers and out into the street. Their joy would only be short-lived; teenage pranks were something I never liked but had to readily accept.

One Friday morning well into the summer, I arrived at the shop only to find a young woman struggling to lift a box from her car. I offered to help by grabbing hold of one side of the box, which was almost splitting with the weight. Just as we got to the shop door the bottom of the box finally gave way and a pile of decent sized books tumbled into the entrance.

"Oh, I'm so sorry," the girl uttered, embarrassed at the state of her mouldy cardboard box.

"No worries," I replied. "It happens, we'll just have to carry in a few at a time." Some of the books were quite heavy hardbacks and I sensed a sharp pain in my left foot, which had been delayed, probably due to the adrenalin. I laughed to myself as I realised that I was so eager to engage with people, any kind of social contact was like a sedative. One of the books on my first pile was titled *The Great Philosophers*.

"Oh, you like philosophy then?" I blurted.

"Yes, I do," she answered, "do you?"

"Yes I do, I used to teach it at the college night school."

"Oh really?" she said with slight surprise in her voice. "Did you teach someone called Chloe Langdon?" she added.

"That name rings a bell," I said. "Though I remember faces better than names. Is she a friend of yours?"

"She's my sister," she said, smiling whilst helping me to place the books at the side of the counter. "Are you Nathan?" she asked.

"Yes, yes I am."

"She used to tell me about you. I think I've seen you before."

"Oh?" I responded inquisitively.

"She said you were a really cool teacher. Anyway, she got an A."

"Well that's good news then."

We started to chat about philosophy as I tried to arrange the books for booking in. Mandy threw me the occasional glare but more in sarcasm than cynicism. Anna as it turns out had also enrolled at the college to study philosophy and sociology.

"Who's your favourite philosopher?" she asked me randomly. The question permeated my past life with a resonance that I welcomed.

"Hmm that's a good question," I replied, musingly. "Though I'm not sure I can remember."

I was tempted to ask her if she would like to have coffee later in the day so we could share philosophical chat, although recalling my past inappropriateness alerted me to withhold any such request. She spared me the shame.

"Would you like to have a drink later?" she asked with a thunderbolt.

"Yes. Yes I would," I answered concretely.

"Are you always so formal?" she added. I could not find an answer so replied through a shake of the head and innocent laugh. "What time do you finish?"

"Well I'm voluntary but I like to work until four."

"That's great. Where would you like to meet?" I didn't have a clue where to suggest but thankfully she took the initiative once again. "What about Blue Bar, say four thirty?"

"Yes, that's great," I replied. "See you then." For the rest of the day I trolled through my duties with one eye on the clock and a few thoughts on my loins, which appeared to have sprung into life. The feeling of arousal became almost uncomfortable. I tried to tell myself that there were no expectations – it was just a drink and a chat. *After all, that's probably just how she saw it.*

Mandy felt the need to jest with me for the rest of the day, insisting that I should be careful of such women. In the few weeks I had worked at the shop she had formed a protective layer over me as though she was my war-child landlady. She knew all about my symptoms and had become like a surrogate aunt; she was a worldly lady in her mid-forties. Mandy was not unattractive though her dress sense belonged to another era; she always wore long cardigans with uncompromising patterns. Her hair was shiny, coal black though I suspected it was often topped up with some kind of colouring agent. Her husband Trevor was a mild-mannered insurance salesman who often called in for a cup of tea. He reminded me of a man from the 1950s, with a balding head with hair at each side leading to a tuft at the back. His round, lily-white face sported a moustache that he probably had from the first ever moment he was able to grow facial hair. His polite manner extended through all his facial expressions. He carried that look of a gentleman from a bygone age and I immediately felt comfortable in his presence. Mandy would always see Trevor's visit as an excuse for a tea break. Her temperament was aloud with a zest for social interaction – preferably chit-chat.

Mandy and Trevor didn't have any children of their own, which is why I believe they all but adopted anyone else a few years younger than themselves who came into their lives.

I imagined their sitting room would be full of memorabilia from the places they had visited over the years. Trevor probably had one of those giant coffee mugs and a drinks cabinet with decanters. I was certain their armchairs had those tacky, plastic trays that clipped onto the arms.

At four thirty precisely, I walked into Blue Bar and ordered a pint of lager. I had to be careful as my tolerance to alcohol was lowered due to the illness. At four forty three, a spritely Anna walked in and came straight up to my table.

"Hi, sorry I'm late," she said.

"No worries." She sat down without ordering a drink. She had changed her clothes and was now wearing a blue patterned summer dress, which came to just above her knees, with white baseball pumps. Her legs looked sporty and tanned just like the female tennis players at Wimbledon. As we continued to chat about all sorts of topics I found it difficult to hide my obvious attraction to her. The waiter came and asked us if we would like any more drinks; Anna ordered a dry white wine and I decided on another lager.

"You okay, Nathan?" Anna asked as the waiter served our drinks and wiped down the table. I waited for him to walk away before answering.

"Yes I'm fine thanks; I'm enjoying myself."

"Me too," she said. "You're a lovely guy," she added out of the blue. I could feel my erection swell under my boxer shorts. It felt like my whole body was bursting from the inside; somehow the compulsions towards sexual activity had not really given me a problem until now. I believe my mind and body had gone into some kind of repressed sexual hibernation.

"I know about your accident by the way," Anna said.

"Oh really?" I replied. "Well it was an illness actually."

"Yes, sorry, I meant that. What is it called that you had?"

"It's called Japanese Encephalitis; it's spread by mosquitos."

"That's horrible!"

"How did you know anyway?" I asked her, probingly.

"I think someone from the college told my sister."

"Oh, bad news travels fast," I joked.

"Well you know how it is – people love to gossip."

"Yes, they do."

"But I think they're genuinely concerned."

"I guess."

It took a while for me to ease myself further into the conversation. After all, it had been quite some time since I'd had the opportunity to be in the company of a member of the opposite sex through my own choice – as opposed to those who were work colleagues or health workers. As it turned out, Anna wanted to chat about philosophy. I was only too keen to offer my thoughts on Descartes and the like. It also stimulated parts of my memory that had not been accessed since the illness. We swapped ideas about life, the universe and everything else, exchanging arguments for our favourite philosophers. Anna was apparently interested in the theories of Karl Marx. She told me how she had been turned onto the study of philosophy through reading some of his ideas in a library book, brought home by her sister Chloe.

"I like the idea that he thinks religion is the opium of the people," she mused.

"So I take it you don't believe in God?" I suggested.

She shook her head and took a sip of her wine. "You've only got to look at all the bad stuff in the world, why would God let it all happen?" I was just about to try and answer her then she continued. "I agree with Marx, that God is a delusion that human beings created to help us through our oppression."

"Hmm you could be right I guess, but I don't see it that way myself." Though my intellect was still fairly intact, I was not able to articulate my thoughts as well as I used to be able to; they were also slightly clouded by blotches on my memory. That, coupled with the effect of the alcohol, meant I didn't feel like a worthy opponent to her debate. It was easy for me to reach overload these days due to my inability for complex thinking. Noticeably, my second pint was starting to have an effect. I felt giddy; if I was really feeling intoxicated then I was quickly brought back to sobriety through an unexpected change of topic.

"Didn't you have a girlfriend?" Anna asked. Astonished by the question, I managed to slur a reply.

"Do you mean Charmaine? Is that something else your sister told you?" I jested.

Anna laughed, "Actually I remember we saw you both in town once; she had really nice dark hair and looked kind of funky. I didn't know you at the time though, obviously."

"I haven't seen her since…" Anna recognised my difficulty with the question and so considerately assisted me with a substitute response.

"Sorry, I didn't mean to pry, maybe my question was a little too personal."

"No, it's not that. It's just, I can't find her. It's like she's disappeared off the face of the earth since I got back… literally."

"Really? That's horrible."

"Yes, In fact I'm kind of helpless about it – helpless and hopeless. I think I would have got through it all better if she had still been here."

"Aw that's sweet," Anna insisted. "But you're doing great; well I think so anyway."

"Thanks, that's a nice thing to say; but how do you know?"

"Well don't take this the wrong way but you wouldn't know that you'd had that… disease."

"Japanese Encephalitis," I interjected.

"Yes that one as well," she jibed.

Our conversation became much lighter toned. Rightly or wrongly I believed that she was flirting with me. My physical reactions once again unravelled my unconscious desires. I began to sweat and feel light-headed; two pints of lager felt more like five.

Anna's question came out of the blue – as straight as an arrow, aimed perfectly at my vulnerable spot.

"Would you like to come back to my place?" As I tried to fathom an answer I couldn't help gazing at her perfectly-cupped breasts; a few freckles were dotted around her chest, dispersing into her shoulders. "You don't have to worry, Nathan. I won't bite, unless you ask nicely." My whole body surged. I wanted to go with her there and then. I wanted to be in bed with her, kissing those pert breasts and thrusting between her tanned thighs. Against my impulses my reply was as surprising to me as it probably was to her.

"Would you mind if I didn't? Please don't be offended."

"Hey no worries; if you want to turn me down I can cope, just." Our meeting ended with more than a hint of sexual tension. However, I was proud of myself for not succumbing to my desire for self-gratification. I had learned enough about the consequences of brain injuries like mine. Impulsive behaviour was normal, yet I had fought it and won. Even though I hadn't had sex for over two years, I resisted the offer. *Why? She was gorgeous; most men would have jumped at the chance. Is there something wrong with me?* I caught the bus back home. Sitting on the bus on the way home I realised there was nothing at all wrong with me. In fact this was a victory. I had just fought a battle with my own selfish desires and I had won back my soul. *Maybe the experience in the church has made me think about things with more purity?* From now on I believed I could choose a path that was a little less diverse; one that would create the least amount of stress.

★

It was winter before I saw Anna again. She came into the shop to donate some clothes that she no longer needed. I offered to make her a coffee, though she said that she had to be somewhere. Winter was a very interesting time to work in the shop. People donated lots of items they wanted to discard, or they just felt charitable in the run up to Christmas. Mandy offered me a paid position as Assistant Manager for the shop. She also advertised for extra volunteers and wanted me to help select them. We had so many letters of application with some applicants preferring to call into the shop personally with their letter. I must have accepted at least twenty. In the end we decided on two college students who were looking for a fulfilling role to help them with their application for university. Rachel was studying for her A-levels and was keen to work in a charity shop because she wanted to eventually get a degree in event management; her eventual ambition was to run her own charitable organisation for animals. Ryan was also an A-level student and he convinced us that his aspirations lay in becoming a fundraiser for a well-known charity. Both of them were very conscientious and caring young people. Ryan was also a member of the youth parliament and Rachel was very proactive with Amnesty International. I felt they were both a credit to their generation. Moreover, they brought an extra special dynamic to the atmosphere of the shop.

The routine of regular work and contact with people contributed to my excellent progress.

Emma's allocated time with me had been dropped to just one session per week. One cold March evening I decided to walk home along the canal. The light was fading and the sunset promised a picturesque scene for my suburbia. A few joggers ran past and couples sauntered home hand-in-hand after a hard day's work. I stopped for a minute to look back towards the town centre. I tried to envisage the person I used to be. The person I conjured up in my mind was very different to the one

I had now become; *he* was hardly recognisable. I liked who I was now – financially less secure yes, but definitely more simplistic with empathy in my soul. I lived from day to day rather than trying to plan the rest of my life. I may not have been quite as capable as I used to be with some matters, though my spirit felt all the more calm for it. I found a niche in the borehole of my previous existence. However, one thing continued to plague me. I hardly dare even mutter her name since that embarrassing night of knocking her door down; I was preserving it for some future reappearance. The sadness of losing her was sometimes unbearable. I had nothing to show for my love, only memories – not even a photograph or a keepsake. I didn't even have a clue where she might be and it seemed no one else did. There was no closure, just a glider hovering over me that had somehow been caught in an updraft, unable to land. I was the one hanging onto it, waiting for landfall.

Two years after my return, I decided to take up a new hobby. Cooking gave me a direction within my own space and time. I learned to cook some international dishes and became quite adept with Indian and Thai curries. My kitchen routine was almost the same whatever the culinary choice; I would turn on the TV and open the lounge door and serving hatch. This allowed me to engage in some sort of discussion with whatever programme I wanted to watch as I went about my work. I would always start with chopping up the vegetables and spices, then place them onto separate plates. Once everything had been chopped and ready I would take a minute, check everything was in order then begin. I came to thoroughly enjoy my new-found gastronomic skills and invited various guests around for dinner. On the whole, I was happiest cooking for myself with the sound of the TV trimming down any unwanted thoughts if my mind started to wonder. The whole process of cooking became a therapeutic interlude.

It was during one of my cooking sessions that I received

another unexpected phone call. Dashing to the phone in the hallway I half expected it to be my mother.

"Hello."

"Hello, Nathan?" My heart jumped at the sound of a female voice I didn't immediately recognise, though it sounded familiar. "How are you?"

"I'm okay," I replied. "I'm just cooking," I explained, buying time to guess the identity of the mystery caller. I was just about to ask who it was.

"It's me, Amelia."

"Amelia. Oh my God! How are you? How did you find me?" My questions seemed to leap out of my mouth and ask themselves before I could even think clearly.

"I had to contact the VOA. They wouldn't give me your details at first. But I told them it was important; anyway they knew that we were in a relationship when you were here. I got in touch with Mr Burrows – he helped."

"I had an accident," I said, piteously.

"Yes I know. They told me. I was so worried about you. How are you now?"

"Well my head is not quite the same as it was," I joked, "but slowly but surely it's rebuilding, like the bionic man." I could hear her snigger at my cheap joke.

"It would be great to see you," Amelia said.

"Yes it would," I answered.

"Is it possible?" she added.

"Well I'm not quite ready to make another trip to the Philippines."

"No, I can come and see you," she declared.

"Really, how so? Do you have a visa to come to the UK?" My questions continued a little more thoughtfully.

"I'm already here."

"What?"

"I'm here already, Nathan," she repeated. "My sister

Rosanna got a job here as a nurse and she married a man from London. They sponsored me to become their housekeeper and nanny."

I suddenly noticed the seasoned aroma coming from the kitchen.

"Wait, Amelia wait please, hold on." I hustled through to the kitchen to turn off the gas ring. Smoke took no pity on me and bellowed around the kitchen. I opened the window wide before dashing back to the hallway.

"Sorry, I don't want to burn my dinner. So, you want to come and visit me," I uttered, regaining my breath and composure, "that would be great."

"Yes it would," she replied. "I've wanted so much to see you ever since I got here." We continued to chat for an hour and Amelia promised to call back one week later to confirm her visit. I was shell-shocked. My feeling of elation was dulled slightly by a tinge of disappointment. I felt a little guilty for even having those feelings. The phone call triggered happy memories of my time with Amelia, though for the first few seconds of the phone call I had wished it might have been someone else. But I would not let that devalue the pleasantness of the surprise.

I'd gone about my usual day-to-day business for a couple of weeks until I heard from Amelia again. She had agreed to come and visit me and so I made sure I kept the house as clean and tidy as possible. My recollection of the time I spent with her was still intact, albeit a little misty. I could visualise her as very attractive with the orthodox look of a woman from South-East Asia: olive skin, dark hair, slanted eyes, high cheekbones and full lips. I also remembered some happy times we spent talking about our different lives, though my recollection for detail of our conversations was limited. Neither could I remember how she felt or smelled; my memory of her was like a stencil of someone I might have invented. I rummaged around my spare room in vain to see if I still had a photograph of her.

On the day of her expected arrival I woke up early; I ran through the house making last minute adjustments to the furniture and various pieces of object art which I had for some reason started to collect; a throwback of my work at the charity shop. I lit candles and turned on the daytime TV to give the house some atmospheric reality. I also bought a few magazines and papers to place pretentiously on the coffee table. *Not bad for someone with a head injury – having the nous to think about that kind of shit.* All I had to do now was play the waiting game. For me this would mean creeping up and down the stairs, peeping out of the bedroom window in order to gain the initiative of her arrival. It was twelve o' clock, midday and she was supposed to have arrived at eleven o' clock. *Typical woman. Hope she can find the house okay.* I redirected my attention by putting the kettle on. As soon as it started to boil, the doorbell chimed like it had done so many times before. Only this time, its din was vibrant. The pang of expectancy soared through me as I walked along the hallway to answer the door. She stood there, sunlit and beautiful.

"Hello Nathan," she said.

"Hello Amelia." I stepped outside to greet her. We hugged lovingly. "It's great to see you," I said.

"It's great to see you," she replied. We looked each other up and down. And then I noticed him; the small boy who had been concealed by her shoulder bag and my slight lack of peripheral vision.

"I want you to meet someone," she said, ushering him towards me with her hands on his tiny shoulders. "This is Jay, your son. Your son, Nathan."

It felt like the air had been siphoned from me. A dark shadow climbed up through my windpipe and spewed out of my mouth into the street. I could do nothing but stare at him, then at her. My breathing became shallow and I began to feel light-headed.

"Are you okay, Nathan? Sorry, I didn't mean to give you such a shock. But I thought about how I would say this so many times and in the end, it just came out." Amelia studied me and gave me time to regain my self-possession.

"Well come on – you need to come in," I suggested, feeling as though we had rehearsed a drama scene right there on my doorstep, with me as the lead, fluffing his lines badly.

I sat down in my chair and Amelia slowly placed herself down on the sofa. Jay stood at the end of the sofa, staring at me. His big, dark eyes pierced my very being as if he knew all along that it was me who first fired him into this big, wide world.

"Isn't he lovely, Nathan? I wanted you to see him." I sat forward with my elbows resting on my knees and my hands in prayer mode resting on my closed mouth.

"Can I ask you something?" I mustered.

"He is yours Nathan, just in case you were wondering."

"Right, right. Well then." The slightly lighter tint to his dark hair and rounder eyes were confirmation. In some ways I was looking at myself through a mirror, a tinted mirror that hides unkind details. I could see that he was a perfect mix.

"So many times, I wished he wasn't yours."

"Why?"

"Because I never thought I would see you again. And, when I heard about your accident they told me you…" she paused and began to cry.

"Told you what? That my brain had been damaged?"

"Yes."

"So you thought I wouldn't be capable of being a father?"

"No Nathan, it's not like that. Because I didn't know how bad it was. No one did. I thought you might not even know me anymore." Jay had started to explore the lounge by treading around the sofa; he came to the arm of the sofa that was adjacent to my chair. He looked up at me and smiled. I smiled back. "He wants to come to you." Amelia said.

"Hi Jay," I said, with some unease at my untrained expertise with toddlers. He walked towards me and clambered up my legs. Amelia was smiling with joy. I lifted him up onto my lap.

"Now then," I sighed, holding him in both arms. I began to cry. Jay continued to look at me as if trying to decipher my inner emotions. I could smell his hair and skin; I held him close and wept. Amelia sat angled towards us with one hand on the arm of the sofa and the other placed flat on the seat. She was spellbound by the moment. I was flabbergasted. Jay fidgeting on my lap immediately beamed new life into my microcosm of a world. My life had woven paths that led to many surprises. The pieces of me that had flaked off were beginning to be replenished. I actually owned much less than I used to. And yet, I knew that at this very moment I had received more than I ever had before, at any time in my life. I would have to adjust once again, but I was becoming an expert in adjustment. We were all going to step through this day and into another new life. I was happy again and I could sense my soul swelling back to its original size and shape – almost.

Amelia and I fell into a very comfortable relationship. She moved into the area but decided to stay with a fellow Filipina called Tess, rather than move in with me. She suggested that if and when we were ready to live together we should start afresh, in order to create new memories. I actually agreed with her; my house carried too many stories – the walls were lined with tears and jollity from a past life. I tried to become a doting father, taking Jay to the park and lake. He also started getting used to staying at my house when Amelia chose to stay over. I turned the spare room into a bedroom for him; I was thankful for Amelia's designs for decoration and requisite toys. I had not fully regained my sense of perception about those important niceties. When I took the actual time to go to the local baby store I over-estimated his age for toys. I of course knew he was eighteen months, but for some reason was determined to bring home a Power Rangers set. Thankfully, the helpful assistant at the store appropriately guided me towards a Playmobil farm.

My favourite evenings were those when Amelia and Jay would come over to stay, and she or I would cook. Jay would play with his toys in the lounge as we took turns to join him in the fun. After dinner we would watch a video, usually a wonderful family movie. We all sat there on my sofa like we had been plucked from a TV advertisement for the latest breakfast cereal. But I felt so happy I had to multiply my senses by ten at least once every day just to check that it was all real. *But what keeps nagging away at me?* I couldn't fathom it and it troubled me. I had been through a hellish few years then arrived in a heavenly dreamland of a life.

I wondered if my slight confusion at how things had evolved were all due to my recovering cognitive abilities. One evening after I put Jay to bed, I opened the cupboard where all my old philosophy books were stored. It was a menagerie of old textbooks, magazines, novels and some of my teaching resources from the college. I tried reading through some of them. Whilst I had no problem understanding most of it, I found it hard to deconstruct some of the philosophical theories. Everything about my rehabilitation and progress since coming back had gone so well, yet all of a sudden I felt inadequate. I was gradually finding out my limitations. That small but important part of me that I believed distinguished me from the man next door had been lost or erased. *It was taken by that fucking mosquito; what good was it to him? Little fuck!* Clutching one of the books to my chest I began to have a panic attack. Amelia must have heard me and came to sit with me. She held tightly onto me, trying her best to understand and console me. She didn't need to say anything.

Just holding onto me, sharing my grief and loss was all I needed from her. She was an expert in compassion and consideration; like most Filipina ladies, caring was in her DNA.

I must have slept late the next morning as the house sounded like it had been active for a few hours. I trod downstairs gingerly only to find Jay tearing out the pages from one of my books.

"What the fucking hell? Stop that!" I shouted at him. His shocked little body jolted backwards and toppled over.

"What's the matter?" Amelia shouted, making her way from the kitchen.

"He's ripping my fucking book up. Why aren't you stopping him? Didn't you teach him to respect people's things?"

"I'm sorry. He's only a baby still. It's just an old book, Nathan."

"It's not just an old book, it's my book. Not his!"

"Look at you," she said. "Please don't get yourself so angry at something like this." Jay was screaming at the top of his voice and the fear in his eyes bolted out towards me with a disapproving air. Amelia lifted Jay up into her arms and walked upstairs. I looked at the remnants of the book. Amelia came back downstairs a few minutes later with one of her bags packed. She placed Jay into his buggy as he continued to cry and shake. They were both in tears as they made their escape. I stood there staring out of the window, then back at the book. When I looked again at the book it was one of my very old second hand textbooks which I had used whilst I was at university. It was smothered in blackberry jam. Some of the pages wilted onto the floor. The video of Tom and Jerry was still playing on the TV and Jay's plate of food and drink were in the middle of the carpet; sad un-owned leftovers of what moments ago was a happy household. My head felt heavy. Thoughts sunk through into my stomach. *What the hell have I done?*

I had no choice but to go into crisis mode. This meant contacting the one person who knew exactly how to help me.

Thankfully, Emma's number was now stored in the memory of my phone. Otherwise I'm not sure if I could have maintained the wherewithall to access it elsewhere.

I left a message on her answer machine asking her to call me back. I sat staring at the cartoon on the TV. Emma called me back within the hour. She could immediately sense my distress and promised to call round in the afternoon. Whilst time stood still I cleaned up the lounge and made some coffee. By the time Emma arrived I was deep in a depressive episode. We sat down in tandem and Emma smiled as she had many times before.

"So you want to tell me what happened?"

"I've blown it! Totally lost it this time," I said.

"Go on," she said. I explained the whole situation to her whilst trampling up and down the lounge. After offering me her comforting advice and listening ear, she asked me a question.

"So how are you going to resolve this problem, Nathan?" I looked at her, then across at the various toys still scattered around.

"I will go and see her and apologise. I hope they will both accept."

"I'm sure she will," Emma suggested. "But Jay is only a baby. He won't be able to understand an apology, so what do you think is the best thing to do?" Emma added thoughtfully.

"I'm not sure?"

"Hug." She added assertively, "give him the biggest hug ever. And tell him you love him. He will understand that because he will feel that you care. He might not understand words so much but he can sense your love for him if you let him." Emma carried on talking for a while as I mulled over her suggestions. Of course she was absolutely right, as usual. I would act on this as soon as tonight.

"So are you making a coffee then, or what?" she joked. I smiled at her and shrugged my shoulders.

"Thanks Emma," I said. "You have been a rock for me since I got back you know."

"Oh I know," she said. "Come on, get that coffee on, I have to get going soon. Besides you've got some serious making up to do, mister."

Rain and darkness can be a discouraging combination. It seemed a fitting scenario for my mood as I approached the house of Amelia's friend Tess. I replayed the incident over and over as I walked. *Fathers do shout at their sons, but I had been in a mild rage. My body language and facial expression must have frightened the life out of him.* It was a ridiculous reaction over something so unimportant. *What happened to my new-found calmness?* The battle was not over yet. I still had to keep looking over my shoulder to spot the demons that would never give up trying to unhinge me.

My tentative knock on the door gave away my feelings of guilt. Amelia's friend answered.

"Hi Nathan," she said, smiling.

"Hi, I'm sorry to bother you. You must be Tess, I've come to see Amelia and Jay."

"Come in," she said, opening the door to its fullest extent as if carving out a walkway of shame for me. Amelia was sitting watching TV with Jay. She smiled at me; Jay's big eyes stared at me and his lips split to offer a much welcome smile.

"Hi," I said to Amelia, never taking my eyes off Jay. Tess asked me to sit down and diplomatically left to make coffee for us. "I'm sorry," I said.

"I know Nathan," Amelia replied. "I know you didn't mean to be angry. It's just you scared him. I don't want him to be scared of you, Nathan."

"No, me neither. I still need to adapt to some situations and I guess having a young son is one of them."

"Yes." Jay clambered onto my knee as if nothing had happened. "You see, he's forgiven you already." Amelia smiled. I hugged him for all I could.

"I'm sorry, little man. I love you. Your daddy is silly!" Though he couldn't understand, I knew he could sense the unconditional love and warmth I held for him. I never wanted to hurt or scare him again.

Tess came in with the coffees. She placed our cups on the coffee table and considerately went upstairs to allow us to continue our discussions.

"Look Amelia," I said. "I've been thinking it through. I want you and Jay to come and live with me. I know it might sound crazy after what happened, but I will work at controlling my anger. I've done well up to now, you can ask my social worker. It's just new situations take some time for me to adjust to." Amelia lifted Jay up into the air as she sat back in the sofa.

"Hmm what do you think Jay? Shall we go to live with Daddy?"

"He says yes," I joked. "Just like the man from Del-Monte."

Tears cascaded down her cheeks; she tried to hide them from Jay through her constantly wide smile. "All I ever wanted, Nathan, was for us to live as a family. I just never knew what to do. When I found out I was pregnant you had already gone to your new post. Then I couldn't decide when or how to tell you. When I finally wanted to tell you, I was already six months and they told me you had gone back to the UK after an accident."

"It's okay," I said. I held her hand and rubbed Jay's head with my other hand. I realised I was touching the two people who I cared most about in the world. I had to embrace them and make them my family. I had to let go of any other dreams I may have still held on to. Though they may tug at me every now and again, I had to cut that rope and let them fall right through the underbelly of my subconscious. I knew this would be an almost impossible task for myself but I had to try, for my son and for Amelia; most of all I had to try for myself. *If only I could know where she was and what she was doing; maybe I could let it be.*

PART FOUR

THE SOUL FINDS A NEW CONSCIOUSNESS

Snow didn't quite manage to fall at Christmas to decorate our new-found life in blissful suburbia.

It waited until New Year's Eve. Amelia had brought a much-needed feminine touch to the house. Jay's toys seemed to adorn every room. Partygoers shouted their elation as they walked home or onto other parties. Amelia closed the curtains and we decided to clean up the room and kitchen after our guests had left us. We had invited Tess and her husband Peter, Mandy from the shop, along with her husband Trevor and a scattering of others such as Ryan and Rachel who made a fleeting entrance before heading off to more exciting haunts. Emma had also called in during early evening and even Brad made a guest appearance with the ever-present Thor. When they all left I realised that my social life was better now than it had been before I went to the Philippines. This tragedy – this assault from an insect and all it had put me through, did bring about some positive outcomes at last.

The Letters

We finished up our tidying routine and hugged each other.

"I love you Amelia," I said.

"*Mahal kita*," she replied. We were both distracted sharply by the sound of the letterbox rattling and what seemed like a few taps on the door. We looked at each other in puzzled angst.

"Maybe Brad is back with Thor nudging his nose at the letterbox," I claimed.

"Yes, better go see then," Amelia hinted; we continued to embrace for a while; it was hard to let go of her sometimes. Seconds later I heard the crash of the front gate as it rebounded back and forth like someone was in a hurry to get away. I hurried up the hallway to peer out of the window in the front door. A shadowy figure disappeared into the New Year darkness. I was just about to turn back to the kitchen when I saw the envelope on the floor. I picked it up inquisitively and headed back into the lounge. Amelia looked worried.

"What was it?"

"I'm not sure. I thought I saw someone but they might not have been the one."

"What's that?" Amelia asked, glancing at the envelope in my hand.

"I don't know. It's addressed to me; maybe a belated New Year's card from someone."

"What is belated?"

"Just means late, hon."

"Oh," she said, smiling. "I will sleep now honey, you coming to bed?"

"Yes, I'll just finish my wine and watch the end of the movie." She kissed me and made her way upstairs. I sat down on the sofa, analysing the envelope; it would have been easy to just open it but somehow I wanted the challenge of guessing what it was and who sent it. In the end I opened it carefully. My eyes denied any attempt to go straight to the bottom of the letter; instead I began reading with trepidation.

Dear Nathan,

I'm so glad to learn that you're back home and making progress after your illness. I can't imagine what you must have been through.

I'm not sure where to begin when it comes to telling you about my life. I left the house about nine months after you went to the Philippines. Mum passed away; maybe you heard? So, Auntie Norma decided to go back home. It was rented out for a short while to a lovely Indian family, however they left after six months and the house has only been occupied by tenants one other time. I'm thinking what to do with it – sell it or let it to another tenant. Perhaps selling it would be best.

As for me, well you would possibly find it hard to believe the path I have followed. I want to tell you though I feel I need to tell you in stages. But first, I feel I should apologise. I know you will say 'what for?' I realise I let you down. Please believe me Nathan when I say this. I wanted so much to go with you to the Philippines. I was tearing myself in two trying to work everything out in my head. Then when I heard that you had become ill I was beside myself with worry. You might not know this but I came to visit you in the hospital over there. Mr Burrows arranged everything for me. It broke my heart to see you lying there. The doctors weren't sure at that stage just how severe the damage to your brain would be. Thankfully, I believe it's minimal, so hopefully you can still do your PhD.

I need to say something important to you. I did leave you because of someone else. I had already given my heart to that

*other person when I came to visit you. You must never think
I decided that I couldn't be with you because of your illness.
My heart and mind were already made up. After all, we had
quite a few discussions about it if you remember, before you
went away. I have so many wonderful memories of our time
together, Nathan. You opened my eyes, my mind and my heart
to something very special. It was through our special moments
and discussions that I came to understand the road I should
travel. For this I will always be forever thankful to you. There
are some people in our lives who are important and special
because they make such an impact on us; you are that person
to me.*

*I will write to you over the coming months. On that, you
can trust. For now I hope you will understand and accept that
I am truly happy, safe and fulfilled, living the life I desire.*

*I wish you all the success in the world for this coming
New Year.*

Take care always.

C x

I was transfixed by the contents of the letter.

"Oh my God, she came!" It was incomprehensible
that she had actually travelled all that way just to see me
lying there lifeless. I began to read again, trying to fathom
the vagueness and mystery. Then, astonishingly another
memory came to me: that she had become so accustomed
to acting enigmatically before I left for the Philippines. I
then wondered if it was really her who posted the letter
personally. *Maybe she was the dark, shadowy figure or maybe she
had someone deliver it incognito.*

I sipped my wine as I eyed specific sentences in the letter.
I felt like a code breaker trying desperately to decipher the
un-decipherable. *Where is she?* There was still no real clue.

It could have been the next town or Addis Ababa for all I

knew. I wondered what type of person she would have fallen in love with. I doubted that it would be some businessman or executive type.

Char would never have gone for the money man. Maybe a scientist? Yes, a microbiologist. I could see it now. He would come home and tell her how close he was to finding a cure for the common cold; then make mad passionate love to her all night long. *I've sussed it. You're rumbled, Char. Ah that's right! There was that man.* I trod upstairs to the bathroom holding the memory of her in my mind, the last time I saw her.

"I remember you now. The man with the tan. So suave and grey. Twat!"

"Who are you talking to love?" Amelia mumbled, half asleep from the bedroom.

"No one darling, just myself."

★

I settled into a very comfortable family life. Despite Charmaine's letter, which had certainly ruffled me, I knew it would be best to segregate it. It was a portion of my life, separated from the realism like a child's secret toy box, hidden away until discovered years later by accident. Aside from my curiosity about Charmaine's cryptic life, mine was quite ordinary. I would go to work every day at about ten o' clock and come home at about four o' clock. Amelia had found a fantastic new job as a part-time nanny in the next suburb, though thankfully she didn't have to live in. She was just required to work mornings or afternoons; any additional hours the family requested were by negotiation. The fact that she was allowed to take Jay with her was a bonus to us.

We planned our dinners the night before, so whoever was home first would cook. I liked the feeling of arriving home, to find Amelia cooking. Jay would be playing in the lounge with his toys or sat on the floor in front of the TV, watching cartoons. At weekends we would sometimes take Jay to the park or the small farm. He was fascinated by the rabbits and guinea pigs running around in their pens. All the staff were so well trained and helpful; they would invite the children to stroke some of the animals. Jay was nervous at first, especially of the goat, but after few visits he couldn't get enough. He wanted to stroke all the potentially dangerous animals such as geese and pigs.

These days filled me with such immense pleasure. Long gone were any thoughts of a career or worries about the future. The feeling of salvation was abundant in me. Even so, thoughts of Charmaine were never far from my mind. The embers of my soul had emerged from the turmoil; moreover they had somehow reassembled from the cinders of Japanese encephalitis. It hadn't happened instantly and it wasn't yet complete. There was still much restoration to my inner-self needed; but I felt it would come with time and patience.

I even made a visit to the college to see some of my ex-colleagues. A lady called Polly was now teaching the philosophy course that I had been responsible for. She wore very bright, pastel-coloured clothes and had traffic-light-red hair. I felt quite plain by comparison. She willingly offered to let me sit in one of her night school classes. I enjoyed watching from the side lines; she was a very good teacher and challenged the adult learners to think about the ideas she presented. The topic was Kantian ethics and the students were keen to express their opinions and apply Kant's theory to modern day issues, such as abortion and euthanasia. I was never a big fan of ethical theories although it was satisfying to be involved, if only as an observer. It certainly stirred up my thoughts on philosophy once more. Though just as my chat with Anna in the pub had revealed, my brain was wired a little differently to what it once was; or perhaps it would be more accurate to say that some of the wires had been disconnected. I found it hard going after a while and would lose my train of thought.

One day I passed a new music shop in the high street. It triggered a real assortment of reflections in my mind – from memories of my old job as a sales rep to my days working with the band in Europe. It was the first time I had reflected on that particular era of my life since the illness. I could remember many of the characters I'd come into contact with, though I wasn't able to recall any specifics regarding my association with them. Perhaps it was a kind of motivated forgetting on my part. Maybe I wanted to shake off any remnants of memories relating to the part of my life that held no importance anymore. I wanted nothing to disturb my inner peace; the sanctum I had found within myself.

I didn't notice the second letter at first. Amelia had placed the morning mail on the telephone table in the hall; her usual rush hour habit. I almost walked past it on my way to open the front door.

The manila envelope protruded from the small pile of energy bills and local junk mail. I just happened to catch sight of the curled up corner that looked as though it had gone through quite a journey. I wasn't sure whether to read it right there or take it to work, though I knew that might make it tricky to read, or wait until I got home; but then Amelia would ask questions about it. It was different in appearance this time and addressed formally to Mr Nathan Blakemore; it had a postmark from France stamped across the middle.

I was fairly early so after getting off the bus decided to walk the long way round to work. I walked around the park, searching for the perfect bench. It was early March and the frost was still clinging to the ground with contempt. Luckily there was no wind so I could open the letter without the fear of it flying into the sky if I nervously fumbled it. I took off my gloves to open it then put one of them back on as I started to read.

Dear Nathan,

I hope you are having a good year so far. I've been so busy, Nathan – guess what with? Can you believe I have been planting trees, flowers and vegetables? I also make natural set honey from the bees we keep here. The garden looks so lovely at this time of year, and it's wonderful to be able to put it to good use. I've also been busy learning lots of new skills. I'm a dab hand at cross-stitching now, though my favourite pastime is craft making. I have made baskets and dried flowers, napkins, tea towels – you name it, I have made it. I can also make my own soup, using very natural ingredients. My speciality is lentil and pea soup. You would approve, I'm sure.

I do hope you are managing to progress with your rehabilitation. I know that some days you will find it very challenging, but I know you Nathan. I know you will never give up. I know this because I know you have the insight to find yourself once again. You are a very special person Nathan, not just to me, but in the way you go about living your life and the way you think about the world. Please always remember this.

Once again I apologise if I seem to be all 'cloak and dagger' about things. I have my reasons. I will write again soon.

Take care of yourself always, love and wishes.

C X

I folded the letter and placed it back in the envelope. I was just about to put my other glove back on when I opened the letter again with more haste. I realised this time that she was deliberately leaving out specific details. She wasn't telling me about her work, or was she? All the things she was describing were more like hobbies than what people did for a living. I pictured her working in a farm shop of some sort, where she was responsible for running the whole shebang. I decided that the professor-scientist husband must have opened up the business for her to run. *I bet he is well off after all, the owner of a vineyard – that's it! Not a scientist; or maybe a scientist from a rich family; a man with everything. Anyway, it's probably set in some idyllic location in five acres of land somewhere in the countryside.* I wondered what happened to her ambitions. *Well I guess we can all change. Look at me. Did you sell out, Char?* Somehow I didn't want to believe that she had. The enigmatic part of Charmaine was what had attracted me to her in the first place. It could drive me crazy at times though it was a trait that we had in common. Without it she would dissolve into an unnoticeable cardboard cut-out.

The third letter would take its time coming. I may have even forgotten about its determined arrival.

By the time the real summer declared its appearance, I was feeling very healthy, in both physical and mental terms. I was still involved with the group meetings at Mind-Set; Amelia had encouraged me to keep attending. Jay was growing fast and now talking quite well for his age. During one of our family outings in the neighbouring town, we were all drawn to a pet shop in the main arcade. The window was fitted out like a small cat den; five kittens lay huddled together in a large, plastic basket. The kittens were all grey striped tabbies with white chests. One of them looked up at us and sprang towards the window, resting his front paws on the glass. Amelia was the first to comment on his feet.

"Look at his white feet."

"Yes. He's the only one out of the bunch with the white feet," I added.

Jay then made a remarkable observation. "He has boots, Mummy." One hour later we were taking the aptly named Boots home. For the next two months the house became a playpen for Boots, with Jay latching on to the high jinks.

Amelia watched the antics go by with more maturity than myself; I was a child again, running around the house with balls of wool, enticing Boots to chase after the trail. Jay would follow on but was often left statuesque, as Boots and I sped past him in the hallway. His infantile intuition led him to try grabbing Boots' tail one too many times; that is until Boots decided to take a retaliatory swipe at him, drawing blood from Jay's finger. The screams nearly brought the house down; Boots was in his bad books for at least an hour. Jay told us he didn't want him anymore. Amelia did a wonderful motherly job of explaining to Jay why Boots had reacted that way. Within hours they were friends again; Jay gliding the wind-up rubber mouse along the kitchen floor, waiting for Boots to pounce like the hunter he was born to be. Of course, his tail was now safe from prying hands; Jay had learned his lesson well.

My joyous humdrum was once again put on hold with the arrival of Charmaine's next letter. I could see it from the top of the stairs glinting upwards at me from the floor. I had come to recognise the purity of the slim, white envelope. We were already well into autumn. Amelia had taken Jay to playschool and obviously left without placing the post on the side cabinet; I surmised this from the way the letters at the bottom of the pile were still trapped half underneath the door. The letter in the pure white envelope lay there unperturbed and undamaged. This time I would read it in the comfort of my own home; accompanied by a cup of coffee and a whining grown up cat.

Dear Nathan,

Nathan, can you imagine the most peaceful place on earth? That doesn't just describe where I live, but also how I feel inside. I live quite high in the mountains; the air is so clear and crisp and I have the most beautiful view of the sea. It is truly a slice of heaven on earth. Have you ever been to the northern part of France?

I want you to see it Nathan. It would be wonderful if you could come and visit me. Therefore I have included the directions of how to find me on a separate sheet. It's not easy but once you arrive here in the area there are plenty of people around to guide you to my front gate. I will be here waiting and hoping you will find the strength to come.

Take care always.

C x

I was disappointed in the length of the letter. I hadn't even taken a sip of my coffee before I had read through the whole thing twice. There was an address on a separate sheet, though it was imprecise; there were no numbers or the name of a fancy house – only what seemed like an area. However, the directions were explicit: *Catch the bus from the ferry terminal signposted for Escalles. The bus terminates here so you have to get off. Look for the sign for Beutro Marc then follow the narrow lane up the hill. You should eventually come to a sign for Chateau d'Eau. Turn left into the wooded pathway that leads up the hills. It's quite a long climb but not very steep. You will find me somewhere at the top.*

"My God, she really does live in a French Chateau." I was talking aloud to myself. Boots cast a look back at me from the window ledge, then continued his gaze outwards. I decided to keep my thoughts from his over-sensitive ears, though he was probably not too concerned with my quandary. *That guy must be seriously rich.* I felt a butterfly floating in my stomach and my hands began to tremble. I sat down at the kitchen table, trying to make sense of it all. As I read through the letter again in what had become my customary fashion, something came to me. I rushed upstairs to my private file where I had stored the other two letters. I opened them all up and laid them out in order on the table. All the envelopes were white but the paper the letters were written on was pale blue. There was something else about them although I wasn't sure of the significance. Each of them had a slight damp spot in the bottom right hand corner; as if she had spilled water on them whilst writing. For some reason I sniffed the patches of damp. It didn't smell like any kind of perfume, but there was a very earthy yet slightly flowery scent to each of the damp spots. I put all the letters back into my private box of memorabilia and headed off to work.

On the bus, I reflected on the letters. I loved my life with Amelia and Jay; I loved everything they had brought to me. But I knew I had to go to visit her. It would be the only way that I could finally move forward without looking back. I still held such a deep love for Charmaine even though it had been three years since I had seen her. Although Amelia was my new tower of strength, Charmaine was my dreams and desires all wrapped into one. She was the suburban soulmate I summoned years before I ever met her. She was the one who was meant to perfect my existence; we were matched physically, intellectually and spiritually. Yes I had changed since my illness, though the person I used to be was in a tug of war with my new self. Although I was winning, at times it made a surge to pull me back over the line I had drawn when my soul began to replenish. *How will I explain my journey to Amelia?*

The November clouds played their usual trick of hiding the sky. I was on my way to a group meeting with Mind-Set when I felt it. The cosmic pins and needles in my hands and arms slowed my walk. I was only a few hundred yards from the meeting rooms. I got down on all fours and crawled towards the door. Through my hailstone vision I could see someone come running over to me.

"You alright mate?" I stretched out my right arm and pointed to the door.

"In there – the people in there – please tell them."

★

For the second time in my life, I woke up in a hospital bed. At least this time I had some sense of awareness as to why I might be here. Amelia was sitting at the side of the bed holding my hand.

I peeped over at the various electrical screens.

"Please don't tell me I'm all fucking wired up again."

"Shush," Amelia said, "please hon, don't use those words. It's okay, you are okay Nathan. It's just a drip, nothing else."

"I wish I could believe that, love. Where's Jay?"

"He's with my sister."

"I'm glad you didn't bring him here. I don't want him to see me like this," I moaned.

A day later the doctors explained to me that I had experienced something called a Transient Ischemic Attack, or TIA for short – a mild or mini stroke. It had possibly been brought about by the vascular weakness in one area of my brain. There was no additional brain damage, though it had left me feeling shattered and worried. It was also possible that I would experience such attacks in the future as well as the chance of epileptic seizures. *Why now?*

Two days later I was back home in the comfort of my living room; Jay played constantly with his toys on the floor in front of me as if trying to coax me out of the hopelessness. Amelia continually asked me if I was feeling alright, and reminded me to take the new medication I had been prescribed.

Over the course of the next few weeks and months, I descended into a depression. It felt like I had the shadow of death hanging over me, taunting me. Amelia insisted that I should visit my GP. During my appointment my doctor insisted she wouldn't prescribe anti-depressants; she felt I had enough medication floating around in my system at the present time. Instead she suggested I attended counselling sessions and kept up my attendance with the group at Mind-Set.

I lost track of time and everything else in my life. From

my chair – that ever present chair – I watched the wind, the rain, the snow and anything else that came into view. The activities of people I used to recognise and keep a mental note of were cast aside; I disregarded them as if they were blurs on my consciousness. I had stopped shaving and hardly went out of the house. If someone had asked me what season it was I would have been unable to answer: *winter, autumn, by the look of it.* Time didn't pass – it was just on hold. My bay window, which used to be my looking glass to the world, turned into a prism of nothingness; a viewfinder to neurosis and obliteration. I'd ignore the rings of the doorbell when people who cared about me called to see how I was. Amelia had to make excuses for me and keep me up to date with who had tried to visit: Emma, Mandy, Brad and whoever. Amelia needed to prompt me to shower in order to maintain my personal hygiene. The black fog descended over me, sucking me in, devouring and devouring. *Is this it? Fuck this!* "Fuck this!"

The loud knock at the door angered me. I headed towards it ready to shout in someone's face.

I opened the door aggressively.

"Nathan. It's good to see you my old friend." Before I could muster enough anger to reply, the stout man reached out to shake my hand and patted me on the shoulder with his other. "Don't tell me you don't recognise me," he said. "It's me – Eddie," he added with a belly laugh.

"Eddie," I uttered. "Eddie!" I repeated gingerly. "Come in. I'm sorry I'm in a bit of a state."

"Don't worry about that Nathan, it's just good to see you matey." I cleared the mess from the sofa and beckoned him to sit. I was still dazed from the surprise of seeing him again. "I'm sorry I didn't recognise you at first."

"That's okay. In fact it's a good thing, proves I've lost weight," Eddie said, laughing heartily.

"Doctor's orders, you know how it is."

"I'm afraid I do, only too well." I agreed sullenly. I sat down in my chair. Eddie also sat back, making himself comfortable on the sofa. I stared at him, rebuilding the jigsaw of his previous demeanour.

"So I heard you've been through quite a lot," he said.

"Yes," I replied, "but so have you." I was pleased that I was able to remember the day he had a heart attack and offer my own empathies. "Well you look good," I said.

"Thanks pal," Eddie replied.

"I wish I could say the same about myself."

"You will, anyway after what you've actually been through I think you look fine."

"How did you hear?"

"You know how it is, word gets around. I've been meaning to get across to see you for a while but it's taken until now for me to feel confident driving again – if it's further than a couple of miles down the road. And, you're not so easy to find, I had to do a lot of asking around." I started to feel more relaxed.

"Oh. So how's the shop?" I asked as I stood up to go put the kettle on.

"Shop's good, I've done a refurbishment. You'll have to come and see."

"That would be nice. As soon as I'm better I will."

When I brought the coffee in I realised that he looked quite soberly dressed. He was still wearing jeans, though he had a long sleeved shirt underneath a V-neck sweater.

"I see the ponytail's gone," I joked. Eddie laughed once again. His face was much more gaunt than it used to be, though a lot less crimson from over-indulgence.

"Yes, I thought it was time to get rid. Sometimes you have to shake off the past."

"I know what you mean." I noticed he was looking around at the photographs on the bookcase.

"Oh, you have a boy now!"

"Yes, he's three I think… nearly."

"Fantastic."

"How's your daughter by the way?" I asked politely.

"She's doing well. She still has the farm. She's into all this organic stuff now, you know."

"Yes, it's the way things are moving." Both of us held our thoughts and questions for a while.

"It's good to see you Eddie," I said after realising my compliment was much overdue.

"Thanks pal, you too. That's the thing you see Nathan," he added philosophically, "you just never know when the last time you're going to see someone might be. That whole thing with my heart attack scared the shit out of me! I thought I was a goner." His words hit me like a freight train, sending a shiver through my whole frame.

Eddie went on to tell me how he had changed his whole lifestyle after his heart attack. He had given up drinking and smoking and had bought a mountain bike. He decided to ban all the dope-smoking cronies who used to hang out at the shop and instead hired a couple of university students who were more into making money than music. Apparently it had given the shop a more proficient appearance, the result being that he could keep his much-loved business ticking over, but introduce new pastimes into his life.

"Yes," Eddie introduced to the silence. "It's like I've had a complete makeover, good to go now, will get a few more miles on the clock now," he added jovially.

"That's great!"

"So I'm sorry, Nathan old boy, but I'm not able to have that pie and pint with you. Been told I have to keep it real these days, you know what I mean? Look after myself a bit more." I pondered on his words for a while then the memory of writing those words in his get well card flashed into my brain. I was astounded at my ability to remember the specifics in such detail.

"Ha ha," I laughed at my recollection. "No worries, we can make it decaf coffee and wholegrain flapjack instead." We continued to small talk for a while, musing about music and the old days; it was a much-needed remedy.

By the time Amelia arrived home with Jay, Eddie was still filling me with stories of his life after his heart attack. Amelia kindly invited him to stay for dinner; she cooked one of her Filipino dishes. I could tell she was happy to see that I was beginning to cheer myself up. My posture and outlook were already changing for the better. I had shaved and showered and felt energised and fresh. Eddie went to get his acoustic guitar from the car so that he could impress us all. He played a song for Jay – 'Hey Jude' by the Beatles. It brought tears to my eyes; Amelia followed suit whilst clapping joyfully as Jay looked on with amazement and delight. He was amazed to see a real life person singing, other than the ones he had seen on TV.

It was around ten o' clock in the evening when Eddie decided to leave. We offered to put him up for the night but he insisted that he loved to drive home in the dark. He said it gave him a solitude and freedom to think. *I remember how that used to feel.*

"It's been great to see you Nathan," he said, packing up his guitar.

"And you my friend," I replied.

"We must do it again soon." He hugged Amelia and Jay and set off down the garden path after shaking my hand sincerely. As I waved at him from the doorway he turned, clenching his right fist in the air. "Onwards and upwards Nathan," he chanted.

"Yes," I reflected. "Onwards and upwards."

Eddie's presence had reinvigorated me. The timing and

nature of his visit was heaven sent. Though Amelia had done everything possible to help me recover, it was an unexpected subtlety that awoke me from the self-imposed exile of my own mind. Eddie had given me a jolt. I couldn't let the course of my life defeat me. He was living proof that we can touch the bottom most rung of our lives, yet rise again to breathe anew. There was always more than just hope; there was the human spirit. It was capable of unearthing new life force; it could find new light where darkness had alighted.

I was able to express my love once again to Amelia. I held her hand as I sat next to her on the sofa.

I also put Jay to bed for the first time in months. One week later, my soul was shining again. I felt the warmth growing back inside, pulling me up to the light of life which I already possessed: my family, my friends and my role in society; I needed to hang onto that notion more than ever. Two weeks after Eddie's impromptu visit I was ready to face the world again. Accepting that I had no control over my mortality was difficult but necessary. Only then could I embrace life wholeheartedly again. Mandy had given me an extra day off in the week. She said I could have it for as long as I needed.

My day off usually began with Boots jumping on the bed and purring into my ear. This was the only day of the week he could do that, because Amelia always left the bedroom door open when she left the house. I could tell whether or not he had been fed, by his behaviour. If he had, he would eventually lie on top of me and go to sleep, still purring. If he hadn't, he would attack my toes when they protruded from the bottom of the duvet cover, then jump up onto the bed and breathe his cat-breath into my mouth. I think he knew exactly what he was doing. The only way to escape the toxin was to get up immediately and feed him. *Who needs an alarm clock?* My to-do list was placed aptly on the kitchen table alongside my diary. I was back in the game of life. I had porridge with banana for breakfast, followed by two cups of tea. The second cup of tea was about an hour later whilst I watched the news. Boots was in the habit of sitting on the windowsill to monitor the goings on outside. He would wash himself first with his forepaws. Then he gawked at the people passing by, as if deciding whether or not to give them approval to walk along our street.

After an hour or so he would get bored and whine to be let out of the back door. Only this time he did the staring thing before he left. He seemed to be spellbound by something in the corner of the room. His wide, green eyes undraped every dimension in that exact spot. I looked across but could see nothing. I even stood up and walked across to the exact point he was staring at, to see if there was a spider or the smallest speck of dust floating down from the ceiling. There was absolutely nothing that I could see.

"What you staring at?" Boots looked at me judgementally before refocusing on the corner of the room where all the action was, according to him. His look was so intense; he would even interrupt his self-preening to continue his gawp. *Maybe he can see something that we just can't see. Maybe all cats have a visual ability to see into other dimensions; or perhaps he is just deep in thought about something he wants to do later.* I was sure that I had read somewhere in the past that the ancient Egyptians believed cats held mystical powers. Watching the curious stares of Boots certainly gave credit to that idea.

"Your consciousness is weird, Boots!" The sound of my own words almost caused me to levitate. I became rigid as my thoughts ran to another time. That brilliant conversation I had with Charmaine in this very room. *My God, I wish I could think like that now.* I could, but only in spurts. *Consciousness!* "Consciousness Boots! That's what it's all about!" I said loudly, "consciousness!"

He leapt off the windowsill, startled, and ran through to the kitchen. He stood there meowing, waiting impatiently for me to let him out of the house, to get away from the mad man inside.

"You lovely sack of fluff!" I bellowed. He licked his nose nervously before he scarpered off for his daily adventure.

The idea came to me there and then. I dashed upstairs into the spare room. I cleared my old desk, rummaged for an old notepad and pen and began to write. Four hours later I was still sat at my desk writing when I heard Amelia come home. She came upstairs tentatively and saw me through the slight gap I'd left in the door.

"Hi hon, what you up to?" She smiled.

"I'm writing a book." The initial look of surprise on her face soon turned into a smile of approval.

"That's wonderful," she said, standing over me and kissing me on the cheek. "It's nice to see you have an interest in something again."

"Yes," I said. "I've woken up from my slumber."

"What is slumber?"

"Like the depression I was in."

"Oh yes, this is good for you to do writing."

"Yes, I'm loving doing it. How's Jay?"

"I didn't pick him up yet because I came home early. Do you want to fetch him from playschool?"

"Yes," I replied. "What time is it?"

"It's still only one, he needs picking up at two; take your time." I took hold of Amelia and held her tightly. We kissed passionately. "Ah Mr Blakemore, you have that sexy look in your eye," she suggested.

"We have time." We made love intensely for the first time in months. The release of my emotion through sexual energy made me feel dizzy. We lay together looking up at the roof.

"I love you," Amelia said.

"I love you too."

I sprang along the road to collect Jay. All the while my thoughts were on my new project.

I was fuelled by excitement. I had come to realise quite

some time ago that I would never have the mental robustness to write academically. In fact I had been in denial of my cognitive deficiencies. Whilst my mental agility was less focussed and precise than it used to be, I felt that my powers of imagination were heightened. I could see things in pictures. Watching Boots had regenerated those powers almost instantaneously.

Amelia was able to get hold of an old electronic typewriter from the family she now worked for. She was much better at typing than I was so offered to copy up my handwritten notes.

"You're not allowed to read the story until it's finished!" I told her smugly.

"Of course," she responded, laughing out loud, knowing full well she would be tempted to take in the story as she typed away merrily. Luckily for me the visual display on the typewriter was small, so it was difficult to read more than one sentence at a time.

"You won't be able to put the sentences into any context," I joked. "So no point in trying until it's finished."

"Correct," Amelia joked back. In some sweet way it didn't actually matter to her. I'm not even sure if she took the whole idea seriously; she was just relieved to see me getting back to my old self.

I managed to wangle some sheets of white A4 paper from Mandy at the shop. I told her I was writing a book about my adventures in the Philippines. She was only too glad to help out and bought me an extra box of paper as a good luck present.

"So am I in your story then?" Mandy jested.

"Well you might just creep in when I get to the bit about the old woman who took me on."

"Cheeky devil, you better make me look good!" she warned, smiling as she tapped my arm playfully.

I became obsessed with my writing, spending every spare minute upstairs in the spare room. Friday especially was my writing day. I spent just about the whole day upstairs, coming down for air and coffee once every so often. I could also watch the antics of Boots when he came back from his amazing cat jaunts. Amelia would bring Jay in to say goodnight at bedtime and insist that I had done enough for the day. The problem was that the words were pouring out of me. My knack for metaphor was certainly intact, if not more superior than ever before. I wondered if it was all to do with how my brain had compensated for the deficits; the left-brain, right-brain concept. I had learned a bit about this during my rehabilitation sessions. *That's it! My creative right brain is dominant now! How cool. Fucking little mosquito – you think you can fuck with me?*

Four months later, my project was complete. I didn't have a clue how to go about trying to get it published, so at Emma's suggestion I went to my local library. The librarian was very helpful and pointed me towards a book that listed most of the publishers in the country. It contained everything one needed to know about writing, presenting and approaching publishers. I wrote a supporting letter and posted four manuscripts. All I could do now was sit tight and hope for the best. I hadn't felt so enthusiastic about anything since my sound engineering days. Those days when the band was trying endlessly for a recording contract, only to end up disappointed by record company executives who promised everything, but came up with nothing. I hoped the publishing world would be different.

After two weeks had passed I started to become anxious. Every morning I would wake up and stand at the top of the stairs and stare down at the front door to see if anything other than what looked like bills or advertisements for Christmas hampers lay on the doormat. About three weeks later I received the first batch of Dear John letters; three arrived on the same morning. I sat down at the kitchen table, dreading the process of opening and reading the first few lines. I hated the way they were worded: *Although we enjoyed reading your story we don't feel it is suitable for us at the moment. We wish you well in future. It was just like the fucking music business.* "Fuck off! Wankers!"

I reacted by posting off another five manuscripts, believing this would improve the probability of receiving an offer by increasing the average number of scripts I sent. This time I genuinely forgot about them. The shop was going through a very busy time and I was attending two sessions a week at Mind-Set. Mandy would ask me politely if I had any luck with my attempts to be published. I would just smile and shake my head. In the end she promised not to ask anymore.

"Tell you what, you just tell me when you get an offer okay?" She had bellowed to me one time whilst we were sorting through some donations.

"Will do." That suited me fine; then I could avoid the feeling of failure thrust upon me through rejection. Over the next couple of weeks or so another two rejection letters found their way onto my front door mat. However, this time they were encouraging about my potential as a writer, giving roster only as their reason for not accepting. The letters did actually include the sentence: 'we have considered your manuscript carefully'. *Hmm, progress.*

On my next Friday off I missed the purring of Boots. I stretched my way out of bed and stood at the window. There he was sitting on the neighbour's garden shed. He looked across at me with an air of condemnation. He then went back to eyeing the birds who were dive-bombing him to ward him off any attempts to raid their nests. There was a small war going on outside; the laws of nature were alive and well in my back garden. It was already ten thirty; Amelia must have fed him and decided to let me sleep. I made a cup of tea and turned on the news as usual. There's something about a phone ringing that alerts me to a wealth of possibilities. I didn't rush to the phone, thinking it might be Amelia wondering if I was out of bed.

"Hello," I answered lazily.

"Could I speak to Nathan Blakemore, please?"

"Yes, speaking," I replied as my head awoke to all kinds of likelihoods.

"Hi Nathan, my name is Angela Barrett from BMA publishing. Well the reason for my call is that we really like your manuscript." My heart leapt up through my chest and out of my mouth, taking most of the words with it.

"Really, wow that's fan… wonderful," I garbled.

"There are a few changes we might like to suggest but basically we want to go with it."

"I'm, I don't know what to say," I said pathetically, yet inside I was about to collapse in a heap of happiness. Angela invited me to go meet her in the London office. I placed the receiver down with great care so as not to alter the authenticity of the phone call; thinking the slightest of shakes could splinter the reality of the telephone conversation. I took a shower and got dressed in lightning speed. I ran to the bus stop and waited for the bus that passed the house where Amelia worked. *Number 21 – this is the one.*

Amelia was in shock when she saw me running towards the house from the front garden where she was playing with the children.

"What's wrong?" she asked, nervously.

"Nothing, nothing my love," I gasped.

"Nathan you're scaring me. Look at you, you're sweating and out of breath, is Jay alright?"

"I don't know, I mean yes I'm sure he is. It's not why I ran here. My book, it's going to be published."

"Wow, Nathan that's wonderful!" Amelia exclaimed delightedly.

"That's exactly what I said," I exhaled, still trying to get my breath back. Amelia turned to the children.

"Oh your uncle Nathan is very clever," she said to them proudly. "Come in," she suggested.

"No it's okay, I want to go back. Maybe I will call people: my mother, Emma, Mandy you know, let them know the good news."

"Okay well be careful, don't rush," Amelia insisted. She kissed me and I walked back to the bus stop. "We will celebrate tonight," she shouted after me.

The fresh air felt brand new; everything I had strived for carried some meaning. It was just about midday and the traffic on the roads was light. I asked a woman at the bus stop what time the next bus was.

"It's due now love," she replied.

"That's fantastic," I replied, grinning. "It's wonderful!" She threw a false smile back at me and looked me over, probably thinking I was drunk or slightly disturbed. The bus came almost on cue. As we waited to climb onto the footboard, I almost forgot my manners due to my over-excitement. I checked my step and stepped back courteously to allow her to board before I did. "It's a great day don't you think?" I said knowing full well she would watch me all the way back to the town centre. For sure she would rack her brains wondering if I was more than just a mere happy extrovert.

It was one of those moments in life where the elation is so fervent you're not sure what to do next.

I could have gone for a pint, called everyone I know with the good news, or listened to my favourite music in celebration. I opted for none of those; instead I sat in my chair with a cup of coffee, pondering on the course of my life. Only this time, my thoughts held a more positive twist. The quiet contentment of triumph was calming; I had started to win the battle again.

Though I knew life would never be perfect from this day on, I at least had something tangible to show for my pains. I had never been a person who could be fulfilled easily or by shallow trappings. This was the only way someone like me could truly feel a sense of accomplishment. It's not a Range

Rover or Laura Ashley sofa that does it for me – it's those things that seep into your soul and burst back out full of colour and joy. People would look at me differently from now on. Not that I wanted or needed some kind of adulation; it was more that sense of *'he actually did it – something worthy'*. It would also be a way for me to leave some kind of legacy.

There was one person I really wanted to tell. During my recent illness and subsequent compulsion to write, I had lost the motivation and will to seek her out. Another letter had arrived but it lay propped up in the letter rack unopened. I had a different reason now to for wanting to see her. I loved Amelia and that would not change, though my quest to play out a finale with Charmaine still loomed. If I could accomplish this big ask, it would not so much be like completing the circle, but replacing a lost relic to its rightful place.

That night I sat and talked with Amelia about my previous life. I opened up the door to a past that no longer mapped to my present existence – and yet a small chunk of it would always cling on to me.

I told her about the letters and offered to let her read them. Amelia was accepting and graceful and said she didn't need to see them. She understood my reasons for wanting to meet with Charmaine and just wanted me to come back safely. That night also unpacked another surprise. As we lay clutching hold of each other in bed she told me.

"Nathan," she whispered, "I'm pregnant." I pushed myself up from the bed and looked upon her beautiful face. Her long, dark hair curled over her shoulders and her eyes reminded me of another night, in the hot sensual mugginess of the jungle. My response was simple and right.

"I love you, Amelia. Will you marry me?" The single tear that leaked down her accented cheek gave me the answer I longed for.

FATE UNFOLDS

It had been some time since I had travelled further than the next town. So even though Charmaine had provided detailed travel instructions, travelling to northern France would present a new challenge for me. However, the trip to London would be a good reconnaissance mission as it meant catching the same train down into the smoke. Other than a couple of misadventures on the Tube, where I ended up going in the wrong direction on the Circle Line, I coped quite well with my short excursion. The meeting with Angela left me feeling excited about the prospect of having a book out there in the world, written by me – Nathan John Blakemore.

When the time came for me to set off on my expedition, Amelia helped me to pack my things and typed me a detailed plan for the journey. I laughed at my own shortcomings. Here I was, a father of one, in fact almost two, about to be a published author yet I still needed slight intervention for day-to-day things.

"That damn mosquito has a lot to answer for!"

"What is it?" Amelia asked, then read my expression and caught on. She put one arm round my waist and kissed my cheek in the way she kissed Jay. "Some things happen for a reason. God's will," she alleged.

I had a four-hour train ride to endure before catching the ferry. Embarking on the boat made me think about previous jaunts to France with the band. Only now I was a lone traveller, with a mission that only I could conclude. I was slightly restless during the journey. I had to keep myself busy by walking around the boat, so spent quite a lot of time on the deck looking out to sea. The thrust of the ship's engines sloshing the waves below made me feel a little dizzy, so I stood holding onto the handrail.

"Are you okay?" a young but quite well built young lady asked me in her American sounding accent.

"I'm fine thanks," I coughed, "just felt a little queasy but better now."

"Not seasick then?"

"No, at least I hope not." She introduced herself as Mumphy, which I gathered was some kind of nickname or pet name given to her by her mother. She was a student travelling around Europe. Mumphy fired a torrent of questions at me; typical perhaps of a young student mesmerised by the intrigue of meeting people whilst backpacking. I ended up telling her half my life story and the reason for my tour. She was actually from Canada though she was studying engineering in the United States. I probably made all the wrong assumptions about her because of her size; she was tall and frumpy with hands like a carpenter. Her hair was limp and straight and her feet were twice the size of mine. But she had a beautiful soul. She was one of those people you would choose to be lost on a desert island with; dependable, trustworthy and acquiescent. We must have chatted endlessly on that deck, almost failing to notice the French coastline coming into view.

"We should be there in an hour," she stated assertively.

"It looks so close," I said. "Like it's just five minutes away."

"It's deceptive, it always looks just a mile or so but we're probably still thirty miles or so from the actual port."

"You sound like an expert."

Mumphy shook her head with makeshift pride and added, "The joys of travelling on ferries around Europe for the last six weeks."

I had one last cup of coffee with Mumphy at the café in the port. We exchanged a few more words of small talk as we both headed towards the bus station; then she dashed for her bus towards Paris which was about to leave.

"Thanks for making my journey more interesting," she complimented.

"It was a pleasure," I responded gratefully. "Enjoy the rest of your travels."

"Good look with everything Nathan," she shouted back. "I'll look out for your book when I get home."

"Good luck with the engineering, I hope you design something fantastic that everybody wants!" With that, I re-focussed on my travel instructions and soon found the bus bound for Escalles.

The single decker bus weaved its way around the thread of narrow roads, which scaled steadily up the valleys. My heart rate accelerated in anticipation of the climax of my journey. I stared out at the vast openness laden with beauty; though my ovation for it took second stage to the thoughts passing through my head. I took out the letters to read the separate sheet that stated the final part of my travel directions. I laughed, thinking once again how enigmatic Charmaine was; *Mona Lisa has stiff competition.*

Three people got off the bus with me at Haute Escalles: a middle-aged lady with a basket full of produce and two teenagers with rucksacks. All except me walked back down the hill towards a steep, paved ginnel, which looked as though it led down to a small, postcard village. I looked at the instructions every once in a while, stopping to re-read them just to make sure I was on the right path.

"Chateau d'Eau," I mumbled to myself in my Yorkshire dialect. What the instructions didn't state was just how far away the signpost was. I had to walk some way along the road before I found it pointing crookedly to the left. The tinder path curved around the edge of a cliff until turning slightly back on itself, revealing huge, wrought iron gates that hung tentatively onto white, limestone walls. There was no one around so I decided to open the unlocked gates and proceed. Limestone footholds swayed gently around to a wider clay pathway, which opened up to yet another pathway of wider, cobbled steps that were sunk into the grass. I was thirsty and noticed a wooden bench opposite. Planting myself down heavily, I took out my flask of water to drink. I was still absorbed. I glanced over at the hill brow. *Surely a few more steps and I will see something, someone.*

Just as I rose to my feet, a small, dark-skinned man appeared from over the brow pushing a wheelbarrow. He smiled and waved.

"Hello," I shouted. "Sir, can you help me? I'm trying to find this place." I bustled towards him, pointing to the vague address on my notepaper.

"Oh, you are here," he answered jovially. He could sense my confusion as I gazed around with a perplexed expression. "There. There!" He said, throwing his outstretched arm towards the brow of the hill as he held onto his barrow with the other hand. "You go up!"

"Oh okay, thank you sir." I had no idea what to expect as I trod up the wide, moss-covered limestone steps: Charmaine's Chateau, or maybe a simple log cabin.

The vision that opened up before me was certainly unexpected. About two hundred metres into the distance was a large, stone building bathed in sunlight. What looked like an orchard opened up to my right, and flowered green fields parted the walk to the centre of the building. Other pathways circled around the perimeter and I could see a few figures pottering around in a gardened area; though I couldn't quite make them out they appeared to be females. *What is this place?* I stood for a while as I evaluated the scenario. I noticed the pathways had wooden benches placed every hundred yards or so. I picked one out and made a beeline towards it. On reaching my chosen seat the ocean came into view over the horizon to my right.

I sat clutching my rucksack and took another swig of my water. I checked the directions and partial address on the letter then looked around some more. I wasn't sure what to do next so I just sat. I stared at the great beyond, which spanned my whole perception. I took deep breaths and tried to relax. For a moment I thought about the Normandy beach landings in World War Two. It was so peaceful – it was incomprehensible to imagine the carnage that once occurred along this coastline.

I must have fallen asleep for a while. The voice startled me at first.

"Hello sir, are you okay?" I looked around at the petite lady stood to my left.

"Yes Ma'am," I replied, re-focussing my eyes on the foreground.

"Are you visiting?" she asked politely. Her tortoise-shell rimmed glasses looked to be from another era.

"Oh no I'm sorry – am I on private property?"

"In a way, yes – but all are welcome here."

"I'm here to visit a friend actually, maybe she lives in one of those houses over there," I added, pointing towards what looked like a block of cottages to the right of the large building.

"Who is your friend?" she asked.

"She's an old friend, called Charmaine," I explained shyly, "Charmaine Laffe." Not for the first time a thought hit me head on, a direct reaction from the words I uttered. "Of course," I muttered to myself.

"Sorry?" the lady asked politely.

"No it's okay ma'am," I added, "I've sussed it at the last minute. I get it now, she's come home. Her name ma'am, it's French." *She's come to meet her ancestors. That's what all this has been about.*

"Oh your friend is French, may I ask what your name is please young man?"

"Yes, it's Nathan, Nathan Blakemore, I've come from England."

"Maybe I can help you Nathan," she said smiling, "would you like to come with me?" I stood up and walked along with her agreeably. "By the way I'm Sister Marie; it's nice to meet you, Nathan."

"Oh yes it's nice to meet you too, Sister." I offered as the realisation of her subtle attire dawned on me. Sister Marie wore a fairly unobtrusive head covering and a fairly normal grey blouse and skirt.

On approaching the building it became obvious that I had entered the grounds of a working convent. I made so many deductions as we walked along making small talk about the weather and gardens. We arrived at what seemed like the front entrance.

"Would you like to wait here Nathan, I'll let Sister Rose know that you're here, I'm sure she will be able to help you."

"Right that's great. Thank you, Sister." I stood for a while before plonking myself down on the stone steps. I waited for Sister Rose, who I assumed might be the Mother Superior. *She probably knows everyone in the local community around here.* I felt a little bit like I was intruding, but then came to the notion that they would most likely be happy to help me find Charmaine. Once again I took in the vast panorama. It really was a heavenly place, in more ways than one. *Why didn't I suss it before? Slow to make that connection – The French connection.*

A flickering orange glow far out at sea caught my attention. I got to my feet quickly, at first thinking it might be a ship on fire. Thankfully I soon discovered it was more likely to be a beacon or a buoy for the shipping lanes. For a few seconds my mind had been diverted. I sensed a presence behind me. I looked sideways to see the silhouette of a nun standing statuesque at the top of the steps. My eyes were still adjusting from the brightness of the ocean sky to the foreground. Her white face etched out a smile. A warm surge swam through me and my heart went into ectopic beats and a waterfall of blood rushed to my cheeks.

"Hello Nathan."

"Hello," I replied nervously. She walked down the steps towards me. Her smile grew stronger and her face became clearer.

"I thought you'd never come," she said.

I was rigid and speechless. "Sorry," I replied, truly flummoxed. I was unable to think of an explanation or reason for my apology.

"Have you got a hug for an old friend?"

"Yes of course, if it's allowed."

"Of course it is." I hugged her cautiously, though long enough to feel the crisp freshness of her white habit. I could not feel any contours of her physique – only the solid, cold density of flesh on bone. I immediately recognised the sublime scent, which I had been able to smell on her letters. "You found me."

"Yes, the Chateau. I guessed you lived in a castle." I was still trying to calm myself as I muttered my way through the ice breaking. I began to sob relentlessly in front of her. "Sorry," I said, "the emotion of the moment, you know." She didn't reply, merely smiled with an expression of consent. Her eyes were still as beautiful and piercing as ever, though her skin appeared to be much paler than before. There wasn't a single blemish on her fresh cheeks and her lips were less accentuated than I remembered. "So…" I began.

"I'm Sister Rose," she interrupted graciously. "It's my middle name, and the one I wanted to use for my vocation."

"Right, yes."

"It's wonderful to see you Nathan," she said.

"And you Char, sorry, Sister Rose," I corrected myself shaking my head and looking down at the ground.

"Shall we walk?" she asked, gesturing appropriately with her hand. "Or maybe you're tired of walking? It's quite a trek up here."

"No, I'm okay, I've been sat on a train then a ferry then a bus, so walking is good. I thought some nuns weren't allowed contact with people from outside, if you know what I mean?"

"Yes that's true, I haven't yet taken my solemn vows. I'm what you call a postulant... or I was, technically I'm now a novice and allowed to meet with people, as long as I have consent from the Mother Superior. But even then we can meet people, with special permission."

"So, you're like a trainee kind of thing."

"Yes something like that," she joked back.

"I guess that's why you couldn't tell me everything in your letters."

"Yes. We're not encouraged to say too much about our devotion, especially after taking our sacred vows. But I also didn't want to tell you in writing. Besides I knew you wouldn't come if I told you everything at once." I didn't respond to her suggestion, so redirected to her earlier statement.

"Oh so you have taken *some* vows already."

"Yes Nathan, I have." We stopped beside a weeping willow tree. Its branches oscillated kindly for us.

"Can I ask you something?"

"Yes, but I know what you want to ask me. What made me choose this life?"

"Yes," I muttered, "as always you can pre-empt my questions."

"It was always there, Nathan. But things grow inside us sometimes, even when we least expect it."

"I agree about that."

"And you Nathan, you also helped me to recognise and appreciate those feelings."

"Trust me," I jested once again.

"You should be happy. After all, each of us needs that special someone to ignite the flame inside us. You did that, because you made me think about things differently. You also helped me to seek the true meaning of life, according to what we each expect and desire."

"Did I say all that?"

"Perhaps not in those exact words, but you certainly guided me towards my decision, through your own ideas of how we should all strive to fulfil our soul and purpose."

We sat down on one of the benches that looked over the village below.

"So you really did have someone else in your life!"

"Yes. He was there all along. I knew I had no choice but to give myself to Him and Him only."

"Well I'm no competition for God!" I uttered, looking up to the bluest of skies. "Not that I would want to be."

"He loves you, Nathan."

"Yes, I suppose. Well actually, I know. Believe it or not I've kind of had a religious experience myself since I last saw you."

"Oh that's wonderful news." She smiled continuously and sat at an angle on the bench, with her hands together placed lightly on her lap. I felt a spiritual honour in knowing that I had contributed towards her quest to embrace God. We both shared the landscape as our thoughts found a way to come alive with discretion.

"I want to thank you," I said.

"What for Nathan?"

"For coming all that way to visit me in the hospital. I just wish I could have been awake to see you."

"Maybe it was meant to be like that," she replied.

"Did you stay long?"

"About three or four days."

"Did you think I was going to die?" She looked at me

then across at the view – keeping her eyes ahead for a while before looking back into my eyes virtuously.

"I knew God would save you," she said with solemnness in her voice.

"Really?"

"Because that room was so full of life and love, and filled with His presence. I just knew you would be safe."

"Your faith was strong, Sister," I said with sincerity.

"Yes it was. It had to be."

"What do you mean?"

"Because God wanted it to be. He decided that my love and prayers would save you."

"Even if it meant we couldn't be together – is it like that was a price to pay?"

"There was nothing to pay Nathan, only gifts to receive, for both of us." Our conversation paused for a while.

"I have a gift for you!" I said, changing the tone of the conversation. I pulled out a pre-run copy of my book and handed it to her. Her eyes almost began to glaze over before she looked at the title, or realised what it actually was.

"'The Comical Consciousness of Coolio the Cat!'" she read aloud. "A story for children by Nathan J Blakemore." Sister Rose rubbed the book with her hands as if anointing it with chrism. She then held it to her chest and inhaled the fresh air.

"It's about a cat with a weird imagination, but I don't want to spoil the story for you," I explained.

"God is so good. Nathan, I'm so proud of you. May I keep this?"

"Of course, it's for you. Look, I signed it inside," I said before falling into an apology. "Sorry, I signed it to Charmaine. Wait, I'll change it to Sister Rose."

"No it's nice the way it is Nathan. Thank you. Let it be, as it is."

"Wait! Let me dedicate it to you as Sister Rose on the back page." I quoted the words whilst writing, 'To my most spiritual friend, Sister Rose'. There you go. By the way it's not even in the bookshops yet so you have the first copy."

"I'm very honoured Nathan, thank you."

"It's not quite a PhD," I added almost defensively.

"It's better than a PhD, Nathan."

"I had to write it," I paused for a few seconds, "for my son."

I sensed from the way she looked at me that she concealed a deeper hurt, though she held on to her dignity with expected reverence. "I know you're a wonderful father."

"Well I'm still learning, but I think I'm getting there."

"We never stop learning."

"No, we don't."

We stayed silent for a while, taking in the sights and swapping the occasional smile with each other.

There were so many things I had planned to say but my words remained locked in, sealed inside my unconscious. It was a beautiful silence.

"What are you thinking about?" I asked her. She turned her angelic face towards me and half-smiled.

"I'm thinking what a beautiful end to a story all this is."

"Maybe it's a beautiful beginning?" I suggested as her smile widened.

"With every end there's always a new beginning," she insisted wisely. Sister Rose stood up and smiled reverently, still clinging tightly onto my book. I noticed that her lips had become fuller and her eyes widely exotic. It was as if God had allowed the blood to momentarily flow to her erogenous zones for one last time. "Will you do something for me please, Nathan?" I replied by nodding. "Pray for me."

"I can do that."

"God bless you," she said. I was surprised that she leaned

forward to kiss me on the cheek. "Peace be with you always," she added.

We spent over an hour discussing our different life paths, though never touching on our past. She gave me a tour of the convent and taught me about the history of the particular order of Carmelites she had joined. I was happy to know that she still held ambitions in her new vocation. I was proud to realise that so much of her work in the future would be regarded as sacrosanct by society.

We walked back around the grounds to sit on the bench that looked out to sea. The wind strengthened, in preparation for our parting.

"It's been so wonderful to see you, Nathan."

"And you, Sister Rose."

"Have you got anywhere to stay for the night?"

"Yes, well I'll just get the ferry later and sleep on that." My eyes wouldn't leave her, though I tried my best not to make it obvious. "I had to come," I said, looking down at her simple sandals, then looking up and out to sea. "I'm not sure what to say now, how to say goodbye," I added.

"Then there's no need to say it," she said softly. "I want you to walk towards the steps that lead down to the gate. I want you to walk without looking back, Nathan. Can you do that?"

"I'm not sure Sister," I replied. We both stood up at the same time. "I guess I'm not allowed to kiss you?" She didn't reply – again her expression gave me the answer. She reached out and took hold of my hand lightly.

"God bless you Nathan, and peace be with you and your family always." The smallest of tears seeped out of the corner of her eye. I looked at her for one last time, as she raised her other hand up to my cheek and held it there for a few seconds. Whatever I wanted to say, I could not. Once again, the words stuck somewhere between my brain and my throat. She let go of my hand and I turned around. Even though my back was turned I knew she could sense my tears.

"Sister Rose, you will always be in my heart," I cried, with a mere half-turn of the head. My legs felt like lead as I broke away from the space that had felt so sacred. As I placed one foot in front of the other I could have sworn I heard her whisper, *'I love you'*. I dared not look back; I had to honour her wish, at least until I reached the steps. It was the longest walk I ever completed; like a dead man's walk to the gallows. My heart didn't pound; it just sunk deeper. When I got to the steps I stood for a while; I thought about turning but was still reluctant to do so. Perhaps she had already vanished from sight. *No*. I didn't want to see her walking back, walking away from me. I wanted that memory of her hand, her tear and her beautiful, pallid face and mesmeric eyes looking at me with such devoutness. I looked upwards at the gathering white clouds and closed my eyes for a few seconds, letting the breeze coat my face; then I began my touchdown.

The ferry was only half-full compared to the outward journey. There was no Mumphy to keep me company, though thankfully the crossing seemed to go even quicker, probably because I was able to get some sleep. I had been anxious on the outward journey, but now my spirit was soaring. I held no feeling of closure, nor did it seem like I had completed the clichéd full circle by meeting with her. Instead it felt more like a union. I would always love Amelia, but a part of my soul would always be shared with another. She had also given me part of hers.

Sister Rose had found herself. Her spiritual journey had been borne out of a harmony, nurtured through precious moments we had shared; the conversations we had created with the aim of finding solitude within. I fathomed something: we were never meant to be together. Some relationships have a greater cause. I believe ours was to create a fate that only one's innermost thoughts can illicit – by asking ourselves questions that demand answering. Even if we cannot find the complete answer, we should always strive for one, because this is just the simple idea we know as soul searching.

I had searched my soul for most of my life. I only began to find it after a mosquito infected me with a virus that changed the way I think. Preposterous, that one of the simplest known organisms on earth can have such a very powerful effect on the most complex. This is the balance of life we all face. Mine had tipped one way then the other, until it perched somewhere unexpected. I knew I shouldn't try to look too far into the future anymore. I would embrace the present, as without doing so, there could be no future.

As I made the last walk of my journey from the bus station to home, the mid-morning sun had started to pour light over my suburbia. I walked along the canal just as I had done so many times before. There was no discontent within me, only a temperate joy that coated my ghost. As if rehearsed for the moment, the couple in the tandem wheelchairs rode towards me.

"Morning," they both shouted, also in tandem, the man doffing his hat with one hand.

"Good morning," I replied heartily. I could feel my smile permeating through my whole body. Two streets from home, the owner of the fish and chip shop was preparing for the lunchtime diners. *For sure it will be steamy in a few more hours and the golden glow will filter through into the street.* Just one hundred yards later, the billboard outside the newsagents read: *England win final test and clinch series in last day sizzler.* I looked up at the skies. *I guess they do get finished, sometimes.*

The final stroll home wrote a perfect ending of its own. Some famous closing lines from movies shot into my mind: *'after all tomorrow is another day', 'there's no place like home', 'you have to have a little faith in people'.* All seemed fitting to my immediate state of flux. From the road I could see into my bay window; the place where I had spent so many pensive hours. Boots was sat on the windowsill trying decide if I had his permission to walk up the garden path. I could see that Amelia was cleaning up as usual, whilst Jay looked to be trampolining on the sofa. I liked those famous movie endings, but not this time. I wanted to write my own. Sister Rose was right about so many things; in fact she was always right. I stepped through the door into my new beginning. The warmness of familial love swarmed over me like a tropical sea waft.

"Hello, my loves. I've brought someone new home, would you like to meet him?"

EPILOGUE

There's a moral to every story; at least that's what we expect. But how many morals could we deduce from Nathan's and Charmaine's journey? Perhaps we search too deeply to derive moral understandings when in truth they are there with us every moment, hanging over us like a halo or a dark cloud, depending on how we react to them. Thus, we are capable of creating our own proverbs before our private history carves them out for us. Unfortunately, our human frailties don't always allow us to. Instead, we approach the journey of life, often without purpose, before the platitude is underwritten. We stumble through, making mistakes − disappointing ourselves and others along the way. But some of us are able to utilise those misgivings and frame the rest of our lives around new possibilities.

Holding an awareness that our lives are not pre-determined as much as we are led to believe can provide us with the unique ability to think laterally. Otherwise we allow ourselves to be led through a life that is linear, with a lack of free will; we then lose the very part of us that is most precious. Yet, if we stand still for moments in our lives, to invite introspection, we can make the journey towards our true self through a more intrinsic perspective.

Nathan and Charmaine are examples of how we can achieve this. Nathan's journey amplified his soul and self-identity, whereas Charmaine was able to transcend unconscious thoughts into a much purer form. I have since spoken with Nathan, and his ability to think divergently has if anything increased; he is even more in tune with the need for us to change our perceptions in times of ambivalence. Whilst his thought processes may be narrower, they are deeper, meaning his thoughts find a way through to clarity despite what he believes to be a fog in his brain.

He has accomplished an inner happiness that he was unable to find before his injury. This proves something about the power of the mind and more importantly, the importance of the soul on our ultimate destiny. Consciousness might just simply be our soul. Or, maybe it is what makes us all unique. Our consciousness is not like that of the cat. It lingers within the realm of the physical and the spiritual; its quantum effects shape our self-awareness, character traits and aspirations. Moreover, it can inspire us to walk through our life with optimism – and meaning.

In the first part of this story I almost presented my identity and my relationship to Nathan. In relation to our chronicle I feel as though I should present myself.

But then something holds me back, hoping that you will decide for yourself who I am.

ACKNOWLEDGEMENTS

The writer would like to acknowledge brief referrals to the psychological and philosophical theories of, Sigmund Freud, Plato, John Locke, Walter Swinburne and Karl Marx.